WORK
NEW SCOTTISH WRITING

WORK

New Scottish Writing

INTRODUCTION BY BERNARD MacLAVERTY

The Scotsman & Orange
Short Story Collection 2006

Polygon

First published in Great Britain in 2006 by Polygon,
an imprint of Birlinn Ltd
West Newington House
10 Newington Road
Edinburgh
EH9 1QS
www.birlinn.co.uk

Introduction © Bernard MacLaverty, 2006
Stories © the contributors, 2006

ISBN 10: 1 904598 83 8
ISBN 13: 978 1 904598 83 1

The publisher acknowledges subsidy from

Scottish
Arts Council

towards the publication of this volume

Typeset in Minion by Hewer Text UK Ltd, Edinburgh
Printed and bound in Great Britain by Thomson Litho, East Kilbride

Contents

Introduction Bernard MacLaverty   vii

With Lamp and Cormorant John Aberdein   1
Housework Sally Beamish   14
Another World Kate Blackadder   24
Shite Lynsey Calderwood   32
In and out the windows Linda Cracknell   37
The Big The Beautiful Nanda Gray Morven Crumlish   46
The Man Who Couldn't Write Morgan Downie   54
Broken Glass Sophie Ellis   62
The Paper Boy Jackie Galley   68
Sea Angel Janice Galloway   73
Escalator Michael Gardiner   94
I Should Have Listened Harder Clio Gray   102
Budding Carole Hamilton   108
Odd Jobbing Nick Houldsworth   115
A Vision Thing Paul Johnson   124
The Menu E. Mae Jones   132
When You Wake Up Peter Likarish   142
A Concrete Dream Sangam MacDuff   148
Brittle James Mavor   158
Strange Fare Brian McCabe   168
Not in the Home Lynda McDonald   178
Coastal Business Duncan McLean   186
What Question? William Sutcliffe   197

Authors' Biographies   205

Introduction
Bernard MacLaverty

It seems self-regarding to agree to be a judge of other people's writing. But this should not be the case because it is something we do all the time, when we think or say, 'I like this writer better than that writer.' We constantly enthuse about certain writers more than others: 'You must read John McGahern. Alistair MacLeod writes monumental stories. If you haven't read Joyce's *Dubliners*. . .' The process is the same when we read anonymously submitted work and think, 'I like that story better than this one.' And so it is that this anthology ends up with a selection of only twenty stories out of the stacks of typescripts submitted for the *Scotsman* & Orange Short Story Awards.

As a writer, I am also a reader. In this case, a very slow and, I hope, careful one. Because there were over 1,500 entries, *The Scotsman* employed filter readers to lighten the burden; otherwise it would have taken me years and I would have been scunnered of short stories for the rest of my life. This means the possibility exists that there was a difficult and obscure masterpiece submitted which did not get through to the final batch judged. Yours, probably. I must stress that another set of readers might come up with a totally different selection. What I would hate to happen is that those *not* selected for the anthology would be discouraged, thinking their work is not good enough.

I don't see much point in trying to define what a short story is. Its form changes all the time. Ali Smith, who wrote *Other Stories and Other Stories*, says, 'If you like, you can disregard traditional structures.' A story is whatever works. But cleverness and craft are involved, as are feeling and form. The great American writer Flannery O'Connor once said, 'I have been writing stories for fifteen years without a definition of one.' She also said another thing which I am conscious of at this very moment (as I write *about* short stories as opposed to writing *a* short story): 'I hope you realise that your asking me to talk about story-writing is just like asking a fish to lecture on swimming.' This is a bit disingenuous. She's more than capable of discussing the craft of story writing – indeed her book of essays *Mystery and Manners* is the first one I would recommend to anyone interested in the form.

There is something wonderful about a work of art that can be read and absorbed in one sitting. You get up with something inside your head that wasn't there when you sat down. Poems on the Underground, for example, is a brilliant idea. Travelling from Heathrow to central London you are faced by a short text for about forty minutes: time to read and ruminate, time to examine and enjoy. The trip becomes also a journey of the mind. The short story is a bit like that – something whole that can be read in one go, something between a poem and a novel.

I remember at school the first short story I paid any attention to was 'The Occurrence at Owl Creek Bridge', Ambrose Bierce's tale set during the American Civil War. It had the thrill of a trick ending – something I'm not so keen on now. But if it leads a schoolboy to a lifetime's reading it can only be a good thing. The tale begins with an execution – a soldier is being hung from a bridge. Somehow the rope breaks and he escapes by swimming through the water. His journey home to his loved ones is described in strange microscopic detail. When he is tantalisingly close to his front gate his neck breaks and we see him swing 'gently from side to side beneath the timbers of Owl Creek Bridge'. What has remained with me over the years is not the twist, but the surreal feeling created by the writing and the preternaturally heightened senses of the escaping soldier.

At about the same time I read less flashy stories written by someone closer to home, a writer from Belfast with a name very like mine: Michael McLaverty. Seamus Heaney praised McLaverty for his 'fidelity to the intimate and local' and I too found his stories had warmth and believability – above all they spoke in familiar language about the community and place I knew. 'To write well,' McLaverty said, 'you must feel deeply and those feelings are the most deep when you are writing about your own homes, your own people, your own backyards. The parochial, the local, if seen and lived deeply enough, is the world. It will jump across its boundaries and become universal.' And on the matter of technique he advised Heaney, 'Don't have the veins bulging in your Biro when you write.'

Years later I went along to hear McLaverty give a talk about the short story. On stage, as he leaned forward and entranced us (he was a great teacher) his enthusiasm was palpable. Tolstoy's 'The Death of Ivan Ilych' was, he said, one of the greatest stories ever written, and when it came to recommending others he was almost inarticulate with enthusiasm. 'You should read Chekhov, Katherine Mansfield and those American women – Flannery O'Connor, Katherine Anne Porter, Eudora Welty.' Everyone in the audience wanted to rush out at the end and start reading stories by these people. And now that time has passed I'm sure he would have also mentioned new names – Raymond Carver, Alice Munro, Grace Paley and, much closer to home, Ali Smith, James Kelman, Alasdair Gray, Alan Spence, Michel Faber, Anne Donovan. The list could and will go on.

After leaving school I read a couple of Hemingway's short stories and thought them slight. There was nothing there; he was bluffing. I don't quite know what happened in the interim but the next time I read these same stories – the Nick Adams ones – I decided they had been written by someone of genius. And they made me want to write. Contrary to what taxi drivers say ('I could write a book – the things that happen in this job') it's not events that make you want to write, it's reading good fiction. I would say that to anyone who is setting out to try and write. Read. And at the same time, look around you. As Morley Callaghan, the Canadian short-story writer, says: 'There is only one trait that marks the writer. He is always watching. It's a kind of trick of the mind and he is born with it.' Having observed, write it down.

Recently I was given a small present, a hardbound pocket-sized Moleskine notebook held closed with a black elastic band. At the back, the end papers make an expandable paper wallet for keepsakes. The advertising tells us that this type of notebook has been used by the likes of Hemingway, Van Gogh and Picasso. What a romantic sell. But it's how a writer might indeed begin, with jottings in a notebook – things they've noticed, striking images they've come across, fragments of speech overheard. 'Everybody speaks an entirely different language' Frank O'Connor once noted, adding, 'If I use the right phrase and the reader hears the phrase in his head, he sees the individual.' That's the act of capturing things in words and if done often enough it will become a habit – what Flannery O'Connor refers to as 'the habit of art'.

For this anthology, *The Scotsman* has also commissioned three stories from established writers. I am unsure about asking writers, established or otherwise, to address a theme – in this case 'work' – even if the aim is the well-intentioned one of addressing an aspect of life much fiction too often ignores. Personally, I think the short story is such a fragile and fleeting beast that to put any limitations on the way it gets born is a hindrance. But having said that, I do think many of the entries handled the theme of work well, as did the commissioned stories.

Brian McCabe's 'Strange Fare' seems to be about an enigmatic man who hails an Edinburgh taxi. I loved the way the story opened with the strange fare 'holding an arm out as if he meant to grab hold of the wing-mirror rather than just hail the taxi'. But gradually, imperceptibly, the story becomes the taxi driver's. 'Coastal Business', Duncan McLean's brilliant story, will make you laugh. The work in question here involves the peddling of boiled sweets and trifles. A lot of the comedy comes from the juxtaposition of modern technology and the homespun. But the story is not simply about confectionery – there is darkness and desperation there too. Janice Galloway's 'Sea Angel' is a visceral and ultimately moving story that begins on an island in eighteenth-century Italy. She has the knack of imagining another age into existence before our eyes, through startlingly vivid descriptions: 'her face went stiff as a sail', 'there was a long moment with only the sounds of gulls in it', 'on the water was a paper boat, turning on its side like a dying fish.' Her confidence and skill as a writer is also apparent in the direct compactness of statements such as 'he ran a dog cart between the gutting tables and the market till the dog died of dropsy and his mother died of despair'.

The entries to the competition impressed me with their range of voices and variety of styles. I liked the unusual device of a monologue addressed to a factory in the historical story 'In and Out the Windows'. A woman suffragette sits waiting for her husband to end his shift and goes over in her mind how she has come to this point in her life. I also admired the directness of naming a story 'Shite' and the energy of its Scots language. 'Budding' vividly evokes a relentless but normal day's work on a Scottish farm – its endlessness, its filth. Told from a woman's point of view, the day involves the work of the kitchen as well – setting the table, baking, making broth, feeding the dog. This is powerful writing which leaves the reader almost at the point of exhaustion.

'With Lamp and Cormorant' is also set in Scotland, but this time on the boats, with their 'pervasive niff of fish and diesel'. Full of nicknames, jargon and sea-speech, the tale centres around a love story. In 'Housework', a deserted wife is taught how to clean her house by her best friend. The middle-aged female voice is perfect: sad, ironic, shocked and self-deprecating. This story is an example of what Willa Cather used to say 'is felt upon the page without being specifically named there'.

And then there are fictions set outside Scotland. 'Escalator' is a story full of wit about a businessman and his pregnant wife discussing the future of their child. Set in Tokyo, the story highlights the dystopia of the city's conformity, consumerism and capitalism – a world which is a carapace for the spirit.

'I Should Have Listened Harder' is a bleak and powerful story set in the lead mines of Siberia. The first sentence establishes the tone: 'It's night at Nertchinsk and here we sleep three deep to keep ourselves warm.' The story has the ring of authenticity, naming as it does the three different winds that blow across Lake Baikal. The people endure Job-like suffering of Biblical proportions, right down to the boils. The writer's gaze is unflinching. There is no redemption except perhaps love – a man finds himself loving a young boy as if he was his son. 'And against all the odds, we were happy.' But things cannot remain that way.

Three stories are set in the USA. 'A Concrete Dream' looks at the end of a man's working life as a road mender. The work he and his squad do is accurately described using striking, clinical imagery: 'Three weeks of surgery and the repairs were finally finished. All they had left were the seals, like butterfly stitches round new grafts.' 'The Menu' is set in Alaska in the 1940s and has a brilliant opening scene in which so much information is adroitly and movingly conveyed. An army doctor examines and fails an underage boy from enlisting, sending him instead to the railroads in Alaska where he will be part of the war effort. 'The Big the Beautiful Nanda Gray' I liked best of the American-set stories. It is a tale of a life lived at full throttle on stage – and off. There's a superb scene when the main character sings out the back of an empty train carriage to the disappearing landscape. You'll catch other epiphanies, large or small, in many of the stories in this collection.

Why do so many people want to write fiction? I see it as an utterly serious play activity left over from childhood. The writer is trying to get to grips with the world by arranging it, or disarranging it.

When I was young I used to like playing farms – setting out the toy animals, placing ducks on the pond (a round mirror taken from an old face-powder compact of my mother's) and moving the farmer and his wife; one day they'd be face to face, the next day standing with their with their backs to each other. I gave a spoken commentary as I moved the figures and animals (along with mouth-made sound effects) around the landscape. Making up worlds. I'm still doing it.

Why? The wonderful American short story writer, Raymond Carver, answers the question well. 'Writing doesn't have to do anything. It just has to be there for the fierce pleasure we take in doing it, and the different kind of pleasure that's taken in reading something that's durable and made to last, as well as beautiful in and of itself.'

Isn't that enough for anybody?

With Lamp and Cormorant
John Aberdein

Ullapool was at whisky, psalms, TV.

The day before work started there was little to do but feast on baby illegal scallops fried in Anchor, and stare up at the crazed caravan ceiling. A pipe of dark Condor, with a sprinkle of dust sent up from London, assisted.

Through a smog of defective rings he sensed direction, and indirection. Wild surgeons shunted to sow rice. Novel professors deployed to collate nightsoil. A Daoist present, with lamp and cormorant, in a shoogly punt. Julia—

He slammed the caravan door and went out on the icy shingle.

*

Next day, being Monday, Jeems picked up his *poste restante*, rammed it in his hip pocket and was out on the pier sharp and early. A slack of local men knotted, unknotted, around him. It was the usual *Aye, aye, piss of a day, see Harold's snubbed him on Vietnam, heard a forecast?* plus a zany or two. Anything to delay.

- Aye, aye, Bart.
- Esteemed Jeems, how's the middle stump?
- Still bowling a maiden over.
- Gink!

To delay opening it—

By ten o'clock saloons and minivans began to arrive from the East Coast. Launches congregated at the pier steps, to take mates rubbing their hands and coughing engineers out to the deep moorings, where painted wood, steel and varnished vessels pointed at the wind and swung. Drifters, ringers, trawlers, purse.

Jeems picked out a gem for Julia. Being a scientist, she always wanted clarity, possibly especially now. He gawked at the posher moorings.

Only yachts, glass, are white.

Skippers in barked cotton ganseys and black shoes disappeared, straight up to the agent's office. Quick girn with Sandy Craw, a joke with Jessie May.

Only yachts, glass, are white.

Whatever a *koan* was, that was probably one.

Four old grizzlers stomped the pier, looking for men.

They chose Oddy, they chose Roy Across The Water, guys that could mend a net and steer. The Venerable Clachy was in monologue, with others. Boats were dumping moorings, and cutting for the pier.

Clachy glowered at Bart, privileged apprentice hippy. Bart lived, not alone, in a furniture van in the Caley car park, ran it on red diesel. Redundant carpets made Eastern hangings.

– Good scalpin an Ah'd mebbe look near ye— said the Venerable.

– I feel for you, said Bart.

Clachy stepped over to Yella Welly.

– They say ye did no so bad aboard *Primrose.*

– No too hellish altogether, said Jeems.

They'd paid him only half a share.

– Ah'm short a man. Davy's got his ulcer again.

– Uh. Aye. Full share—?

– Catch her rope then, mannie, dinna stand aboot!

Green *Fidelity* was gliding in, loops of terylene tossed up. Jeems hauled round the bollard, a couple of hitches, as she churned in reverse. In slid her pair boat, red *Roselea*, next berth along. Time for oil and water, diesel, sacks of veg and mince in boxes.

– Say, before it slips me, said Bart, here's that book of yours, *Low Cost Chassis Maintenance*, I got it filthy you'll be glad.

– Cool. Havena seen you in yonks.

– Need the dough, man, big-time, said Bart.

The March wind freshened from the nor-wast as they heeled around the shingle spit, abandoned the neatness of Ullapool, and headed out Loch Broom. Jeems squirmed into the timber wheelhouse for the first watch with Clachy.

Halfways butted across the Minch, seas severing, *Fidelity* bucking, Jeems felt rough. The day was ripping grey from itself. Palms braced on opposed panelling, his bum, with Julia's missive, wedged against the door. His sole job was to check astern for *Roselea* and the other ringers, you'd catch no oily fishies on your tod. He craned around.

Head burying and answering, *Roselea* was there, Bart aboard her.

The radar warmed, soft emerald figuration sweeping the night for the coast of Lewis, and Jeems came off watch and went below. Half-doubled in the spare bunk, minding fine maidenhair, when the dank pillow, salt quilt, pervasive niff of fish and diesel, brought him up on deck again. Bellied over the rumpled ring-net, he retched his no lunch into the wake.

– Sma wattir, Jeems.

Jock Patience, mate, dropping the wheelhouse window on its strop.

Sma wattir.

After a tea of washed-out tatties and pale speldings, *Ta, Chic,* sluiced with a mug of Typhoo, they found themselves hunting amongst Lewis's northern lochs, Seaforth, Brollum, Lemreway and the like, the Venerable following his muckle nose, Jock alert for *smudge-smudge* on the echo-sounder, Dod the Driver checking the

Gardner, cookie hashing the reject titbits. Sixmaniac with a swift one (fag) behind the mizzen. Hunched in the bow, threading the thoughts of a guy with frozen paws, Jeems clutched the Aldis. Posted to gleam on sudden skerry, follow-spot a fleeing herring—
Pas une saucisse.

They let *Roselea* precede them into Rodel, their last chance in a loch before the waste and confusion of the Sound of Harris. Often the herring would choose to be there, because of plankton, shelter, whatever, a lucky loch. *Roselea*'s red light went up—
– Ringin!
An hour later they had thirty cran, neither here nor there. *Roselea* naturally took them aboard, six long scoops of her butterfly brailer.
– Catch you later, shouted Bart, they hadn't been hauling side-by-side.

There was nothing for it but the Sound of Harris.
On passage, they were allowed down the engine-room, for a shit or a heat.
Nothing for it but Julia's letter.
He hoisted up his oilskin smock.
The Gardner was clattering away.
Inside the package there was a folded sheet and a second envelope.
Dear Jeems, nothing much in the ecstasy line, it was a *Dear Jeems* letter.
Dear Jeems,
Yes, it's confirmed, I am pregnant, marvellous! I went to the doc yesterday and she confirmed. Due at the start of November, but I don't know. I don't feel like a mother, but I do feel different. Thank Evolution for David Steel! I'm going to a planning clinic on Tuesday to have a chat.
Don't open the next envelope till you've had a chance to digest. Do you fancy being a dad? It's not you, is it? Kisses, Julia.

*

They were tacking, rev up, rev down, reverse, amongst the one-sheep continents and sunken *bo*'s of the Sound of Harris—

Jesus, Julia!

– Shine on the rockie, bawled Clachy.

– Whatna rockie? yelled Jeems.

– The lang rockie!

– Nae lang rockie here!

– Well whaur in the name are we—?

That's where it all begins.

Be clear. Trees and savannah, that's for the birds.

By four in the morning, in poor vis, they had rung thrice for a few horse mackerel.

The sea's where it all begins.

Julia!

– Jeems, said Bart, a time they were shoulder-to-shoulder, hauling empty black glisten. Jeems, you struggling, man?

– Need to talk. Later—

– Stay with it.

Roselea steamed to Skye to land at Uig.

Fidelity went to Maddy to lie.

*

Tuesday came in as they lay at the empty pier. Clachy had said a grace. The men were sitting round, unshaven, half an inch of tea in the mug. Now Clachy passed an ample hand across his face, consecrating boredom.

At last seaboots on the deck above, and Jock the mate came down and joined them.

– *Roselea*, fiver a cran.

– Home market? said Clachy.

– Aye. But *Gratitude* got klondyked tae the Poles for three.

– Oot Gdansk way, aye, they fairly snap their *sledz w smietanie*, said Clachy. Ye'll no ken what that is, lad? *Herrings in cream.*

Jeems just looked at him.

Rat-tat, rat-tat-tat on the cabin skylight. Jeems got on deck to see hail jiggling on glass like angel shot. He hiked out Julia's package, might as well. Inside her second envelope there was a card with a cartoon. A stork, all pelican, with snug slung nappy.

> *Jeems!*
>
> ?
>
> *Hugs, Julia*

He dug out a pen, the better to express, under this guise of weather, aegis of scenery. The last of the hailstones pinged the card.

> *Hail, that timpanist o tents, timber, tin,*
> *Tattoos ma hert but ~~can it~~ ^it canna^ get in—*

It canna fitted the rhythm better.
– Up the road, Yella? said Sixmaniac.
Disturbing.
– Deaf or what?
– I'm gone, said Jeems. Can ye haud on, something I gotta read?
For there was a third.

Lochmaddy Hotel, summer haunt of rocket trackers, trout men, the odd tandem, had winter fire in its grate, two dud coals and a flat peat.
– Drink, Yella? said Sixmaniac.
– Treble, three pints.
– Kind o whisky?
– Hundred Pipers.
– We could chance the one.
– Heavy, then, said Jeems. It's okay, I've heard what the skipper's like.

– Sixty noo, an just remairried.

– Hea-vy.

– Erse on him like a maul hemmir.

– Cheers.

– Aye, so ye can count, said Sixmaniac to the barman, as he got his change. That is five fingers plus a thumb ye're seein.

– An accident I take it, said the barman.

– Genetic, said Sixmaniac. Inbreedin.

The barman put on the test card on TV.

Jeems, I know you're trying to save up, to save us, whoever us is, US, but it's not that simple

  O yes, however complex, we are still simple—

    there's somebody else

  Millions of the muckers—

    who's very nice

  Somebody Else always is—

    and I think you know, I know you know, him

  Whoopee—!

– Get me a dram if ye've nothin tae say, said Six.

    so I hope it won't be too big a shock

– What—what was that?

– Dram.

– Still giving Julia one? said Jeems.

– Who's effin Julia?

– Good question. Pint an a nip for ma pal, barman.

He hadn't read the rest. Maybe he was just caught in her creel, part of her prawn research.

– Why did ye tear thon letter up? said Six.

    and don't be sad, for my sake.

– Because. A letter shouldna be *a letter*. No when ye're at sea.

– Got ye. Bird dropped ye, is it?

– Drink your beer.

– Worse things happen at sea. Seen ma Dad?

– Cook on the *Roselea*?

– Yep. Huntington's. Gets the shakes worse every year. Good for spreadin loaf, murder for pourin tea, ma ain Dad. Fisher inbreedin, like I said, death sentence.

– Really?

– Death sentence. Nane of them live past fifty.

It's probably Bart, he thought.

– An it's handed-doon in the male line. I winna ken till I'm thirty-five.

Bastardin Bart.

– Terrible. But she's that academic, ken, she needs real connection, Julia—

– Shame. Like I says, ma Da's real trammelled wi these shakes—

They had another, and took a wander.

That night, *Roselea* didn't return. She teamed with *Gratitude*, while *Fidelity* steamed south to pair with *Sapphire*.

He's avoiding me, thought Jeems.

They worked Wiay under a scud of cloud, a few small rings. *Sapphire* went off to Mallaig with fifty cran.

Fidelity poked up into the lee of empty land.

– So if she's this great marine biologist, why's she wastin her time in London? said Six.

– Boys, get your anchor! bawled Clachy.

Sixmaniac and Jeems ran forrard to unlash.

– Interviews, said Jeems.

– Fancy.

– Loads o interviews. Nae lyin at our buggerin anchor in this forsaken hole, are we?

– Lie aa day, as like as no. Clachy's on til us.

*

Fidelity mended net in the morning, Jeems scrubbed around, getting stray scales off the mast and casing. They worked back up the coast during the afternoon, looking for signs. They saw a gannet or two plunging off Barra, a whale sendin a whiff into the cold air off North Uist. As they crossed south of the Shiants, they had their tea.

– Full o rats, said Jock Patience, the Shiants. Full o them.

– Where's *Roselea*? said Jeems.

– Tryin up Loch Ewe wi *Gratitude*. We're meetin *Sapphire* north o Raasay, then it's Shieldaig. She only got fishmeal in Mallaig, waited half the day.

– We've had the best o the winter, said Dod.

– Aye, said the mate, mebbe so. No wantin the rest o yir mince, Yella, heave it ower here. Enough tae feed a bloomin convoy.

In the shallows of Shieldaig Wednesday night they got but a scalping of ware and stones, and six small skate. Chic fried them up, they ate the wings.

– Convoys, said the mate. I mind we were on destroyers ae night, at the heicht o the U-boats, and boy, were we hard on the auld zigzag! Weil when we swang the wheel, here's this white liner, pure white liner, port-holes glintin, lichts ableeze—

– Typical, said Jeems. Idle rich.

– Na, she had a big swarmin net doon her side, said Jock. Tourin aboot on her lonesome, can ye imagine? Huntin here an haltin there—

– Daft— said Dod.

– No as daft as us an the Germans. She was neutral, ye see, Swedish. Last ditch hope for men on rafts, them black wi ile and gey sair frozent.

– Tell me, said Clachy, tell me what ye young lads get up til?

They were steaming up north on Thursday afternoon, past Priest, heading for Stoer. The wind had faired away, there was still a swell.

– The usual, said Jeems.

– No in ma day, said the skipper. Ah think ye ken Ah like til preach.

– Preach?

– Well Ah do preach, every Sunday night, back in Avoch. At the street corner, til aacomers or nobody.

– How can ye preach tae nobody?

– God's work, boy, God's work. Life's no aa drinkin an whurin.

– Apparently, said Jeems.

– An will ye tell me true? said the Venerable.

– Mebbe.

– Dae ye ever snuff—?

– What?

– Thae cannibals' raisins.

*

The four boats rendezvoused at last in Eddrachillis Bay. They purled around, prowling for marks, keeping their distance as they rose and fell.

The herring stayed deep till it got dark anyway. The men said they were afraid of light. Julia said the better theory was they were just following plankton.

They were standing by the stack of ring-net. A big steel boat, the *Vanquish*, came between them and the sun.

– Pursers, said Six. Bloody millions o cran. They'll kill wir fishin.

The *Vanquish* throttled for deeper water.

– Try the wire, lads, give it a go, said Jock, his head out the back of the wheelhouse. A smudgie here, I'm seein on the sounder—

Six began to unwind, from a fish-box end, first a plumb-bob, then yard upon yard of piano wire.

It plopped, disappeared, went deep.

– Feel a haud o this.

Jeems put his palm to the thrum of the wire. It was – *bip* — bip-bip – *bipbipbip* — bip – urgent, imperfect as all Morse code.

Sun scarce dipped below the horizon, *Fidelity*'s light went up.

– Ringin lads, ready tae ring, said Jock Patience.

Sixmaniac spat on the winkie and passed it to Jeems.

– Your turn. Mak it good.

Jeems held the polythene buoy and flashing wooden winkie in two hands, waiting for Clachy's command.

– Chuck awa!

He did, and Six helped with the first few fathom of heavy net. It dragged the rest of the ring-net sawing over the stern, in a great sinking wall of meshing.

Wonder who'll pick our end up, thought Jeems.

Dark *Sapphire* and varnished *Gratitude* were further off, so red *Roselea* came curving towards the winkie. Jeems could make out the straggly locks of the guy with the boathook.

A splash and Bart drew the winkie aboard, still flashing as it was passed aft.

In half an hour they had towed, closed, clashed their bows together, let four of the second crew come leap aboard, and ranged a row of ring-net men, like ten skilful daffodils along green *Fidelity*, to tackle the corks, the wide, the dripping small mesh. With moon coming up, the net was down.

Roselea, with a rope to *Fidelity*'s bitts, towed her abeam, off the invisible desperadoes in the bag.

– What the – bejesus – is going on? Bart—? gasped Jeems.

– She's full of fish.

– Not the net, said Jeems, bracing between mast and scuppers, and gripped on to the straining cork-rope. Our beloved—

– Oddy? Roy—?

– Julia.

– Thought she was off.

– Supposed to be coming back – staying with me – when I rent a place.

– Think not. *Sarawak,* I think she said.

– Gerraway, man. *Sarawak*—!

– What Julia said, said Bart. Her research here's finished. It's tiger prawns.

– Excuse me?

– Yeah it's bad. They're going to muck up the coastal mangroves for tiger prawns.

– She can't, she's totally pregnant for chrissake!

– You jest?

– Quit gassin like lassies, said Dod.

– Backs intil it, lads, said Jock.

– I don't believe you.

– Ditto.

– I do not believe you.

Jeems' corks went down like iron.

Bubbles frissoned the surface. The trapped herring were releasing bladder-air: *en masse* now they would plummet, lump and burst it. Only with a winch running hot, and every heave of swell's advantage, could such a net be budged, towards the zone of light and profit.

Pale intimations swirled, way down beneath them.

They bent and heaved.

A score boasted in the centre, a hundred bulged at the wide.

They hauled, and better hauled—

Thousands of fish appeared, to thrash.

And cracked their collective back.

Flaying, from the bluegreen flanks, flew irises of sharp confetti.

Jeems absorbed the mad, bright bounty. Gulls gathered for fat at the silver table.

Roselea relinquished her yoke, came alongside, and the net was slung between them.

Waiting to load, a few of the guys lit up, old geezers with their lidded pipes. Six reached under his smock, and offered Bart—
– Christ, Da! Watch oot—!
His frail Da, unsteady night had nigh cowped into the rich seething.

– Poor gink, said Bart quietly, his puff travelling sideways on the breeze.
Outside the scope of the net, a moon glinted on belly-up fish the snakeneck darkish birds were claiming.
– Sorry? said Jeems. He had a *koan* coming.
– Poor *gink.*
– Who?
– Not sure. Kid I suppose.
– Yeah.

They were brailing herring, winch groaning, five thousand a lift.
– One thing though, said Bart.
– What? He had received, of the *koan,* only a phrase.
– How do you tell the difference, said Bart, between a shag—
Grizzled, glad, unsteady men stood round them, counting.
– And a cormorant—?
– Don't push it, said Jeems.
– You don't usually smoke after a cormorant.

*

He was walking up the pier with his share. The *koan* was still drafting itself.
One for Julia.
Something something – *the mind swims free*
Up through the unembraceable fish of the sea.

Housework
Sally Beamish

I am getting to know about dirt. There is the kind that rests, solid, in a hammock of cobweb. Twenty years of particles like a crumbly charcoal eiderdown.

There is the spotty kind that clings to walls. Splashed and showered there by passing dogs and children. A textured build-up of different-sized dots, variegated browns, greys, a few pinpricks of black. Approach them with a wet sponge and they smear and spread into tracks of mid-brown.

There is the sticky kind on top of white kitchen appliances. Clinging to the fridge and washing machine. You try a damp cloth and it persists, greasy and hard. But return ten minutes later and take it by surprise, and it comes away, leaving the calm, white, shiny surface, throwing patches of unaccustomed light onto the ceiling above.

And then there are the fingerprints. Years of different sizes, on door frames, around light switches. These are the stubbornest of all.

Today is Monday, and Sue's taxi has just disappeared round the corner. I turn from the window to the bucket of soapy water she carried upstairs before she left. To start me off.

'Leave me be,' say the prints of my eldest child on his bedroom door. 'Once I was two years old, don't rub me out; remember, remember . . .'

The room crowds in on me, and I know I am defeated already.

I look at my own hands and see something new. The sides of my forefingers are lined and ingrained with black. The skin is hard and cracked. The nails uneven. Have they always been like this? Manicure – something other women have time for. And how is it that those manicured women are the ones who also clean their houses?

I've spent twenty years dreading visitors. But even then, I hadn't realised the extent of the neglect. I am learning things. That other people clean not only floors, but skirting boards too. Really. That they clean not only the inside of the loo, but also the outside. That you have to dust the Hoover. If I list the tasks that most people take in their stride, I am overwhelmed. How have I brought up four sons without knowing what most people seem to know instinctively? That every inch of the house is supposed to be regularly serviced.

Why have I only realised this now?

Sue has been to stay. My oldest friend, who never criticises me, to whom I can tell anything, anything at all. She came because Pete left. She came all the way from New Zealand, and put the kettle on. While she was waiting, she took a cloth and cleaned a small area of the kitchen tiles. She was smiling, gently rubbing, head on one side, as if she loved my tiles. We stood and looked at the shining patch together. 'I was dying to do that,' she whispered, not blaming me, not meaning anything by it.

I didn't want her to leave. The empty days stretched ahead. What does a middle-aged art teacher do in the school holidays, when she no longer has a husband, and her children are gone?

I know what I do, Sue said (although, of course, she does have a husband, and her children remain around her, because they want to). Sue said, I clean. It's such a great feeling.

Give it a week, she said. You'll see.

Every day of her stay she cleaned something. I felt it was hopeless. The more she did, the more I saw there was to do.

Don't despair, she said as she scrubbed. This is the first rule.

Don't look past the next job. Just one tiny corner, on a vulnerable day. Don't set yourself something you can't achieve.

Today I am low. I look in my son's grimy mirror; my sagging face gazes back. Today, being low, I will simply clean the mirror.

Sue had never been here before. For thirty years we have talked every week on the phone, and I miss her so much it aches. Once we met at Heathrow for lunch – she was on her way to visit her parents in Scotland. She always said she would come again, when she had more time. But somehow it never happened.

I have a plant – a grape ivy. It was a present she gave me when we left school. It is, I realise with a shock, thirty-two years old. It is a little bit of her, and I look after it. I can't count the number of times I've repotted it. A few years ago I had to put a trellis on the ceiling to accommodate the spreading dark-green tendrils, and now it sits in a massive tub, obscuring the dining-room window, harbouring little bugs that drop from time to time. Pete hated it. My mother asked me how I could clean, with that thing all over the walls. Well, we don't really use that room, I said.

Tuesday
Today I'm a little brighter. Today I'll clean out a drawer. One drawer, in the bedroom, and I choose it carefully. It's a very small drawer, in a very small wooden chest, purchased from IKEA in a half-forgotten attempt at reform. A chest to organise my life; a small price to pay at six pounds. I open it slowly, and it sticks. I shake it, prise it out. It is full to the brim.

The contents of a small drawer:
one earring
a plastic hospital bracelet for a new baby
some holiday photos
a Peter Rabbit book

picture hooks
four pairs of nail clippers
several packets of spare buttons
Other things. I don't even know what they are. Bits of metal,
bits of paper. A press cutting with a tiny black and white photo
of . . . oh, someone.

I arrange the items on the bed, and pick up the tiny plastic baby-tag. Which baby, though? The date is worn away, and there is no Christian name. An unnamed joy, mine, his, ours; celebrated then, and now as much part of our lives as our own skins. That baby is contained in a young man several inches taller than I am. Do I need his (or is it his brother's?) plastic tag? And yet – I can't throw it out. Can I?

The photos. A holiday we didn't enjoy. Would it leave jagged holes, to throw away a bad memory?

Could the book be a first edition? It could, but half of it is missing. I lift it and my hand hovers over the gaping black bin bag on the floor. Did I remember to read them Peter Rabbit?

I should keep the picture hooks. Somewhere, there is a pile of pictures. My paintings from college. I was going to make frames . . .

The bits and pieces from the bottom of the drawer are covered in something sticky. I should wash them.

All the buttons belong to garments I no longer wear. Monsoon, Laura Ashley . . . I have never, as far as I can remember, sewn on a button. And yet, here are all these neat packages, stashed away for a woman who might, one day, mend things.

The press cutting. Why have I kept it? I have accused Pete of deception, of duplicity. But here, in a forgotten drawer, is a picture of someone I loved.

Do I keep things because I like them, or because I might need them? Why is it so frightening to put something in the bin? I put the cutting in my apron pocket to deal with later.

My sons have their own homes now. They are all, surprisingly, very tidy.

Did they mind the mess? They never said.

Wednesday

Why is it only other people who have beautiful homes? I call them the Good Housekeepers. They don't give away their secrets, but they have the kind of homes where you can wander through the master bedroom and into the en suite during a party, and it is perfect; fragrant, tranquil.

I do have one friend who is not a Good Housekeeper. Abigail. She's an actress, and her house is a tip. She comes round for coffee, and sits cross-legged on my sofa, flicking ash onto the floor. You know, I love coming here, she says. It's the only house that looks worse than mine . . . still, I'm an artist. A Bohemian.

I've never told her it's art I teach. She's never asked.

A good day today. I tackle the high shelf in the laundry room. Climbing onto a stool. I clutch the shelf with my fingertips and peer over the edge. Softened and smudged with a layer of light grey dust, I make out the shapes of . . .

the contents of an inaccessible shelf:
light bulbs (some are used, some new – but which?)
empty light-bulb boxes
biscuit tins
shoe-cleaning equipment – never used
A basket of craft accessories for decorating picture frames (the
names – ah, the names, that was what inspired me – Antique
Brass, Cracked French Provincial. A roll of gold leaf. White
wood stain.)
Dust.
Dust.

Thursday

I am – happy. I have cleaned the hall. The first thing you see when you come in. I went out to the shops, just so I could come back. It's the first time I've been out since Pete left. I step into my house, and it welcomes me. Some of it is clean now. I have discovered for myself the greatest secret of the Good Housekeepers. The one Sue told me, and I didn't believe.

Housework makes you happy.

I am tired. I sit at the computer, nursing a cup of tea. I've heard that you should clean out your computer, too. The desktop is solid with icons.

Should I delete my old mail? I open the file. It goes back eight years. The very first mail on the list is from Simon. 1998. I bumped into him at Waterloo Station. My art teacher at school. We all loved him. He was . . . something different. He asked us to call him by his first name. The others did; they giggled as they said it. I never could. That day in 1998, in the midst of the rush-hour mayhem, I was suddenly fourteen again – embarrassed to be talking to him as an equal. I still couldn't say his name; in fact I couldn't think of anything at all to say, so I told him we just got a computer, and e-mail. He asked for the address, and when I got home, there it was – my first message. Welcome to the e-world, it says. I never answered it. I never deleted it either.

In my apron pocket I find a bit of crumpled paper. It's the press cutting. I open it out; it's about an exhibition. Not far from us, but I never went. Simon. I say the name out loud.

Friday
The kitchen. I've finished the tiles, and I am dazzled. I begin to empty the cupboards. At the back of one, there is a large Tupperware box, containing:

the top layer of our wedding cake

I remember my mother saying she'd put it somewhere safe when we were on our honeymoon. For the christening of the first baby.

But we never got round to having the boys christened. I lift the cake out; it's heavy, dry, solid. The icing is greyish, and the sugar flowers have lost their colour (they were yellow). There is a sweet, musty smell. I catch a glimpse of my reflection in the dusty window, dishevelled, grubby, greying at the temples.

I've thrown away photos. Even Sue was a little shocked when I told her on the phone, and she is a fully paid-up Good House-keeper. (Not your wedd . . . she began, then stopped.) I looked at all the photos, and if they made me feel bad, they went in the bin. Most of them have gone. After I'd done it, I buried my face in my hands, and wept.

I still have the press cutting though, in my pocket. I have to decide what to do with it.

Once I took my class to a lecture of Simon's. Some of them had heard of him. We sat near the back, and I watched his familiar features move – I didn't take anything in, really. Then he saw me. At the end of the lecture he looked over and smiled. People were crowding up to him, but he still looked at me. I waved my hand and left quickly. I didn't want to speak to him. I didn't want to tell him I had never had an exhibition; that I don't even paint any more. That I've been an art teacher in a secondary school for twenty-five years, passing on his wisdom. I think of him often as I teach, and his phrases come back to me. Little jokes, witticisms. The things he said that made me feel I could do anything, that the sky was the limit. 'You're good,' he would say. 'You know that, don't you?' Mind you, he could teach anyone to draw. 'You're not looking. Learn to look. Trace what you see. Forget it's a face; draw a map. Look. Look.'

I have learnt to look. At my house.

Things that need cleaning (I didn't know – no one told me): *the inside of windows (window-cleaners do the outside; I thought that was it)*

that ledge half-way up the window
the leaves of house-plants
curtains

I think curtains have to be dry-cleaned. Chair covers are meant to be, but I've put them in the machine. If they shrink, I'll get new ones.

Items found under the covers of the three-piece suite:
a mouse, quite dead, and flat, like one of those dried ducks in a
Chinese restaurant
a raw potato, with roots
Pete's watch (He lost it two years ago. He got very agitated.
Looking back on it, I realise it was probably a present from her.)

How do you clean a marriage? Maybe some marriages are dry-clean only. You wear them till they get too dirty, then they hang in the wardrobe because you don't have the time or the money to take them to the cleaners. Best to choose an easy-care marriage. Even then I expect you should really dust it down regularly, keep it smelling fresh.

Pete has chosen another relationship with a 'delicate' label, I think. She's young – the same age I was when I met him. Starting again with a new garment. He met her at the school sixth-form art display. I wanted him to come; I wanted him to show an interest. He never saw the point of art. At first he stood around looking awkward. I could tell he was longing for a cigarette. Then later I saw her chatting to him. I felt immensely grateful.

Saturday
I woke at five this morning. Today is the day for the dining room. It used to be my favourite room. Sue's ivy. Simon's painting. The antique corner cupboard, with the crockery. I never liked the cupboard, but the dinner set I adore. You can't see it now, because of the ivy. I fetch some secateurs, begin gently cutting. I free the

door of the cupboard, open it, and take out one of the plates. I rub away the dust, and the pattern reveals itself. Little red flowers, with dark green leaves. A cream background.

Once, about fifteen years ago, I suggested Pete invite his boss to dinner. Really? he said, are you sure? Why not, I answered, other people have friends to dinner. Why not us?

Pete rang me from work before he left, to check. I was hysterical with panic. I had seen the house for what it was, and knew that ten years of dirt cannot be removed in a few hours. Let alone with a meal to cook as well. Shall we go out? he suggested, and I loved him for it. I loved him for never saying, I told you so, for never, ever, complaining about the mess. For never complaining about anything. After that neither of us ever suggested inviting people.

I have cleaned Simon's painting. I bought it years ago. Pete was furious. If you're going to spend money on useless things like that, he said, I can have that golfing holiday. He did.

When Sue saw the painting, she smiled. One of Simon's! she said. You know, we were all so jealous. He's a genius, I murmured. She laughed – No, jealous of you! We all had such a crush – and it was only you he ever took notice of. Well, you were the best, of course – but it was more than that.

I was too surprised to answer.

Simon didn't stay in teaching long. It was just a stop-gap after university. Then the world claimed him, and we watched.

Sunday
I have found my art things, in the cupboard under the stairs. The paints are covered in sticky dust. I wash them, dry them, and lay them out on the dining-room table. The table has nothing on it, perhaps for the first time since we bought it, and is ready to receive a neat row of acrylic paint pots. I prise one open, and the paint is still good. A brilliant yellow, full of possibilities. I arrange the brushes. There are several unused canvases, and an easel.

I have cut away the ivy from the dining-room window and the

morning sun is streaming in. I set up the easel. The light is catching the shiny leaves, and dappling the canvas.

Look. Look.

I started the day by throwing the press cutting in the bin. I've made a cup of coffee. (I have discovered that kettles need cleaning). I take my coffee to the computer. The New Zealand holiday people have got back to me, and I feel a flutter of excitement.

The file of old mails is almost empty now. I'm going to delete Simon's email.

After I've answered it.

Another World
Kate Blackadder

The loch is holding the mountain upside down.

Liam can see it below the surface of the water on the far shore as he steps into the boat. Alarm sweeps over him at the thought of rowing into its rocky slopes and although he knows that this image, this mirage, will disappear if he gets closer, that's alarming too. He never saw a mirage himself, but he heard about them from some of the guys who saw green places and wells and palm trees vanish between blinks. Now, hundreds of miles away from the desert, his is a world where mountains can vanish.

The rope is heavier than he expected and the oars feel the way he remembers them as a small boy, too big for his hands and full of splinters. Pulling one is difficult, two almost impossible. All he's doing is moving round in pathetic dizzy-making circles. He rests the oars and sits back. It isn't a race. He isn't letting anyone down. Just Liam Fraser. He takes a deep breath, shuddering as he lets it out.

He wanted to come along to the jetty by himself. Anna followed on, and now she's walking along the bank looking out over the water. She'll be able to see the looking-glass mountain too, see him go right through it. What might he find in the looking-glass world on the other side? A world of nightmares? Of all his demons coming after him at once? Of sleeplessness, and the memories he doesn't want to be memories any more going round and round in his thick head? Or maybe he'd find a world of possibilities, when he'd be a child again, his life before him. Is that the world he would choose, if there was a choice?

He looks over at his sister. Anna waves but he doesn't want to let go of the oars and hopes she'll see him lifting up his chin in returned greeting and in – false – acknowledgement that he's doing fine.

As he dips the oars in the water again the rhythm of the strokes comes back to him, briefly recapturing the joy he used to have, not just in his strength and skill, but in those early summer mornings long ago before anyone else was awake, when he would slip down to the loch, jump into the boat, row the mile down to the village and back, always trying to beat his own record. On those mornings he was Christopher Columbus discovering the New World; he was Adam in the Garden (to be Eden there must have been a loch with a slate-blue mountain on one side, and a stony beach on the other, with trees dipping their toes in the water, and startled birds flying out of ferny undergrowth); no – on those mornings he was God himself at the dawn of creation.

Now, although in his head he's gliding through the water, his palms feel burning hot and rough and his arms and legs jerk as if strings are attached. Should he try to reach the looking-glass mountain or go back to Anna, waiting with his jacket and his lunch, and wearing that sympathetic face?

She's being a real star, his little sister, but he wants to shout into that face. He doesn't deserve her sympathy, doesn't want to be grateful to her for leaving her husband and children to spend a week of her summer holidays with him. He doesn't want sympathy from her or anybody else, and the more he backs away from it the more she treats him the way she treats her two-year-old when he has a tantrum, with a hug and cajoling words.

Being a parent has softened her, the feisty sister he scrapped with through childhood. She is two years younger than him but she always punched above her weight. In those days, Anna would argue with a table leg if there was no one around to take her on – about anything, from whose turn it was to dry the dishes to the iniquities of the bull fight they'd seen on holiday. He would retaliate before he could stop himself, find his arguments bundled like a fly into a web. Unlike the fly though he was able to go, leaving her speaking to an empty room. He would hurl himself out of the house to walk the dogs or climb the hill, and behind him he would hear a window being flung up and her voice, determined to have the last word, would reach him across the garden. *Liam, it is your turn, I have dried the dishes for the last three nights. Bull fighting is not exciting, Liam, it's barbaric and it should be banned.*

That was the girl. Now there is a woman of twenty-nine who suggested they come back up north, to a holiday cottage near their old home, so that he can *get some peace and quiet, decide what he's going to do next*; a woman who never raises her voice and who seems to have infinite patience with his grumpy self.

His legs are like bendy drinking straws under his lightweight trousers. It's hot enough for shorts but he doesn't want to see his bare legs, doesn't want to see them ever again, tries not to look at them when he showers or has physio. The thought of them, thin and white and scarred, make him shudder. They had evidently made Rachel shudder too. She had hung around long enough to enjoy the drama of being the wounded Captain's brave girlfriend, and then it was goodbye Liam.

As a test to see if he is fitter than he looks, this is a failure. He'll be lucky if he makes it back without toppling himself into the water. The looking-glass mountain is not to be scaled today.

Anna has reached the jetty. He can see she's longing to help him secure the boat but thinks he'll be offended if she tries – which he would be, but he longs for her help because it's hard, the hugest effort, just to climb out and tie the knots.

'I've found a lovely place to have lunch,' Anna says, chattering so as to pretend she isn't aware that he is breathing fast, incapable of speech. 'Over here. It's out of the sun, but I can't guarantee it's midgie free. They're always worse near water. Do you remember we used to jump in fully dressed just to get away from them?'

She's been doing that for the last five days. *Do you remember the bramble jam Mum used to make? Do you remember when Fluff had kittens in the ironing basket? Do you remember the night you spent on the hill looking for one of the dogs? Do you remember when you and Dad went for a swim in the loch on New Year's Day?* His brain feels woolly when he tries to reciprocate. She's talking about a time that he seems unable to remember during the day but finds haunting his restless nights. A looking-glass world.

Why does he keep thinking 'looking-glass'? It isn't an expression he ever uses; who does now? It's from *Alice* and Lewis Carroll, dimly recalled, of course, but better than any other description for those other worlds, that other mountain under the water. Mirror world isn't nearly so mysterious . . . shaving-mirror mountain?

'What's funny?' Anna leans forward. 'It's nice to see you smile. What was it like, being back in a boat?'

'Like I'd never been in one before. What's for lunch?'

Anna hands him two bottles of sparkling water to open.

'Cheese, the onion tart I made last night, raspberries, strawberries.'

So that's what she was doing after he had gone to bed, annoyed with himself for being tired after a day of doing nothing, and for snapping at her solicitous questions. He'd heard the low murmur of the radio and her moving about the kitchen. They'd spent the morning having a slow walk along the lochside – that was when he'd seen the boat and arranged to borrow it – and the afternoon sitting in the garden, Anna with a pile of paperbacks she said she never got time to read at home, himself with a book of First World War poetry he'd found on the sitting-room bookshelf in the cottage. It was probably not the best choice he could have made.

What passing bells for those who die as cattle?
Only the monstrous anger of the guns.

'Anthem for Doomed Youth'. Wilfred Owen, 1917. A hundred years ago, near enough, and still no end to 'the monstrous anger of the guns'. Or of the bombs.

And for those that are dying as cattle now not one single poppy flowers in the desert.

Anna has plonked a sun-hat on him – as if he were her

two-year-old – but his head aches in the thundery heat. Ironic to be complaining about the heat in Ross-shire, after Iraq.

As if she reads his mind Anna says, 'Dad would never have gone to live in Australia if it was as hot as this all the time! We're thinking of taking the kids out for Christmas. Do you want to come with us?'

Apart from having to decide about going back to work, whether to go back to the army or not, he can't think of anything he'd like less. Christmas on the beach? That would be another looking-glass world. And Dad being tactful and not asking questions but looking worried and whispering with Anna in corners. His brother-in-law not knowing how to talk to him, their usual male bonding over sport and Liam's love life, being out of bounds; his nieces and nephew being hushed so they don't disturb poor Uncle Liam having his afternoon nap. No, thank you.

'Remember that winter,' he says in reply, 'when the roads were blocked and we couldn't get out for a week?' He longs suddenly to be his joyful nine-year-old self, reprieved from school, making tracks along crunchy white roads in black Wellingtons.

Anna nods.

'It was like the Snow Queen's palace. Another world.'

So many other worlds. If he could just lie down and sleep maybe they would all go away.

Anna is handing him a plate – a china plate – which holds a slice of tart and a wedge of his favourite cheese. He leans against the bank and drinks some water. A frond of fern tumbles over and tickles his face. He picks some earth from the bank and rubs it between his fingers. It smells good. From here he can see the mountain rising high on the far side of the loch but its upside-down twin is out of his sight.

Anna produces a book and looks at him apologetically, saying she wants to finish it before she goes home.

The tart is savoury and delicious, and the cheese Anna has brought from Edinburgh has gone runny, just the way he likes it.

She has put the berries in a bowl and packed ice blocks round it. They burst on his tongue, frosty sharp and sweet. He feels as if he is tasting food for the first time in ages.

He looks at his sister, her fair head bent over her book, and feels sudden love for her. They haven't seen much of each other since university – Glasgow for him, Edinburgh for her. Then the army for Liam; teaching, marriage and children for Anna. Mum dying, Dad moving to live near his brother in Sydney. He knows he's always welcome at Anna's house but months go by without them meeting, or even talking or e-mailing when he's out of the country. When he's back he finds it hard to relax, to take an interest in the things everyone else seems to be talking about. There's no common ground. Except there is, he realises now. He and Anna share a history; whatever has happened since can't take away the childhood they had together.

'Do you know what I'd like right now?' he says abruptly.

Anna raises her head. 'What?'

'A glass of wine. Cold white wine.'

Anna reaches into the coolbox.

'You haven't brought . . . ?'

She looks sheepish. 'I've been dying for one too. But you've refused it since we've been here, I thought maybe you weren't allowed to drink.'

'I wasn't for a bit and then I didn't want to. After the hospital, and then Rachel leaving, opening a bottle on my own, going to the pub . . . well, I didn't want to end up a drunk as well as a crock.' The slippery slope.

He watches her take the bottle from its insulated jacket and deal with the cork.

'How come you got so efficient? You should join the army. You'd make a wonderful quarter-master.'

Anna doesn't laugh.

'What are you going to do, Liam?'

He takes the tumbler from her.

'No wine glasses? You're slipping. What am I going to do? I'm going to sit here and enjoy this and look up at the sky and watch that big black cloud that's heading our way.'

'You know what I mean. What are you going to *do*?'

'Do I have to *do* anything?'

Anna puts her book down.

'Yes . . . you . . . do.' Her voice is mild but there's a flash in her eyes and she leans across and beats a gentle tattoo on his leg with her fist.

He's no longer her two-year-old, to be patted and persuaded.

'You're a bossyboots, Roly-Poly, you always were,' he says. 'Why don't you join the army? Take my place at the front line. Get promoted to sergeant-major.'

'Don't be daft, Ginger.'

The old childish nicknames. He feels laughter somewhere inside him.

'Roly-Poly, Roly-Poly.' He plucks a bit from the fern and throws it at her.

Anna catches it and throws it back.

'Liam?' This must be the voice she uses in the classroom.

He crumples up the fern frond. Without looking at her he says, 'They've offered me a desk job. I have to decide soon. I don't know. What's teaching like? I might try that.'

'It has its moments. Well, why not? A bit of army discipline in schools. We could do with it for our lot.'

'I'm just kidding.'

'And you wouldn't have to cut your hair. You suit it longer. Remember Dad had a fit when you came home with a pony-tail?'

Liam reaches over and picks at the tart.

'That's a very good reason for not staying in the army. I can have a pony-tail again. Thank you, Anna. My mind's made up.'

'Ha-ha. Seriously though?'

'Seriously, I don't know. I'm having another session with my CO next week. He's a good bloke. Though I never realised how much I'd missed being up here. Maybe I could retrain – be a forester or a conservationist or something.'

'A tree hugger? You?' She dodges as he throws another piece of fern at her.

'Tree hugger yourself. Stop grinning, woman, and pour us another glass. Hey, is that all I'm getting?'

'We'll finish it later. I don't want to have to carry you back.'

'Do you think I can't hold it any more?'

'I'd rather you were sitting inside if you were going to put it to the test.'

He clinks his tumbler against hers. Later, he thinks, I'll talk to Anna about her life, pick up the conversations she's been trying to start since they arrived.

'Thanks, for everything, Roly-Poly.'

'Don't be daft, Ginger.'

As their smiles start to turn into laughter, the black cloud is right overhead and thinks this is the moment to join the conversation while Thor, up there in the heavens, decides he's been quiet for long enough.

Anna dives to pack the picnic stuff away. She throws Liam his jacket which she's been sitting on. He picks it up and puts it round her shoulders, pulls the hood up, ignoring her protests.

The rain is heavy now, chandelier crystals bouncing on the surface of the water. Liam takes off the hat and raises his arms to the sky, feeling the wet drops like a benediction. Maybe tonight he'll tell Anna about the world he's just been through, that desert world – tell her about its danger and pain, its excitements and comradeship. Or maybe not. For the first time in months it all seems very far away.

He wipes his face and looks across the loch. There is the mountain above the water, ageless and solid. And there is the mountain below the water, the looking-glass mountain, being broken into thousands of shimmering pieces.

Shite

Lynsey Calderwood

Ma da's goat a new job. He's startet cleanin the toilets across the road fae the swimmin baths that ah go tae wi ma pals. He quite likes it but he disnae really get paid that much (four poon twenty an oor), a lot less than wit he wis gettin when he worked at Babcox. Yir no really daein that much though, he said, yir maistly jist sittin in that wee room watchin the wee portable telly an then every so often yi gie the flairs a mop an check tae see if thir's enough bog roll.

Charlene burst oot laughin when ah tolt her. Haha, she said, your da shovels shite. Laura Kyle tolt her tae shut her geggy. She said, At least Kirsty's da's goat a joab. Yeah, said Harpreet, thir's nothin wrong wi shovellin – Harpreet bit her lip an went aw quiet, an then Chris Rice jumped in an said, Aye well at least Kirsty's goat a da.

The guy that used tae clean the toilets is some auld fart that ma da knows; ma da caws him Big Davy fae the lavvies an it's cos ae him that ma da goat the job. Big Davy's only fifty-five, said ma da, but he's goat a bad heart so he took early retirement. Haha, said Charlene, magine cawin enubdy a name that rhymes wi lavvy. Who cares, ah said tae her. Haha know wit ah'm gaunny caw your da fae noo oan, she said, Big Jamie the jobby jabber.

Me an Charlene wur in the school toilets at interval the day, doon daein a pee, an Charlene went intae a toilet where the plug hadnae been pult. Ayyy naw! she shoutet, Kirsty moan see this! She dragged me in behind her an pointet doon at this big jobby that some clat bag hud abandoned, that wis noo bobbin up an doon in the pan like a wee broon monkey. Aye wit a mink, she said. Aye ah know. Aye magine yi could never ever flush it away cos it wis aw pure stuck. Ah don't really want tae magine it, ah tolt her, it's awready gien me the boak. Aye but jist hink, she said, cos Missus Auldhill's the cleaner, it wid be her that has tae pit her haun doon there an fish it oot.

Aw the lassies in the school wur called intae an emergency assembly durin third period. We aw thought it wis gaunny be the heidy that wis takin it but instead it wis jist Missus Auldhill staunin up on the podium wi a sanny bin in wan haun an ah pad in the other. Can enubdy tell me wit this is fur, she said. Naebdy answert. Come on don't be shy, she said. Still naebdy answert. Charlene startet sniggerin an diggin me in the ribs. Well, said Missus Auldhill, ah'll gie yi a wee demonstration will ah. She held the sanny pad up (it wisnae a used wan or anythin). This goes like this, she said, an she pushed it through the wee flap on the lid ae the bin. Some ae the fourth-year lassies that wur sittin up the back startet clappin an whistlin. Missus Auldhill jist smiled. Noo, she said, ah don't want tae find anymair ae these cloggin up ma toilets.

Ah said tae ma da, how d'yi no go fur that job roon in the paper shop? Wit paper shop? he said. Iqbal's paper shop. Ah don't think so somehow. Aye but how no. Cos ah don't want tae work fur Iqbal, he said. Aye but how no, ah said, ah thought yi liked Iqbal. Ah've nothin against him, said ma da, ah jist don't want tae work in a cornershop.

Ma da didnae have tae say it. Ah knew it wis nothin tae dae wi workin in a cornershop an everyhin tae dae wi workin in a paki shop. It wisnae exactly racism as such, but it wis kindae. Ma da hud never said anythin bad against Iqbal or his religion or anythin before; he wisnae like some ae the wans roon oor bit that sprayed mentions aw ower his waws or cawd him a black B when he didnae sell the young team thir cairy oot. It wis awright fur ma da tae buy bread an milk an a lottery ticket aff the guy an take the Christmas card he gied us every year, but when it came right doon tae it it wis embarrassin fur ma da tae have tae rely on a paki tae pay his wages; far mair embarrassin than shovellin shite fur a livin.

Da's pal Davy went intae see him at the toilets the day. Him an his wife hud been at Blackpool fur the weekend an they brought back boxes ae broken biscuits fur ma ma an da an a big chocolate dummy each fur me an Karen. Ayyy! Know wit that looks like, said Charlene, it's like a big turd oan a stick. Ah went an flung the chocolate dummy doon the drain ootside oor hoose, an when ma da ast me if ah'd ate it yet ah felt dead guilty so ah said it wis lovely.

Ah spoke tae Iqbal in the shop the day. Wit've you been tolt? said ma da. Ah wis only talkin tae him, ah said. Aye an ah bet it wisnae aboot the price ae butter. It wis aboot aniseed balls actually, ah tolt him, ah wis tryin tae find oot if they hud additive E wan twenty in them but Iqbal didnae know.

Ah don't know why ma da hud tae take a job as a toilet cleaner. How could ae no've been a road sweeper or a windae washer, or how could ae no've jist took the job wi Iqbal or even went an did a course at Reid Kerr College till somethin better came alang.

Ma da worked at Babcox since he left school at seventeen. Nearly sixteen year an he's never hud another job. Yi'd think he'd be glad ae the break; yi'd think he'd want tae go tae college or somethin tae learn new skills or even tae jist meet new people. But naw, no ma da, aw he wants tae dae is sit by himsel in they toilets aw day, wi his face trippin him, an nae company bar Big Davy an his shitey wee portable telly.

Ah wis feelin pure depressed the day, an Harpreet wis away tae the dentist at lunch-time so ah went an jist sat ootside the tucky by masel. Charlene wis away doon tae the chippy wi Laura Kyle an Nicola Buchanan (they'd ast me tae go wi them but the chippy's right next tae the toilets) but ah didnae want tae chance bumpin intae ma da; ah could jist imagine him seein me fae across the road an then pure wavin at me in front ae aw ma pals wi a big pishy mop in his haun or somethin.

Missus Auldhill opent the tucky early. Ah didnae even see her at first until she shoutet me in. She ast me wit wis the matter; ah said nothin. She said, Ah hear your da's goat Davy Clark's auld job in the toilets up by the Victory baths. Ah don't know wit ah wis mair shocked at: the fact that Missus Auldhill knew big Davy, the fact that she cawd him somethin other than big Davy fae the lavvies, or the fact that she knew ma da wis noo a toilet cleaner. She musta thought it wis the first yin cos she said, Aw aye ah know Big Davy, ah worked beside him when he wis in the fire service. Honestly, ah said, an ah couldnae keep the surprise oot ma voice. Yi didnae think, she said, that we cleaned toilets aw wur days did yi? She laughed after she said it an ah tried tae laugh an aw but ah couldnae imagine Missus Auldhill daen anythin other than cleanin an runnin the tucky never mind bein a firewummin. Aye, she said, Big Davy Clark wis a good firefighter an ah met him when ah worked in the canteen there. Aw. That boy disnae keep well, she said, that's how he'd tae gie it up an take the job in the toilets.

Ah spent ages talkin tae Missus Auldhill that afternoon: we talked aboot her wee granwean an how he'd be gaun tae school this year; we talked aboot ma da when he wis a boy an how he used tae help her run the tucky an aw; we also talked aboot how Missus Auldhill hud jist cleaned aw the latest mentions aff the lassies' toilet doors an how she knew it wis Charlene that wis daein maist ae them. So yi'd better warn her tae rap it in, she said. We didnae really talk aboot Charlene that much though; ah didnae want tae talk aboot her tae Missus Auldhill cos ah knew ah'd jist end up gettin upset an thinkin aboot aw the nasty stuff she's been sayin recently; ah also didnae want Missus Auldhill tae think ah wis a snob fur wantin ma da tae be somethin better than a toilet cleaner.

Charlene come lookin fur me wi Laura an Nicola jist as the bell wis aboot tae go an ah wis jist leavin the tucky. AW RIGHT CRAPPER

NAPPER! Charlene shoutet. Chris Ross an Chris Russell wur walkin past, an Charlene hud obviously tolt them aboot ma da's new job cos they startet makin really loud fart noises an lookin ower at us. Ah don't know wit goat intae me at that moment but somethin inside me jist snapped an ah pure flew fur Charlene; ah hud her pinned up against the waw at D stairs an ah'd ma haun right roon her throat; ah think ah mighta actually strangult her if it hadnae been fur Laura Kyle pullin me aff her. Don't you EVER say anythin aboot any member ae ma family again, ah tolt her, or ah'll kick seven shades a shite oot yi.

Big Davy fae the lavvies died ae a heart attack this mornin; his funeral's this Friday but ma da's been tolt he canny get the time aff work cos thir's naebdy else tae open the toilets. He's talkin aboot packin in the job anyway. Yi should see aw the mess the school lassies leave, he said, thir far worse than the boys.

Charlene's been actin as if the tuck shop incident never happent; she's no said a thing aboot ma da since then, an she's been suckin up ma arse like naebdy's business.

In and out the windows
Linda Cracknell

Come on my china, give me a keek of that husband of mine. What have you done with him then? I don't see him framed in his usual window, bent over the loom. I've to show him this, see, come in this morning's post. It's got a crest that my finger bumps over. A crest, aye. And it's addressed to me. To me.

Maybe you don't hear me, with all that great rattling and jumping going on inside you, and the engine outside puffing and panting to keep up with the machines. Never as keen for a blether as me, eh?

You've a face like a keekin glass the day, all your watery eyes catching at the falling sun. Does it not make you feel a wee bit in danger, all that glass? But you've your bell-towers to make you feel important. One for east and one for west, bringing the whole village to squeeze like a swarm of bees into that door and up your stairwell. Oh aye, you're the rare wee tyrant.

And I'm here waiting again. On my bench. But I'm early today, right enough.

I know them by heart now, your windows. Nine across the top floor, then nine from right to left on your third, and so on to the bottom corner of you. Counting's a fine way to pass the time – to take my mind off the cold that's eating my fingertips.

> In and out the windows
> In and out the windows
> In and out the windows
> One, two, three.

I know your lines and wrinkles, too, by sight if not by touch. Those patches of oil staining the sandstone blood-red next to each of the lintels. The wee curve in the stonework at the top of each window. It's just how I've got to know the laugh lines of John's face. It's from staring into it each night by the fire, when we measure our fingers against each other's. Under his nails there's aye the wool-grease to scrape out, and under mine, the bannock-dough, terrible stuff that sets solid like stone. It goes with this rattle. You hear? Aye, a box of matches in my apron pocket to show the proper wee country wife I'm becoming. We laugh about that in-between talking about meetings I've been at. Like Miss Parker and Miss Christie, come last week to Perth from Dundee, and getting pelted with eggs and men's crude words for their trouble, all as if they were prostitutes.

Aye, then, play me your tune while I wait. Now, is it a jig or reel? We've the looms two-stepping on the first two floors, and then the whirr of the twisting frames above. But the spinning mule, there on the top floor, that's harmony, eh? Making its wee dance with the operative as they glide in and out.

And there's the river all solemn and slow behind you, not seeming to mind what you steal from it for your lade, and the splashing wheel that turns and turns at the same speed all day, till I find myself inside it, my eyes dropping shut with the turn and splash, turn and splash.

What a joke, eh? That we chose you instead of a ship to Canada? Glunchy old you, sat still and sour-faced. I could just picture myself, when I read the adverts, on a sleek, shiny, new ship. I'd be the one stood at the prow, cutting though the waves, the first to spy the land of opportunities.

We went down to the Clyde even, saw one of them away. Folk were cheek-by-jowl on the decks, greeting and waving, and the noise was rising off them across the water. And the hankies all like wee blossoms shaken about in the March wind.

It's you that's our ship now. A big square red stone ship. So where is it we're sailing to?

I mind the windows back in Neilston, too. Alexander's Mill, sunk down below the line of the hill with its zig-zags of climbing stairs clinging to the outside walls, and all its different faces, and windows different shapes and sizes. It was as jaggy as the Paisley skyline itself with all its towers and chimneys.

And we spinners running along, singing and shouting up at the windows. A river, so we were, with our bunnets catching the sun to make a field of flowers. Aye and the polis trying to push us back. Five thousand we were according to the papers. And all because five girls were doing the work of six. And that damn feartie Mr Hough hiding in the railway station for his precious life.

Hearken to this part. A wee lesson for you. There was a woman, stopped the flow. Aye, and she had a great rock in her hand, heavy and rough. It wheeshed high over the heads of the lassies and the polis helmets, clattering through a first-floor window. Then she caught my eye, said she should follow it in with a burning clootie, eh? And then there was shattering and shrieks, and ducking heads as we all followed her example. Aye, but later we got the assurances we wanted from the bosses. It worked, see. And all they could do was put wire mesh over the windows.

You're no so big and bold as a cotton mill in Paisley, but still, for a wee village stuck here in the back of nowhere, you're something. And right enough you dwarf the white cottages on either side of you. Even the hotel and the hall down the road, the church, almost everything in the place. You squeeze them quite breathless.

But don't you go thinking that coming here was my first choice. It was John's mother, aye, and the sisters, wanted him back here at the weaving, after his da and his grandpa. Stone dead they are in the graveyard down the road but. John couldn't resist coming to see, when he got the offer from your Mr Knight. And that was the once I was allowed inside. For the guided tour. Once!

No one warned me about the smell of you mind, like a clootie in my face, smothering my words. You could sink your fingernails into a smell like that – greasy and thick, like the sheen you send home on John's clothes, and on those rows of tweed samples in his precious pattern book. He says he doesn't smell it anymore, but I do. I've noticed as well how his forelock's grown, so it limps over his eyes.

Aye, don't think I've not noticed what you're up to.

After our wee trip to the country, he came on that persuasive, said we can live in new ways, Catherine, amongst old ones. And we can carry the new ideas, out to the provinces. We don't need to go to Canada for a new start. And I wasn't so sure.

But that's when I told him of that other idea, seeing as how we both believe in a woman's right to work, married or no. The idea that's smouldering here under my shawl. And he said aye, why not, we can talk about it once we're there.

Is it that your Mr-Knight-Sir's caught him into the office? He must come out soon, eh? I've his favourite tea waiting at home. We'll walk back together arm-in-arm, you watch. I'll wind a skein of your finest wool around his shoulders, reel him to me until his eye's matching my eye, his smile to my smile, and I'll show him what's been burning my hand all day. A wee keek at it and I'll be on the road to a proper training. I'll be making myself into a nurse, and I'll be the one to say what happens to my person and my time and my money.

All I need is his signature.

It's dark so early in this winter village. All your rows of lit windows are glowing brighter, the lassies on show up on the third floor, their heads bent like they're praying to the spinning frames. No idea, those lassies, eh? No notion of that fairy hill, with its daft wee point way above their heads – the rust, purple, and the steel-grey rock all fading into the gloaming. Not one of them's taught themselves to read and write, I bet. Perhaps they've not heard yet about the labour movement, or even about suffrage.

They'll still be jangling, no doubt, from the swarry on Saturday night, all the flushed faces from the dancing and the whisky, the pretty gowns ballooning out. We were reeling till two in the morning. There'll be new clicks to giggle about, I'll bet. And you'll be leaning in your great fat red walls, souking up their whispers between the spinning frames.

The 'happy family' Mr Knight cried us from his platform.

The happy family. Jings!

'Hand-in-hand, the proper relation between employer and employee,' he said, 'so we can prosper together.'

Hold my John's hand, I thought, and you'll get yourself a slap.

And then one of the foremen was up on his hind legs, thanking them for inviting us all and for their kindness through the last year. Aye, the kindness of oppressors and capitalists I thought. So out of me comes a snort, like I was that Krakatau.

It was quite the dig in the ribs John gave me. And just after that he was piping up himself, and I thought the good socialist, he's going to speak up just like he did at those Glasgow meetings when I fell for him. And what does he do? He proposes a toast.

'Long life, happiness, and an increasing gathering every year!' he calls out.

My words clashed and clattered in my head, but none came out. Then he sat back down and whispered to me the news, that he'd been made a foreman.

My mouth hanging open, I'm pushed into the parade for the Gay Gordons. We step the backward bit inside our cradle of arms, and then I'm spinning, spinning, spinning, all dizzy and catching for my breath under his raised arm. We stride off thigh-to-thigh for all like our days marching under the banner in Glasgow. We're reeled together into the polka and match each other, step for step. The rough edges of him catch on my wrist and chin, and there's a wee spark in his eye that promises we'll be awake a while back home.

I mind my hands on his cotton shirt, after the dance. I get one of they wee hot skitters to think on it. His breathing coming faster in my ear.

'You're not turning soft, are you, agreeing to be foreman and all?' I noticed the waxy look of his face then. 'You're not bowing to the bosses?'

But he whispers something about it being different here in the country, a family affair, and how there's growth in the market what with the demand for khaki and that. Coorie in, and I'll whisper you what happens next. Your lanolin keeps his hands soft as a wean's. I've no complaints there. So maybe I should thank you, eh?

You're not shocked – blushing your sandstone pink? It's a secret between us, because we share the man, me and you. But you can't say you need him more than me just now, you mean old scallywag.

You'll not reply? You don't hear?

You'll tell me next you never heard those men earlier. That'll be why you did nothing to stand up for me, eh? Those beasts. Swaying and surly from the public house.

'Suffragette. Suffering yet?' Calls out one of them.

I can be strong. Breathe, breathe, chin up. Like Miss Parker with her grace under fire, aye.

'You nothing to do at home? Go and mind the bairns,' he says.

Snap. Snap goes the anger, and my tongue free as a snake.

'Aye. I could be a mother. Or a nurse, or a mill lassie, and yet not have the vote. Whereas you're a useless drunkard, and you still have it.' My face afire.

'If you were my wife, I'd give you poison,' the drunk one comes at me again, leering round.

'If I were your wife, I'd drink it!' Spitting. Tongue rattling.

He lunges, but the other one cleeks his arm, and they roll away.

This village. Look at me, stuck with just you to talk to. Aye, even the mill lassies look away when they pass me, and I heard John's mother tell him he should catch my dress in the mangle, to stop me gadding off to meetings. And there's his sisters asking when I'll be with child. It seems John hasn't told them what we agreed, how bringing weans into the world means women lose their lives to domestic labours.

I have to shut my mouth before that rhyme escapes.

> Holy mother we believe
> without sin thus didst conceive:
> Holy mother, so believing,
> Let us sin without conceiving.

We're a united front, him and me. We are so. Don't give me that look. I'll hold him to it. When he came home the other night asking if it was pie or mince, and it wasn't there yet because I'd been away at a meeting, I felt his arms around me slacken a wee bit. I had to laugh. How can I change the world between cooking lunch and dinner, John Devlin? I said to him. And he kissed me and changed from talking pie to the betrayal of the Reform Bill.

It's me he has kisses for, not you, see? And kisses make me forget how I'm feart what it is you and Mr Knight are steeping him in. He's my John, eh? Mine, not yours. You hear? And you can stop lanking his hair with grease, and sagging him with that tiredness he brings home.

He minds me of the effigy of Mr Hough the men marched onto the football field behind Alexander's that night, his arms cleeked between them, feet dragging behind, head bent and bobbing. There was thousands of us gathered, and that wee one with a red face stood up on a platform spitting out 'Is he guilty?' as he shook the jointless, flopping man with its suit and tie and hat and a blank for a face. Three times he shouted it out, and every time the roar came up from the crowd. 'Aye! Aye!' Louder and more hungry each time. And then the last. One great roar it was that joined us all together we were so set for justice. 'Aye!'

And then the paraffin was splashed, and great flames licked up and the wee jointless man was hoist onto it, and you've never heard such monstrous cheering this side of hell, and the bonfire a great mountain pointing up into the sky that you could see right across Scotland I'd say.

Aye, it's a fine warning to the bosses. These days John looks up a bit sharp-like when I says that.

You'll make me into the shivering ghost waiting for him at the end of the world on this bench. You old bitch.

I've made a wee picture of you in my head. You think you'll go on for ever, don't you, just like the turn and turn of that water wheel, so long as the river runs? But. I see you become a decrepit ruin, abandoned by everybody, your roof fallen in, and your walls tumbling down, your two bells fallen into the mud so they can't even peep. The land'll rise up and swallow you, take you back. I see it, I see it.

There's crows, too. Come to hang about on your roof, clanking their great feet on your head, singing you heeshie-baw. And I hear them because you're so still, your machines silent. And I can make myself one of the crows. It helps me wait. Flying in and out your windows. How many of the gaping black gashes can I soar through, where the glass used to be?

It wouldn't take much. A hurled rock could set off your downfall, or a wee spark out of my apron pocket, if you get too greedy – the night shifts there's been talk of, the 'efficiency'. I know what it is that word means.

I'm a spinner, mind, like the spider. You might think yourself a grand thing but I can snarl you up with cords spun as tough as steel.

Give me my husband back, sly witch.

What's that? You holding your breath?

Looms. Clattering to a halt are they?

Spinning frames whining down. Aye.

Heads moving between the machines, heading for the stairs now. You spit them out into the half light, the men swinging onto bicycles, the girls' heads bent in a blether. I tuck my ankles under the bench as they pass me. Here's my shawl pulled in against the shivers and under it the paper's crisp.

At last! My man's shape flickering between the looms. A shadow of his face under his arm at the window, looking out for me, the wee darling.

The gas-light fades in each of your eyes, and you begin to shiver yourself down for the night, just like you're a wee dragon curling up under that mountain. Ach, perhaps you're not so bad. I could almost sing you a wee lullaby.

And the hand-held lamp flickers his silhouette across windows;

the greased forelock bobbing, unfamiliar. Down and down he comes, down the stairwell.

And then the door finally opens. And as it swings, it unleashes a great storm of beating wings in my throat, and so I stand up to give them more room. I'm ready for the new road ahead of me. Ready to walk home arm-in-arm. Ready to slide that pen into his hand.

The Big The Beautiful Nanda Gray
Morven Crumlish

She knew some tricks, that was something. People had always said about her, well, then, you sure know some tricks! And even earlier, well, you sure are tricky, a tricky little thing. The funny thing was, she never meant to be tricky, she just did whatever came to her, it was as though her body knew the best way to make things easy, to make people like what she did.

They could call it what they wanted: tricks, or magic, or genius, either way she couldn't take responsibility for it, whether it was in her blood, or clinging to her skin, or in some pre-destined path of fortune, though she found it hard to think God would be that much on her side. All she knew was that it wasn't just the cosmetics she wore on stage which fooled her audiences into thinking she was striking, or even stunning, there was more to her allure than mere disguise. Besides, everyone wore lipstick nowadays, even the nice girls sitting around the back tables with their boy-friends, the ones who, especially in the later shows, grew flushed and loose, and ended up sitting on all kinds of laps. You could spot them, they would be dressed up to their necks with their mouths closed and their eyes wide open as they came in, and they would start twitching as the trumpet slid and built, twirling their ankles, until they began to find their skirts too long, too constricting. By the end of the show these were the ones who would be up, shaking and swinging, and making fools of themselves in scenes which would return to them in fractions over the next day or two.

Nanda knew about that, the slow layering of delayed embarrassment of those who drank, but in order to keep drinking you just had to learn to live with it. She shrugged expansively, as though the audience was already here, in her dressing room – little more than a closet, but she had got them to put up a star on the door, and there was a mirror framed with electric bulbs, and a rail for her costumes, and even a washbasin and a comfortable chair – and continued to examine her reflection in the unforgiving light. She outlined her eyes with black, and filled in her lips and her cheeks with red so that she resembled an expensive doll staring unblinking through the window of a Fifth Avenue toy store, propped up between the fire-engines and jigsaw puzzles. Now that she was rich, these were the kinds of fragile, oversized gifts Nanda bought for her nieces and nephews, her godchildren, and mostly her own children who had never actually got round to getting born, fate and certain accomplished medical professionals having come between them and any useful daylight. Which was a good thing, she would remind herself, as she dimpled the cellophane window of a box containing a flowered china tea set, because how could you ever have a child, and raise it in any decent way, when you had never even been one yourself?

This doll-face, though, laughable as it was among the creases of worry and joy, imposed on her loose, tired-out skin, was an improvement on the first days when she was let up on stage. She was too ugly to sing as a white girl, they told her, and too fat, but as a negro, then just maybe she wouldn't get laughed off stage, so she blacked up, smearing burnt cork across her face and her chest, and she found that far from laughing they whooped her and cheered her, and when she jiggled herself around, and sent her voice scratching down low to catch the bass notes, or panted across some line about a faithless lover, they didn't act as embarrassed as they had done when she was white. These audiences, in the smaller clubs off Broadway, they liked to think they were being adventurous, they had the jungle sold to them in the fronded entrance halls, and they lapped it up, and would've believed it if you'd fed them apples and told them they were bananas.

Nanda had known she wasn't going to stay underdressed and invisible in the shadows, any more than she'd been intending to make a life out of turning tricks back in the Midwest, all of it had only ever been a stepping stone, a note on a scale until she reached the shattering, perfect pitch of the life she knew she deserved. She used to lie there, staring over the hairy shoulder pressed up against her ear, feeling the spreading, unlovely slab of belly suckering off her own, damp skin, shifting her legs up, rolling her pelvis so that it would be done with that bit quicker, and she would calculate how many miles she would get out of each thrust and groan. The best ones were the Catholics, who yelled apologies to Mary and whoever the hell else, right at the last minute, as though hoping this would count in their favour; they always tipped her extra.

In those days her arms had been thinner, and her hair had been thicker, and it hadn't been such a bad living to make, better than staying at the farms, stinking of chicken shit, and popping out a kid a year, and married to some dumb, heavy-skinned farmboy whose only musical ability was to make instruments out of things that you could pick at the side of the road. At the time, she shrugged off a lot of the bad things which were done and said to her, thinking of those screaming blades of grass, and guessing that it could be worse.

She had spent several weeks riding the railroads, criss-crossing her parents' great and ambitious country, picking an unsteady path east, sometimes buying a ticket between two towns she had never heard of, other times waiting for the train to slow before swinging up through the tall, wide open doors of one of the rear cars. To Nanda, an empty wagon resembled a stage, and if she had the place to herself she would stand right at the edge, clinging on to the door with one hand, hurling her voice out into the passing landscape, and hearing applause and praise in the rhythmic, repetitive phrasing of the train's movement – the-voice-of-a-star, the-voice-of-a-star, you're-so-great, you're-so-fine, you're-so-great, you're-so-fine, and, of course, the steamy whistle screaming youuu, youuu! Which meant, I love you, and was the other kind of appreciative, non-paying audience Nanda expected to find in the city.

For a long time after she started getting well known, and even now that her name was painted up over the club, and people took cabs out to see one of her three shows a night, she would get up there sometimes, and the light would shine in her eyes, and she would see nothing, and the music would swell in her ears until it sounded like the static on a radio, and the only way she could pull herself back was to press her toes over the edge of a railroad car, and let the wind whip her hair all out of its pins, and send her first, soaring, drop-everything-and-listen note away over the disappearing, endless plains, right out to where the sun was sinking over at the edge of the earth. And at the end of that first song, with the band keeping up as well as they could be expected to, the whooping and the cheering and the nice things said about her were real, and she would open her eyes, and take in the view, and nod, because she had come out at the right place.

Now she stood up, and turned towards the clothes rail, narrowing her eyes with the pre-emptive disappointment of a woman who should have bought a new outfit for the occasion. Tonight was her Anniversary Show. They had taken out advertisements in the newspapers:

The Big The Beautiful Nanda Gray!
Twentieth Anniversary Performance!
Tonight, Miss Gray will be taking requests from members of the audience, and singing from her repertoire of well-loved favorites.
NOT TO BE MISSED!!!

And above this, was a photograph of her, glancing backwards over a naked shoulder, the doll-face among heavy features softened and improved with the graininess and slight smudging of the newsprint. An old picture, too. A necessary vanity of showbusiness.

Nobody clarified what this was meant to be the anniversary of, maybe the anniversary of them realising that February was a slow month. In fact, she had arrived in New York City twenty-five years ago, right after her fifteenth birthday, at the height of a summer which was so hot it took her weeks before she could find a man with the energy to tell her he loved her, one rich enough, and with clean sheets, because she had already decided that she would not be a whore in New York City, which somehow seemed more dispiriting than being a whore on the road. She had lived with this little man, and still thought of him fondly, and spent days hauling her perspiring self around the clubs and the music stores, and nights with the little man climbing over her, getting himself lost among her breasts and thighs.

Sometimes in the stores she would get paid to demonstrate the sheet music to the customers, she could bang it out well enough on the piano, and her voice carried her over rough patches of accompaniment. The pay was just change, she would go to the drugstore and buy a soda and sit on a high stool in the window watching as New York carried on without her, before launching herself, somewhat refreshed, back out among the knees and elbows.

At last, one of the clubs took her on, as part of a cabaret, and she was able to exchange the little man for a musician – and she could still laugh at her youthful innocence for thinking that this was an improvement! – and so it carried on. In twenty-five years she had gathered up and disposed of four husbands and numerous lovers, all the time edging her way up the bill. She had thought that nothing would beat headlining, but that was before the recording contract, and that was before the day she took out the lease on this place, and watched them paint the sign above the door, starting with the middle letters, so for much of the day the sign was a cryptic code, puzzling passers-by, but at last, TE N transformed to TE-NITE NAND, and finally NITE-NITE NANDA's was there in front of her, and she was breathless as she realised this time she was not dreaming it.

Her mother, on one of her infrequent visits to the city, had asked her, in a plaintive, apologetic tone which irritated Nanda, why she couldn't just have used her given name, the name with which she had been baptised, right in front of Jesus, and the town. Who was Nanda Gray, anyway? What a strange choice. Nanda had explained that no one would want to go and see someone sing with a name like that, they'd expect some greenhorn in an embroidered dirndl, straight from the docks. She did not tell her mother that she had found the name Nanda in a newspaper, a scandalous story involving bigamy and dead and hidden babies; and had liked the sound of nandagray all in one word, though now she sometimes wondered if she should have gone with something with a little more colour.

Nanda's robe hung open at the front, revealing the feat of engineering that was her underwear. Nanda had never been one of those people who wondered how skyscrapers stayed up, she figured if her breasts could defy gravity then a fifty-storey building was the next, logical step. She was strapped and bound and redistributed by unfashionable garments made of silk and bones and strong laces, which enabled her to wear some approximation of the flimsy, loose hanging dresses which were the style of the moment. She ran a hand along the edges of her costumes, like a child drawing a stick through long grass, aimless and dissatisfied. There were sequins and fringes and gold and silver thread, and all the things which would generally make her feel glamorous and fortunate, but which tonight weighed down her limbs with weariness. The fourth Mr Nanda Gray had recently left her for a girl nearer his own age, there had been tears and apologies, but she had been guilty of smothering him, coddling him, treating him like a child, he said before graciously accepting a car and an apartment in the divorce settlement.

She did not like going to bed alone, waking up alone, eating breakfast alone; nor did she like the contortions which were necessary to entice a new man into her life, even just for one night, and at her age she should have something more permanent than that, you would think all the hours she had put in, the times she had held her tongue, and soothed this or that ego, you would think one of them could have stuck it out, but even though she knew she was worth it, she never could do enough to keep a man from falling through on her, as though he had run out of breath, or collapsed from exhaustion.

Eventually she settled for a dress which dripped with black sequins so that from a distance she seemed to have been recently soaked, to be emerging from deep, dark water, which poured down her, causing the dress to cling heavily, and shine with a muted, stolen light. She attached her hairpiece with an ornament made of jet and ostrich feathers, and stood before the mirror, her hands reaching down her front and up her skirt; she was her own, frustrated lover, but her satisfaction came from suitable readjustments of flesh and fabric, until she recognised the woman in the mirror as the same woman who stood on the stage every night. She practised smiling, and there she was. Nanda Gray.

She checked the small travelling alarm clock which rested among the strewn cosmetics and jewellery, the magazines and emptied glasses, and saw that so far she had kept her audience waiting for eleven minutes, not too long for such a special night. They would be extra keen to see her by now, even more likely to forgive her, or to choose not to notice if she slipped or slurred. She poured herself one last drink, and toasted herself in the mirror, before leaving the room.

The dingy passageway which led to the stage seemed endless, her feet felt that they were walking uphill, her head swam, who would believe she could live with these nerves three times a night, six nights a week? At last she was up in front of the audience, waiting for the cheering to die down a little, but stirring it up at the same time, raising her arms, and shimmying her body, and slamming her hips, each movement accompanied by a shirring of drums, a clashed cymbal. The band had been playing for over an hour, their faces shone with sweat and glee and booze, and they had reached that glorious state of synchronisation, where the music seemed to exist by itself, and all they had to do was pull it down out of the air. Nanda knew that her appearance pushed them apart for a few seconds, as though she was a shape cut out of their dough, but soon they would fit round her snugly, clinging to her curves, soaring and breaking with her, until you could tell that all of them had the same heartbeat.

'Well, hello folks, I'd like to thank y'all for joining me for my twentieth anniversary . . . I guess you didn't know I started singing when I was one year old . . . Thank you! Well, I can tell you've been having a great time with Benny and the boys out here . . . Can I have a little show of appreciation for Benny and the boys now, ladies and gentleman . . . Honey, I said *ladies* . . . Thank you! Well, I'd like to start with a little number that's always been one of my favourites, I hope it's one of yours too . . .'

And Nanda Gray nodded towards the piano, and began to sing.

The Man Who Couldn't Write
Morgan Downie

Once there was a writer who could not write. Of course the world is full of such types, those who do write but have no ability, those with the desire but not the time and the others for whom simply the act of putting pen to paper engulfs them in an anguished past. This writer was none of these. His published works, works published in as many languages in as many countries, were ample proof in themselves that he had not only been able to write but written in such a manner that his books were a staple feature on the bookshelves of a certain class of reader without regard to borders. Further, should the curious visitor or student be lucky enough to be admitted to his house, he or she might browse the walls of annotated volumes, decipher years of notebooks, kept since the writer had been a boy. In his own country he was known simply as 'the great man'. It was a title he had neither sought nor asked for but now, at this certain time of life, he allowed it, with a slight wave of the hand, an inclination of the head, and felt the glow of a deserved satisfaction.

This satisfaction derived not solely from the act of writing or even his success, but from the fact that he had used his fame to advocate those causes that were dear to him and which found a sympathetic ear among his contemporaries. Naturally he was a champion of the poor, whose cause he espoused, at least meta-phorically, and who, in his books might escape from the many restrictions of their circumstances. Though he was careful to avoid stating any political allegiance, a position known to have raised some eyebrows in a country where allegiance runs in the veins like blood, he was widely regarded as a liberal. He was outspoken in the cause of other writers who could not write, not for the reasons detailed above, but because they were forbidden to do so. More than one of these, though acknowledging his support, noted on their release, that this support did not extend to actually visiting them in prison. The great man, however, was his own first critic in such failings. That he was just a humble writer was a phrase that frequently tumbled from his lips as he appeared in public with political dignitaries from foreign countries, wealthy visitors, or with any of the string of actresses with whom his name was so often associated.

These are the things the great man thought of as he lay in his bed, morning light flooding through the long windows. Outside he could hear the stirrings of the students and the soft instructions of his amanuensis Apollonia. He allowed himself to dwell on her voice, imagined the softness of her skin, the dark falling of her hair, yet, although he recognised the inevitability that he must take her as a lover, he felt no accompanying physical stirring. It disturbed him that these days such opportunities were more often than not passed by, ever more the duty, and he found himself reflecting on loves lost rather than those to be gained. The exercise of memory he felt, in these days without the pen, would help him to find his way back to writing but that morning, like so many mornings before, the day stretched before him white and empty. He sighed. He was the creator of great sagas, of the rise and fall of families, haciendas hacked out of the verdant jungle, waterways cut to the parched plains but these days the fields were barren, the bowls of the fountains split and open to the sun. To such deserts no liberation would come.

As he came down the stairs he heard one of the students talking. It was the Japanese, the one they called Idoru. 'But he doesn't really turn into a panther. The transformation is purely metaphorical. He is returning to his roots, turning his back on the society he has helped create, giving up on a present which is merely an imago of the colonial state.'

'I think it's too obvious,' said Angeliki, the Greek girl. 'The panther represents a talismanic masculinity. After the destruction of the revolution he cannot accept the feminisation that he associates with the creative act of reconstruction and so gives himself completely to a purely phallocentric mode, the lion in retreat.'

He paused for a moment on the stairs. They were discussing his first novel. It pleased him to hear his novels discussed, but recently he felt as if they were doing so as a means of passing the time, waiting for him to write again, to produce the next great work. Or to die. Even when Apollonia looked at him he felt there was an expectancy.

Angeliki smiled. 'We were just discussing the transformation of man into panther.' She laid a fresh cup of coffee in front of him as he sat. 'We were debating the significance of the change.'

They waited as he composed his thoughts. 'It is La Rochefoucauld, I think,' he said finally, 'who says that our actions, in this case my work, can be fitted into whatever meaning one chooses. When I think of the panther it seems, to me, to represent an area of mythological intersection, a realm which is both the past and the imagination.'

The German gave a slight laugh and glared pointedly at the Greek girl who returned his look with equal ferocity. So, thought the great man, it is you two who have kept me awake these last few nights. He raised his cup. 'But that is only what I think today. Tomorrow it may be different.' He nodded at Angeliki, whose eyes flashed at his acknowledgement.

Apollonia dropped him at the city's central park. 'Do you want to me to pick you up later?'

The great man shook his head. 'I'll walk.'

While he enjoyed the Mercedes, and especially the sensation of being driven by Apollonia, he had begun to resent its air-conditioned comfort. More and more he found himself lowering the electric windows so that he could smell the carbon monoxide, hear the relentless torrent of car horns, yet at the same time when he looked at the faces of the occupants of the vehicles stuck in the same traffic jams, he found himself looking at strangers. In the park at least he felt somehow more at home. He enjoyed watching the tourists, cameras at their hips, the nervous glance as they took their photographs, watching for the street thieves for which the city had gained something of a reputation, not totally undeserved. Sometimes he wore dark glasses, more as an affectation than as a precaution against being recognised. He was after all a writer not a movie star, but there were occasions when he might stroll by the areas where the retired men played chess or backgammon in the afternoons in order that they might call his name or tip their hats, gestures he found more satisfying than guest appearances at any number of international literary conferences.

He sat himself on one of the stone benches. Almost immediately one of the street urchins appeared at his feet, dirty-faced, bare-footed. 'Shoe-shine, sir?'

The great man waved his hand but the boy was persistent. 'Don't be so quick, sir. The shoes, like the eyes, are windows to the soul. A freshly shined pair of shoes reflects a certain balance but yours . . .'

'But mine what?' questioned the great man.

The boy flashed a smile. 'Your shoes, it has to be said, seem troubled.'

The great man laughed. 'In which case I must let you ply your trade in order that I present to the world a more acceptable face.'

The boy rested the great man's foot on his stool. 'I think there is more to the world than face,' he said, spitting into his cloth. 'You, for instance, even with these shoes, it is not obvious what it is that you do. What, may I ask, is your occupation?'

The great man thought for a moment; he was, after all, just a boy. 'I write stories.'

'Very good,' said the boy, his head bent. 'Tell me one.'

'I cannot.'

The boy looked up. 'You claim to be a storyteller but can't tell stories. Perhaps one day I will become a shoe-shiner who doesn't shine shoes.'

'I told stories once,' said the great man.

The boy shrugged. 'I was a boy once. Now I am halfway to being a man. I can make no claim to that former state. As you no longer practise your profession is it not the same for you?'

'It's different.' He saw himself at his desk, the paper in front of him, pen in his hand, but the words would not come. Either the paper was left entirely blank or all he produced were scratchings, scrawlings, sentences deformed and broken. The months of this were steadily becoming years and he was forced to admit that now even the thought of the act of writing claimed him with a state approaching panic.

'Why is it different?' said the boy. 'I have shone the boots of a certain general, the name of whom, for both our sakes I will not mention, before he went off to make love to the wife of the man he had just murdered. If I could make those boots talk that is the story they would tell.'

'A book is different.'

The boy shook his head. 'One can't walk far on a book that sits on a dusty shelf.'

The great man laughed. He remembered himself, he remembered how easy it had been, in those times when he was the same age as the shoe-shine boy and his escape from the oppressive heat of the summer had been simply to write in his journal stories of water, pirates on the high seas, explorers in the frozen North. And later he wrote of beautiful women he could not have or who came as shadows from his dreams, and men who were better than those around him, less frail than he.

'Can you read?'

'Can I read!' exclaimed the boy, jumping to his feet. 'What a question! Have you sons, daughters? If you, a stranger, met them in the street would you ask them such a thing?'

The great man gestured as if to apologise but the boy ignored him. 'Of course I can read. I could read almost before I could walk. As a child I read books through pictures but my mother, an educated woman, encouraged me so that I could create the pictures in my own head. Not only can I read in our language but I can read the language of the tourists in the books they leave behind.' The boy glared at him. 'Yes, I can read. I have read many things. Including you.'

'You know who I am?'

'I live in the park,' said the boy. 'How could I not know you, the great man, champion of the poor? Was it not here you wrote the story of the man who turned into the panther?'

'Yes,' said the great man, 'it's true.' He was on the cusp of adulthood, of becoming a man, and the revolution was in full swing. He had written here in the park as the sirens roared around him, the air stank of tear-gas and the sound of tanks and gunfire could be heard in the distance. Somewhere he knew his friends from the university would be waving placards in the face of water cannons, some would die at the roadside, others would simply disappear, seen briefly in the arms of the security forces, then nothing. He talked to those who had been released, trying to find out something, anything, but all he could see on the faces were the marks of an unspoken horror, and he turned away. Yes, that was why he had written his book, because he was not brave enough for the barricades, feared even the thought of torture, so he had created a man who would stand firm in the face of such things, a man who was not him.

'It's my favourite,' the boy was saying. 'The first book my mother read to me. The first book I was able to read by myself.'

'What was it you liked?'

'I liked what all the poor people liked,' said the boy. 'I liked the characters. The old woman who cooks the corn.' He pointed across the park to where the hawkers' braziers burned. 'She's still here. And if it isn't her then it's someone like her, and beyond her there are those who work in the fields, her own family perhaps, and the priest as poor as they are, able only to give them the hope of Jesus. All the minor characters were like that. The bus driver, he is all the bus drivers, he could be sitting over there, with the other old guys, playing chess right now, and if it isn't him he could pretend to be. It's why I still read that book, because I can see you, sitting here, writing, and I know that you see us.'

The great man did not speak. He remembered the simple joy of standing on a street corner, his book opening, his pen flashing across the pages as the people walked by, no thought, only the story forming under his hands, warm as a clay pot.

'Your mother?' he asked. 'What happened to your mother?'

The boy spread his hands and looked upwards. 'She is with God.'

'The new regime?'

'Of course.'

The great man felt a familiar pang of guilt, as if he had survived what the boy's mother had not, but he knew it was a false guilt, a work of fiction. 'And the man who turned into a panther,' he asked, 'why do you think he did that?'

'What does it matter?' said the boy. 'A revolution happens but all that concerns the poor is whether they have more or less to eat. A man turns into a panther and we realise there is still magic in the world. Any more debate is for those who inhabit the universities and have their eyes closed to us. This man has played his part, his time in the story is over. He turns into a panther. What else could he do?'

'What else could he do?' echoed the great man. He remembered that he seemed to have run out of words, when the new regime had just come to power, and, even in those early days, seemed to be trying as hard as it could to mimic the behaviour of the old. His character lay still on the pages. He sat day after day in the park, pen in his lap, unmoving. What was he to do? Make him don the clothes of the dictator and become what he most despised? Have him hide, wait in the shadows watching his hopes and dreams shrivel until he became the enemy of what he had once fought for? He watched one of the park's feral cats stretching in the sun, paws extended, ears flattened against its head and suddenly, without thought, it was done. He had written it. The man was a panther. He could be nothing else. The story was finished in his hands, his story of the revolution, his part. It was done.

The old man and the shoe-shine boy sat through the hours of the long afternoon. Perhaps the old man told the boy the story of the cat, perhaps he told another. The boy told the old man secrets which are best kept between shoes and their owners and the old man laughed at the scandal. Finally he got to his feet and readied himself for the long walk home.

'So,' said the boy. 'What will you write about next?'

'I don't know,' said the old man. 'I don't intend to think about it. Perhaps I will tell a story about a man who closed his eyes once and forgot how to open them.'

'Will there be animals?' asked the boy.

'Why not?'

The boy smiled. 'Who hasn't dreamed of becoming a panther?'

Then he dropped to all fours, his shoulders sprouting a rude, tawny fur, nails knotted into claws, irises narrowing, eyes pale and yellow as those of a jungle cat, before giving the astonished old man a last look and bounding away into the traffic, his long tail vanishing amongst the taxis. The following day the papers were full of it. 'Panther Sighted in Capital!' The police were mobilised, hunters were called in from the country, grim-faced men who posed for photographers with their rifles cradled intently in their arms. Pet lovers wisely kept their cats inside.

The old man returned home. He walked around the table where the students were working and closed each of their books in turn, then laid out wine and glasses. 'Please,' he said, 'this house is far too quiet.' And kissed Apollonia with a twinkle in his eye.

Closing the door to the rising sound of music below the old man sat at his desk and reached into one of the drawers for a journal. He picked up a pen and without hesitating, began.

Once there was a writer who would not write . . .

Broken Glass
Sophie Ellis

It was a deceptively simple piece. A constellation of broken glass – shards, chunks, slices, glistening fragments, all forming themselves around some sort of centre. There were countless pieces sparkling under the bright lights, splintering and defracting the overhead glare. It was intended to dazzle, I thought, and it did. Somehow, this field of broken glass was a tribute to its own destiny, a monument in memory of its own intent to shatter; it seemed to tell, in its mischievous glaze and random geometry, the story of its fall from grace. Mesmerised by those glassy surfaces, I thought I almost recalled the moment of suspension, the unbroken glass loose within the air. Petrified. It hung there, not for a split second but somewhere just outside of time, in its own frozen moment. Then its contact with the floor, where the potential of the glass was realised, the momentum of its fall broken, its energy transformed.

This exhibit was all trouble, gorgeous trouble. It declared the artist's bravura. I stood perfectly still and stared.

It was just a few hours earlier and the rooms were beginning to fill with people. The stark, white-walled, wooden-floored emptiness gradually infused with expensive perfumes and intelligent con-versation. There were already several groups scattered across my view, not quite knowing whether to focus on each other or the exhibits on offer. I was positioned at the furthest end of the room and had aligned myself perfectly with a painting mounted at the opposite side. Possibly the symmetry pleased me, the direct relation between me and it. Both of us static, waiting patiently at either end of this impressive space. I stared harder into the distance. Perhaps the painting wasn't unmoving. It was a kind of vortex, a whirlwind of different colours splayed outwards from the central 'eye' onto a circular canvas. I say 'eye', it only appeared to be an 'eye' from where I was standing. There were many shades of reds and greens, and a wonderful back-to-front yellow 'C' which seemed to offset the rest. I could imagine paint canisters being harnessed to a wheel and spun with relish. Child's play, I thought. A firework to remember.

The harder I looked at the image the more I could see – whoops and swirls soaring in front of me, vivid bands of paint spread in every direction. Some of those bands were like birds of prey, falcons perhaps, diving in or bursting out from their sea of red and green. Their wings were embattled and their feathers flayed, as they struggled to emerge from their circular page. Caught in motion they were. Captured and transformed into delicately splattered paint. Unless you looked hard enough, of course. Because the harder you looked the more the painting moved, as if it were secretly insisting that stasis is always a lie. This Catherine-wheel of colour seemed to deny its status as painted surface, and forced recognition with all those suggestions of its depth. I still hadn't moved. The 'eye' of the painting held my stare: watching me watching it.

My arm began its dull ache.

The pain always progressed in the same way, travelling from the wrist joint where the weight was most concentrated, into the fingers and along the forearm. That's where I felt it now, on the underside of my wrist, the main point of contact. In the beginning it only felt like an inconvenience, a slight unfairness perhaps, but the discomfort would always mutate into something else, some deeper shade of resentment. The tension was physical at first, until the strain on my arm began to distort my vision, coloured my way of seeing things.

There were two women reclining against one of the immense white columns which formed the entrance to the room. They both seemed implausibly tall and thin, draped in luxurious fabrics which moved with the light. Something in their stance, the way their bodies inclined towards each other, was both creaturely and conspiratorial. Their lipstick mouths returned to self-satisfied sneers in-between their whisperings. Later, when I came to collect their glasses, I would surely be able to distinguish the meanness of the crimson half-moons staining the rims. Perhaps it was the fact that my right arm was beginning to buckle, or because I had been nailed to the same spot for what felt like an eternity, but I became convinced that the two women were glancing in my direction, muttering, giggling, then glancing again. I was suddenly conscious of my own appearance, my tired black shoes, black trousers, the ill-fitting black shirt with the company name branded back and front. My cheeks began to burn, the champagne glasses looked more precarious in their arrangement at the end of my arm, their liquid bubbles tremored in anticipation.

But of course the women weren't discussing me, or regarding me with interest, because no one had spoken a word to me, or glanced in my direction since the evening began. I was being foolish. I was forgetting that I wasn't really there. We were black shadows, negatives; we were the circular trays at the end of our arms, our visibility buried beneath our function. It's just the way things are. Everyone always says, 'That's just the way things are.' But tonight that statement seemed lazier, more insufficient than ever. Something was different, there was something more ominous about my agitation, something more significant about the build-up of pressure in my arm. I looked across at the beautiful 'C' at the opposite end of the gallery. Although the colours were still bursting and spinning their circular round, the 'eye' remained completely still, its unflinching gaze intent on me. It made me restless, it made me want to move, it made me want to dance, to be alone in this generous space and leap and spin and turn about. It made me conscious of myself: 'I am, I am, I am.' The 'eye' held my stare: watching me watching it, watching me watching it watching me.

The room was much fuller now, larger groups were flooding through the columns at the entrance, milling about, chattering. Yet, despite the number of people meandering past me from exhibit to exhibit, my tray remained completely untouched. The nine champagne glasses waited patiently in their three-by-three formation, exactly as they had been all evening, except heavier now. Much heavier. I watched with envy as I glimpsed other black shadows darting back and forth to refill their trays. All I needed was a moment to recuperate, to allow my arm to breathe. Perhaps people could sense my mood, the aggressiveness of my stare, and were deliberately keeping their distance. Silly. I was forgetting again, forgetting my own invisibility. But the waves of pain creeping into my bicep, up into my shoulder and down my back seemed to insinuate that my overlooked tray was more than just a coincidence. 'It's a conspiracy,' the pain whispered, 'a conspiracy.' As I looked back across to the entrance, where the two feline women were still licking their fuchsia lips and purring with self-delight, I knew my aching arm was right.

Time wouldn't pass. I needed the evening to be over. Appraisal was my only means of distraction.

My attention roamed back and forth between different groups of people, trying to pinpoint the abstract quality that united them. It wasn't necessarily money or good taste, or even the love of modern art, but more a powerful self-consciousness regarding all these things. It's as if each group were a separate installation, out to exhibit. They each invested fully in their own false image, stamping out anything which might betray them, or portray them, depending on which way you look at it. Theirs was the kind of self-awareness which feeds off a constant comparison with others. And somewhere very hidden, in some subterranean part of their consciousnesses, they bothered to compare themselves to me, and were thankful for my shadowy presence, because I made them feel good about themselves.

Although none of the sideways glances and empty gestures were directed at me, I felt every single one. Each affectation was made even more palpable, more nauseating, by the vast dimensions of the room. Every hollow laugh ricocheted off the elegantly varnished floor, onto the lofty white ceiling, into absolute nothing-ness. I amused myself that I could see this entire circus reflected nine times over in the glasses I held. Nine times the forced smiles. Nine times the feigned interest. Nine times the mock excitement. Each gesture made more grotesque by its distortion in those glassy spheres. I can see you, I thought. I can see through you. At least transparency was a two-way street. But the distraction didn't last.

I still hadn't moved, I mean I hadn't moved a single muscle.

The room was chock-full of people now. Everyone had gathered for the closing speech. I strained my eyes, desperately trying to locate the 'eye' of the colourful storm. The canvas had been obscured by the sheer volume of assembled bodies, stolen from view by a series of broad-shouldered men and big-bottomed women. My pupils narrowed, refining their search, and there, ever so faintly, through a multitude of shoulders and handbags, I was just able to make out a black mark in the far distance. I only saw a fraction, but it was enough.

Someone, somewhere, *tinged* on their glass. The shrill note echoed impatiently round the room. Gradually, a restless silence fell, begging to be broken. The director cleared his throat, adjusted his glasses, waited for the right moment. Confidently, he began: 'Firstly, I'd like to mention our enormous debt of gratitude to those involved in this truly marvellous exhibition. A round of applause, please, for our team, who have worked tirelessly on tonight's display, and, of course, a warm hand for the artists themselves.'

There was a smattering of polite applause. The joints in my fingers groaned. The weight tore through my fleshy palms. The director continued: 'So, what have we gained from tonight's event? What have we learnt? Well, I believe this contemporary display is all about surfaces, our need to invest in surfaces. And when I say "invest" in surfaces, I'm talking about our need to see through them, beyond them, be capable of dismissing them, in order that we might discern; in order that we might arrive at a fuller under-standing of the human condition. And so, ladies and gentlemen, I offer you an exhibition which is superficially about surface, but irrefutably about depth, nameless depths, mine and yours. With that in mind, I'd like you all to raise your glasses. Here's to "our depth". Here's to "the beingness of our being".'

The applause was more emphatic this time. Everyone loved it. The clapping wouldn't stop; it grew and grew and grew like some enormous conceited bubble waiting to be burst. The applause reverberated through my body, hammered at my ear drums. The young women squawked their approval, the suited men gave knowing nods, the circus clowns stamped their feet. Across the gallery, the cats reclined lazily in their corner, just milking the applause, lapping it all up. 'Here's to our depth,' they purred. 'Here's to the beingness of our being'.

Some things can't sustain themselves, I thought, as my face cracked into a dry smile. I wanted to be seen, to be heard, to break through the applause and create a silence which would allow me to exist. My muscles started to contort. The champagne fizzed as the glasses wobbled on their long stems. I willed my fingers to loosen their grip, I longed for my arm to tilt and the tray to slide from reach. The 'eye' was perfectly still – watching me, watching it. It willed me to do it, the pain along my arm whispered for me to do it. 'Things fall apart,' they said, 'things fall apart.'

But I didn't drop the tray. There was no moment of suspension, no frozen moment. Nothing shattered into countless pieces which sparkled under the bright lights.

No one ever drops a tray on purpose. That's just the way things are.

Later we collected the empty glasses. Some were abandoned in corners, or left carelessly in the middle of the floor. Others had unthinkingly been placed on top of sculptures, where the surface was flat enough to act as a table. We washed the glasses, dried them, boxed them up. They waited there patiently in the darkness, unbroken, unfulfilled, ready to be used the next time.

The Paper Boy
Jackie Galley

The miners' strike had a big impact on me. The few quid that I brought in with my paper-round made all the difference in our house. I was glad to hand it over to my ma, it felt like blood money burning into my palm each Saturday. I knew I was as bad as the rest of the scum that left the line or took up another job or turned their backs on their mates. I was only fourteen, but I was already an expert in betrayal.

Each morning in the first dawn light I would see the oil drum fires, newly made up and doused with petrol, with legs of chairs and bits of fencing protruding above the flames. The black smoke, heavy with fumes, rolled down the road towards me. The number of drums lit, the intensity of the smoke, was a code that I understand all too well. One drum and it was just the local men, two or more drums lit and they were expecting reinforcements. I used to see them arrive sometimes, the flying pickets. They came in coaches and parked in the Main Street. Men would disembark, obscured inside overcoats and donkey jackets and heavy, scuffed work boots, tossing short greetings to those already assembled as if words, like the money, had to be carefully rationed. And then they all stood there, at the end of Muir Road, waiting for the police vans and coal lorries.

The final bit of my paper-round was the row of miners' cottages at the end of Muir Road, right beside the picket line. To deliver the papers there, I had to thread my bike through the groups of men, past my own da, standing with the rest of them. In the beginning it was fine, they would josh with me and ruffle my hair.

And one of them would always ask, 'Have you come to join us?'

And I would nod and say, 'Soon.'

But then the men would look away, turn back to the oil drums and mutter, 'Aye, if there's a mine left.'

And my da would get his funeral-face, all serious and drawn. But it was different when the flying pickets came. They never said anything like that when there were outsiders there.

The mine has always been part of our family. When I was small my ma used to take me and my sister on picnics. She would lay out this woollen tartan rug and we would all lie down on it, staring straight up at the sky and we would wait. Then, faintly, no more than a gentle rumble, we would hear a blast and the ground would tremble.

And my ma would whisper to us, 'That's your da doing that.'

My sister, still in nappies, would giggle as if ma had let her in on some huge joke. I never understood. Still can't understand why my ma would want to go and wait for the blasting. Once it was over she would hand me a glass of pop and a roll, and we would spend another hour or so playing games or sometimes, if the wind off the hills was raw, she would wrap us in the blanket and read to us. That bit of the day I liked.

I did tell my da once that I thought it might be scary, being near when the blast went off.

He said, 'You'll soon get used to it.'

I had run the paper-round for Mr Starkey for a year already. I told him then that I was fourteen. He knew I wasn't, but I was reliable, I always turned up on time. The town's a different place at 6 a.m. All space and quiet and no people. Maybe the occasional light on in a bedroom and a cat sat huddled on a doorstep. I could hear the hiss of my tyres on the tarmac as I rode around the roads. I could hear blackbirds calling in gardens. I could see for miles. I liked getting out of the house. And at Christmas Mr Starkey gave me an extra week's wages and a selection box and he called it my Christmas bonus. I was chuffed.

But, as the strike lengthened and even the cash to buy a newspaper began to run out, the men would watch me silently as I pushed the folded daily through the letterboxes. A group of middle-aged men envious of a paper boy's wage. And I started to give my paper-round money straight to my ma.

She said, 'Don't tell your da, say that you're putting it in your savings account.'

The strike had been going on for months now. It had begun to seam itself through our town like the coal in the rocks beneath us. Even the launderette was closing down, no dirty pit-clothes to clean. My paper-round was shrinking and the bag was getting lighter and lighter. The only bit of the paper-round that remained hard work was the Friday local rag run. It was as if every house now took the weekly *Chronicle* instead of forking out some money each morning. And the *Chronicle* always carried the news on the strike. Mr Starkey quickly learnt to order in extra copies if there were any significant developments.

So when I went to school on the Thursday morning and the place was buzzing with the news that the strike leaders were coming, all I could think was that it would make my Friday paper-bag an extra heavy one.

'They're coming to show solidarity,' my mate Ian said, emphasising the word 'solidarity' in a way that made him sound just like his father. 'Coachloads of pickets are coming and the police scum will have to be there so there's bound to be fighting. Who wants to go and watch?' he asked, as if he were arranging a trip to the football.

We all said yes.

'We'll go out at lunch-time.' Ian said.

I went, because you had to, although I already did too much hanging around Muir Road to actually enjoy it. I saw the police vans draw up, followed by the telly crew with their cameras. All the people seemed to merge into one amorphous mass that pushed and heaved and left police helmets – like rugby balls – lying in the road. Their collective breath was visible in the cold air as a miasma of anger. I had never seen men fighting before, not close enough that I could hear the smack of fist on flesh and the rushing out of air from crushed lungs. Above the shouts and cat-calls, there was the revving of engines and the constant low hum of bitterness that seemed to be coming from the ground itself.

I arrived back at school ten minutes after the start of the afternoon period and got detention.

I went in to the newsagent on Friday morning fifteen minutes early. My bag was already full and Mr Starkey was making up a second pile, pencilling names on the top of each paper, marking them up on a second list as a record for his bills.

'I've split the round for you,' he said. 'This pile is the scheme, you can do it last. In your bag is the Main Street and on up to the end of Muir Road.'

I put the bag across my shoulder, I felt as if someone was trying to weigh me down with sandbags.

There was never any discussion about what I would do when I left school. It was just sort of assumed. And I was never that brilliant that I was an obvious candidate for university. When I said I wanted to do art as one of my Standard grades, my da shrugged his shoulders. But I knew what he was thinking – he was thinking that art wouldn't do me much good down the mine.

I think my ma always had an inkling, she looked over my choices and nodded.

'Mr McDermot says you're very good at the technical drawing.'

'Graphics, ma,' I corrected her.

'That, too, I expect,' she said, loyally.

The mines have always been part of our family. My da assumed that they always would be.

The heavy paper-bag hung off my shoulder and pulled me down. I went towards the picket line with reluctance, as if they might see inside my soul and know.

There was not much banter. I noticed a few people were missing after Thursday's run-in, I had seen Ian's dad bundled into the police van on the telly last night.

'Let's have a look at the headlines, son,' my da said.

So I parked my bike and handed him over a copy.

Standing in amongst the group of men I got a hint of what it might be like to be one of the miners. There were some things that even I understood. These were not just my da's mates. They relied upon each other. They had stood together. They risked their lives together.

They wouldn't like it. I knew they wouldn't like it. Da held the paper up.

'See what they're saying!' he yelled. 'They're saying we've caved in!'

And in his disgust he threw the paper towards the heat of the oil drums.

The *Chronicle* fluttered around the men as the wind off the hills lifted and swirled each page till it caught in the eddies from the oil drum fires and the news flew, like kites, over the houses.

My heart was soaring, too. I had read the front page. It said the mines were to close.

A few weeks later the strike began to crumble and one morning, when I cycled down Muir Road, the oil drums were cold and the dew was caught in the cobwebs of the spiders that had already claimed them. I dropped my bike and went to investigate. It was like walking between ancient standing stones. In the quietness of dawn the only things that called out were the curlews on the fields. The drums were set out in a line and around them the earth was trampled bare and littered with cigarette stumps ground into the soil. Inside each drum the ash held a treasure-trove of nails and hinges, all distorted by the heat that once simmered in this space. I took a few as souvenirs. And, for a little while, the men walked around the town again, smelling of coal. But it didn't last.

It broke my da's heart.

I knew I was as bad as the rest of the scum that had left the line or taken up another job or turned their backs on their mates. I was only fourteen, but I was already an expert in betrayal. Every day I had prayed for the strike to cripple the mines. I wished my da out of a job. Anything, so long as I didn't have to work the coal. I never told my da, but I think my ma had an inkling.

Sea Angel
Janice Galloway

Mrs Broschi, who kept house for the priest, had heard something. She ruffled Lucca's hair, chucked his cheek and looked into his face with her head to one side like a chicken. Was he not beautiful? Lucca edged away from her to the gutter and Mrs Broschi, as if seizing an opportunity, turned back to his mother. *Lots of people,* she said, would hear sooner or later. And whatever anybody else might think or not think, she wanted Mrs Benigno to know that she at least thought it was *the right thing.*

Mrs Benigno's face went stiff as a sail. Speranza noticed. Mrs Broschi didn't. She just went on talking as though the child was not there. Hardly anyone spoke to Speranza. She was used to it by now.

Thinking of the – Mrs Broschi flicked her eyes to Lucca, flicked them back – *immediate requirement* was not pleasant, perhaps. But it happened all the time in the Papal States. It was not a crime.

Speranza saw her mother clutch the fish basket so tight her knuckles changed colour. Mrs Broschi hardly paused for breath.

Present pain for future benefit was entirely Christian. And it was for Lucca's sake, for his eventual gain. If she had three girls to feed – she rolled her eyes at the tragedy – and one so sadly disfigured, she would do *just the same.*

Speranza watched her mother pull away from Mrs Broschi, a movement so sudden it looked like a slap. Even Lucca, kicking nothing at the side of the road, turned round. There was a long moment with only the sounds of gulls in it. Then Mrs Benigno walked away. Only Lucca said goodbye.

Next day, Mrs Benigno looked up from the table, her face dusted in flour, and told her children that Mrs Broschi had no family. She was skinny and stupid and no one had wanted to marry her. The *Mrs* part fooled nobody. She had no children and no love and it had made her soft in the head. She turned back to her dough, pounded it hard against the dusty table. Mrs Broschi, she said, her lips a line, should be remembered in their prayers.

Trust was vital. Trust in God to know his own, those to whom he had given great gifts, and trust in the boy himself. Didn't he deserve more? Wasn't that voice incomparable? If he took steps to preserve it, to safeguard it against change, how could he fail? What was in front of him if he stayed here? He would grow up, he would have no trade, he would grow older but no wiser. He would have nothing all his life. Like his father.

Lucca was named for his grandfather, a fisherman who drowned. Caught in the mildest of storms, the sky full of low, thunderous cloud, his boat had foundered on rocks he should have known were there. He was pitifully close to home, but bad light loses a man his bearings, his experience counts for nothing. He made a mistake. By way of apology, perhaps for the family's sake, he had hauled his boy, a thirteen-year-old who couldn't swim and who couldn't tie a knot to save himself, onto the torn and upturned keel. Then he caught in his own nets and there was nobody else to do the saving. The body of the man stayed tangled to the rocks and the boy floated across the bay to home shores. The whole business took a few hours.

Old Lucca was a big man who asked no one's help. If he hardly spoke, he was good-hearted and fearless. Sometimes, solitary in his boat or in his cups, he sang and the sound carried far. He had a true voice but used it only for himself. Marco, the boy he chose to save, did not sing. He had been born with a club foot and a predisposition to being carried, like a burden, by his mother. He survived what killed his father with a chest wheeze and never much recovered. Hauling sails or fish crates made him breathless. He turned his hand to other things and those other things, one by one, turned away. The goats he milked dried up, the lambs he tended wandered off, the turnips he guarded were eaten from beneath the soil by worms. Thrown out of farming, he ran a dog-cart between the gutting tables and the market till the dog died of dropsy and his mother died of despair. Finally, he turned his hand to gathering rushes for a basket-weaver who, out of kindness, taught him her skills. He earned enough to marry his teacher and ensure an income, of sorts, for life. He was gawky and sixteen, she was plain and ten years older and did not say no. By the age of twenty-four, Marco had a wife, four children and bad lungs. He never reached twenty-five. Lucca was six, Paola and Innocenzia, four and two years old.

None remembered the funeral save the eight-year-old Speranza, hidden behind her mother's skirts all the way through. Speranza had a hare lip and hid habitually, but her eyes were keen. Mrs Broschi, seeing the writing on the wall for both husband and daughter, had already taught Speranza to weave as well as, if not better than, her father. When he died, she took his place easily, almost without question. God gives everyone work to do, her mother said. And that work is our service, our duty to God and to others. All of us, no matter how humble, have something to give. It had always been true and now it was truer. Weaving was Speranza's duty to God and family. Lucca's, since he was small, was to gather sticks and draw water. Without asking, he did more. He brought home eggs and rabbits from the hills, scavenged shellfish from the harbour. Sometimes, he brought home milk and no one asked any questions. He could charm a living, Speranza thought, out of thin air. The littlest of his sisters found kindling and sorted reeds into bundles and plucked feathers from birds Lucca found. They schooled themselves not to stray too far from the door. God had given her obedient children and Mrs Benigno tried to be grateful. They were healthy and Lucca could sing. It was a blessing to be able to sing. He sang for company at first and something to do. Then for his own pleasure. He sang his sisters to sleep at night and to keep his mother in a better frame of mind. The priest came and he sang for the priest who insisted he sing in church on Sunday and gave him a chemise to look the part. The chemise reached to his knees, but it was linen and smelled of incense and Lucca was keen to wear it. He had aptitude. People looked up from their feet in church, sought out the source of the voice. Sometimes, fishermen asked him for a song at the harbour side, the way they had asked his grandfather, but the boy did not know his grandfather's songs. He sang God's songs instead, and they gave him bread and fish and sometimes, remarkably, money. They smiled at his dirty hair, asked after his sisters and called him *piccolo angelo* while he turned the coins over and over in his hand. *Little angel.* Already giving.

One day, after mass, the priest drew Mrs Benigno into the corner of the church and told her he had been thinking. Had Mrs Benigno considered training the boy? He was good enough for any choir she cared to name on the mainland but – he sucked through his teeth as though he had wind – in Naples, no one sang for long or for money without training. Had she considered, however, that he might be trained now?

Mrs Benigno told the priest what he knew already. She had no money to train a voice. She needed Lucca at home. The priest shook his head. Perhaps she did not understand, he said. There were ways and means for these things. In no time at all, Lucca's voice would be splitting like a tree and the sweetness might run out like spilt honey. Would she consider talking to someone who might – he paused, picking his words as though he was picking brambles – assist in this regard? Someone from Naples?

Mrs Benigno looked at him. The priest sighed.

Your son has a fine soprano that shows great promise. He already has all the grounding I can give him. With the right attention, he could be better still, develop a *special kind* of masculine voice, much in demand on the mainland. There are ways, Mrs Benigno, for your son to develop such a voice.

Mrs Benigno was aware she was not catching something. Something important. The priest pursed his lips.

I am not making myself understood, he said. We will talk again. I have a suggestion, Mrs Benigno, one that might help your son to earn a great deal. And discover the best within him for the service of God, of course. God wishes us to develop our talents. With a voice such as his, it is surely his duty!

He turned his eyes to heaven as rain touched his fine woollen cassock, his broad felt hat. Have no doubt, Mrs Benigno. He started to run, calling over his shoulder. God's plan for Lucca will soon come clear.

She did not, perhaps, realise what was at stake here. These voices were like no others. They had saved people from death. The priest of the Sant'Onofrio had proof! And the wound would give the child connection to the Son of God himself! God would not forget those who were wounded in his service, who only wished to sing for His glory all their lives. The cut was nothing, less than nothing, a matter of moments. She need have no fear on that account. There was everything to fear, however, from prevaricating, allowing time to gain the upper hand. He was – what? Almost eight years old? A year, maybe less – there would be no second chances. Most students began younger. Mrs Benigno should have courage. Her son would be educated, boarded and cared for at another's expense. It was more than anyone of her station in life could have expected. Would she rob him of his chance? To keep him at home and gather rushes? Of course not! All she had to do was agree. To sign. To think what the money would mean for the girls. The time to act was now.

The man arrived for the second time when Speranza was shelling beans. She remembered him, or at least his coat. It smelled like an animal, like something freshly birthed in a field. The last time he had come, Lucca was sent to fetch milk though no one they knew would give them any and Mrs Benigno bolted the door to keep the girls inside. Speranza had heard nothing, only a faint sound like laughing or weeping through the wall. Like chickens. This time

Lucca was not sent away. His hair was brushed and he was wearing one of his father's belt-buckles. If he had had shoes, he would have worn his father's shoe-buckles too. The man, whoever he was, was important, and he had come to see Lucca. Speranza was told to go to the well and take the little ones with her, not to return for an hour. When she came back, Innocenzia tugging on her skirt hem and Paola clutching a bunch of herbs in her fist, the man was still there. Mrs Benigno stood and pushed one foot into the fire, pressing down on the embers. Lucca coughed and his face was flushed. He looked as though he had been sitting with them the whole time.

Well, the stranger said. He stood up and his mouth flashed gold when he yawned. He shook Lucca's little white hand as though Lucca were a man. He nodded to Speranza, turned to Mrs Benigno.

Tomorrow, he said. He reached into his pocket and fetched a leather pouch, weighed it briefly in his hand, then took it back again. Tomorrow. He placed the hat squarely on his head with a puff of wig powder, smiled broadly at the girls and dusted his lapels. They were, Speranza noticed, very fine lapels and she might look all she pleased. He did not look once in her direction.

He came back before dawn when the little children were still asleep. It was cold and Lucca shivered. His mother gave him a shawl. Only the man, his collar high on his throat, looked warm. He avoided looking at Speranza's mouth but this time at least addressed her. His name was Fazzi, he said, in the general direction of her ear. And he was a barber but not an ordinary barber. He smiled. He had found Lucca an apprenticeship.

Speranza nodded. She already knew.

The Santa Maria di Loreto, Lucca said. He had said it last night, as though it was the name of a deity, and now he said it again. Speranza had thought the Loreto was a poor house but they taught music, her mother said. Good music. Speranza didn't care what they did. What she knew was that Lucca was leaving. He was leaving for a long time, and he was leaving now.

I will send money when I am trained, Lucca said. His voice rang in the cold air and he placed his hand on Speranza's arm. This is my offering, he said. He looked quite calm while her chest was tight, brittle. His fingers, still fat and pink against the woollen sleeve of her dress, were ranged with long, dirty nails like a beast's. No one was asking her opinion, nothing was going to change. Signor Fazzi coughed and said they should be going.

Lucca had a Bible, a tiny bundle of clothes, bread for the journey. Signor Fazzi nodded to Mrs Benigno and made a little speech. She must not worry. He had signed what needed to be signed, paid the fees, had the necessary letters. He reached into his pocket, showed her a sharp-cornered slip of manuscript, firmly sealed. Everything was in order. He placed a little cloth bag of money directly into Mrs Benigno's hands. Lucca, he said, would make her proud.

Speranza watched Signor Fazzi put an arm around her brother and turn him to the road. Before it was too late, she pushed forward and opened her palm. She wanted to give him something but had nothing, or nothing much. Just a few clam-shells still smelling of the sea. One was hinged and perfect, like two hearts. Take them, she said. This child who almost never spoke. She pushed out her hand. He took. He touched her cheek and traced the line of her broken lip. Then Innocenzia ran out in her nightshirt and Speranza went inside without looking back.

Well, yes. In the strictest sense, her son would not be, since that was how she cared to phrase it, as other men. But he would, in other ways, be more. Even people on this small island had heard the name of Farinelli, the name of Caffarelli and Senesino. How they sang the hero in the finest of theatres, the finest of operas. They travelled all Italy, Spain and France, the German states, to Russia and England. The sopranisti, whatever their background, on the strength of their incomparable voices alone,

lived like kings! And they learned their art here, in the schools of
Naples. Durante was a master famous throughout Europe! In
due course, with such a master, her boy would travel the whole
world and the whole world would, deo volente, fall at his feet.
He would never know the anguish of having an ungrateful
child, never be merely another cuckold. He would become a
special being, above the concerns of the flesh. He would be a
member of a third, purer, sex.

He was sick on the boat but had an uncomplaining disposition and
recovered well. On the mainland, Signor Fazzi hired a cabinet to
take them to the edge of town, then they walked down the side-
streets, through strung-out washing and runaway geese, till they
reached his house. It was not grand, but grander than many, the
street outside noisy with people. It was quiet, Signor Fazzi said:
cities took time. He said they would stay here a few weeks,
becoming accustomed, allowing the time to prepare for the
Conservatory. They would take only ten boys each year, and
Lucca could be proud that he was one of them. He would sleep
one night and tomorrow – tomorrow, there were things to attend
to. Signor Fazzi brought two cups from a shelf, poured wine and
pushed one toward Lucca. It was dark and thick. Signor Fazzi cut
bread and cheese. For later, he said. Once they had talked.

Do you understand my meaning? He sat forward in his chair,
pulled it closer to the table and raised his own cup. Confused,
Lucca drank. It tasted bad, choking as wood smoke, but he
swallowed it down and hoped he had not made a face. He looked
at Signor Fazzi who was merely looking back. My meaning, he
said. You know what to expect? Lucca was not sure what he meant.
In part he knew something, in another part, nothing at all. His
mother had told him about *barbering* the night before, something
to do with letting blood but nothing clear. She had been upset and
he had comforted her and let well alone. And Signor Fazzi had
talked to him on the ferry, shown him the priest's letter of

approval of Fazzi's guardianship and decisions. Lucca could not read, but he recognised the hand, the wax seal. Now, while Lucca sat silent, he told him what his mother had tried to say and failed. Lucca, he said, had had an accident when he was barely more than a baby. He had been sitting outside near the solitary olive tree, defenceless, and had been bitten, no one knew why, by a wild boar. There had been terrible bleeding, fear for his life, prayers to the Virgin, a miraculous recovery. It was a near miracle for which Lucca should always be grateful.

Lucca was grateful. He took a little more of the wine. It was awful, but soothing once it passed over. Signor Fazzi clinked his cup and took a sip himself.

But, Signor Fazzi said slowly. There was also a price.

He looked into Lucca's eyes, put a hand on the boy's shoulder. To this day, Lucca had a hidden infirmity.

Lucca stared at Signor Fazzi.

An infirmity that could not be mended. Which could prove dangerous as the processes of manhood began. Did he understand? And while Signor Fazzi explained, Lucca stared into his wine and listened. He heard the injury was silent, insidious, not yet ripe. Already it was likely he could never father children, for a wound to this place – Signor Fazzi placed his hand between his legs, drew it delicately away – seldom meant anything else. But severed ducts, the little vessels inside his body that attached to these parts, might become infected as he matured. Unless, of course, a good surgeon came to his aid. Fortunately, Signor Fazzi could perform such an operation – a bath, a drink to make him sleepy, a tiny incision he would not feel – and the threat would be gone, definitively and for good. He had done it before and for the same reasons. It was a fine thing, he said, to be able to save a life. What's more, the operation had one more magnificent benefit. Signor Fazzi let the air grow silent before he spoke again, so what he said would resonate in Lucca's fuddled little head. The operation meant his perfect voice would never break and leave him.

Lucca thought of broken things: a reed, a cup, an egg. He tried not to think about the place between his legs and blushed. Wild pigs attacked children indeed, he had heard of such things. He could not remember, but no one remembered babyhood. He would not have children of his own. He might fill with invisible poison poured from invisible vessels. It made no sense. His mother had not said for fear she frightened him; the priest, to save his feelings, but Signor Fazzi was telling him now.

If you are afraid –

No, said Lucca suddenly. His seven-year-old face was pale but earnest. I am not afraid. He raised his cup, and though the taste of the wine disgusted him, he drank again. He cleared his throat and thought about his service to God and the world. He thought of his voice and looked Signor Fazzi cleanly in the eye. I do not want to be broken, he said. I want only to sing.

This, Fazzi thought, his eyes filling, had the feel of destiny. This time, and for much less money than he could have hoped, he had stumbled upon gold.

It took a deal of heat before the bath was hot enough. But Signor Fazzi did not stint. Heat encouraged drowsiness, the necessary looseness of the skin. The boy was shy to remove his clothes before a stranger, and turned his back. Signor Fazzi removed his own coat, his collar and stock. He rolled back his sleeves. He was delicate enough to sharpen the coltello in another room, to hide it so the boy would not see, to soften bread and linen for dressings under cover of heavy cloth. He flavoured the oily, almond suffusion of opium with honey to make it palatable. Sunk to his neck in steam, the boy grew slack-shouldered almost immediately. His eyes closed before he had finished the cup and Signor Fazzi felt sure he had no time to think or fear. He poured milk to aid softening and made sure the boy's head rested securely on the rim of the tub. Then he plunged his hands into the scalding water, felt for the loose sac of skin and stretched it taut, his fingers sensing the cords inside. At once, he tilted the knife, careful his sleeves did not fall as the water bloomed pink as sunset. It was, more or less, over. He checked the testes, foraged out of their hiding place and into his hand, were whole. Like blind eyes, ravelled, intact. There would be no sepsis. The boy's purse would knit together again in a few days with only a fine scar. It would be painful, certainly. But not for long. And Signor Fazzi had his herbs, his tars and poultices, his hard-won ways. A week with good bindings between his legs, with soup and milk and he'd be, almost, his old self. He looked down at the boy, his smooth, unconscious brow. This was the part he liked best, the short time when the boy was innocent and grateful. When he would turn to his mentor out of fear and pain and cry for his mother. It passed, however. It always passed.

Music and philosophy, the heart of all learning, would be his main studies, of course, but the school would provide a firm grounding in dogma, religious observance and literature. He would learn Latin and one other tongue. If he chose to enter religious orders after his time, there would be no impediment. The Loreto also valued modesty, obedience and strict observance of decorum: he would wear a chemise and drawers at all times, even when bathing, his white surplice and sash within and without the school's walls. Talking would not be permitted save in his recreational hour. She should know the castrati were well-fed – two meals a day – and had extra blankets. Not one eunuch had died at the Loreto from malnutrition or cold. Unlike the other boys, they did not riot, so he would never be flogged. He would be kept busy and mindful of duty. He would sing seven hours a day: the Loreto believed it moulded the mind. He would sing for public feast days and holidays, all church and saints' festivals, all masses. He would sing as a cherub at children's funerals; as a senior boy, at those of monks, priests, dukes and even, if his voice deserved it, of kings. Royalty of other nations, particularly the Germans and Russians, often bought boys for

short periods in the course of their studies and treated them
handsomely. At the end of his tenure, he would be paid six
ducats a year for his fidelity: in Lucca's case, some sixty ducats –
not a fortune, but not inconsiderable. And all this time, Signor
Fazzi would act as his guide and mentor, his confessor, his
trusted advisor. The boy should think himself blessed.

He had thought it would be huge, a white palace guarded by stone
lions and weeping angels and pillars big enough to hold a ship.
Dun-coloured and of medium proportions – four of the island
churches might fit inside, not more – it seemed, if not welcoming,
at least bearable. Naples itself was too big, too full of wigs and
door-wide dresses and hawkers and beggars and strays. The
palmed courtyard of the Loreto was soothing. If most of the
governors were stiff in their long wigs and high stocks, one at least
offered him water. If they asked him questions that caused him
pain – how his father died, if his family were truly penniless,
whether he truly loved God – he had ready answers. He remembered Signor Fazzi's advice and was agreeable. When required to
swear that he was truly castrato, that his calamity had a natural
cause, he kept his face steady. He remembered what he had been
told and repeated it word for word. He had been bitten by a wild
pig as a baby and was his mother's only son. It was wholly true.
The music master tested his singing without saying a word and he
was accepted finally, formally, required to make his mark. Outside,
in the cool of the corridor, a painted Virgin that had seen better
days observed him from the wall. Scales and runs and arpeggios
echoed from every corner tangling together like wool on a spindle.
On the dome, he saw white gulls. He heard them, calling.

There were times when he cried and times when he wished the
masters dead, but Lucca served his ten years' contract largely
without complaint, entirely without bitterness. From the day of
his reception, when they dressed him in his white sash, his white

surplice, when the other boys sang fit to shatter the window glass, Lucca had been filled with a sense of rightness and gratitude. He had been saved from death not once but twice, and God had his reasons. He did not mind the tomes of rules or the cramped dormitory with barely a window to air the room at night. He did not mind singing morning devotions even while he washed and made his bed or the wait till noon to eat. He did not mind the silent meals, the silent prayers, the silence in general, for he never had much to say. Least of all did he mind if the educandi, who had fathers who paid for their lessons, looked down their noses at him or when the older boys, the integri with their balls still snug in their drawers and whose voices were broken into their boots, refused to be served their meals by *the fat little eunuchs*. Those boys did not have chicken broth to stave off the cold in winter. Who cared if the educandi caught colds, if the integri were consistently, mutinously, hungry? No one. The sopranisti were particular and everyone knew it. Everyone inside these walls, at least. The spite of envy meant nothing to Lucca. Signor Fazzi told him that boys such as he did well to keep their own counsel and never walk singly. It was good advice. Some of those in his dormitory were arrogant and others were no good. One stole and fought and blamed others for the consequences. But they stood by their own kind, even those who wept for being the kind they were. He did not have family, but he had kinship. He was a disciple at the Loreto, where Porpora and Farinelli had trained, his teacher was the great Durante who had entered the Sant'Onofrio at the age of seven just like himself. The feeling this gave him, one of purpose and continuity and simple use, was something to treasure. If he felt lonely, he searched for the shells Speranza had given him in the bottom of his little box of belongings and held them to his ear. He fancied that way he could hear the sea.

He studied notation and scales, harmony and composition, counterpoint and structure, Handel, Scarlatti and Provenzale. He improved his flexibility with arpeggios over three octaves, decorations, trills, ornamentation and extemporised cadenzas. He spent hours a day on breath control, lung expansion and phrasing. He learned in his own dormitory and in a cramped room with seven harpsichords, seven boys and seven masters, all singing a total of seven different things, where the cacophony taught him how to focus, to chisel the sound clean. He learned with the contralti in the cloakrooms, the young tenors of the integri in the hall, the string players in the side-passages and the trumpets, his favourites, on the stairs. He learned without a desk or a private space of any kind and did not miss what he had never had. He met boys with resentments and regrets, boys with rages that led them to gloom and alcohol without betterment, boys lustful for a future of adoration as revenge upon those who ridiculed their condition. He was none of these. Lucca, as he always had been, was a solitary soul whose thoughts remained his own. As his sense of duty and devotion to the music grew, his voice, like the rest of him, became a thing apart. By the age of twelve, his sound was resonant as the after-tone of bells; a child's pitch but cavernous, layered with sinew and latent muscle. It arched and swooped in the air if he told it to with a reach like the cry of a wolf over snow. He began to grow taller. Much taller. By thirteen, he was alarming. His fingers turned spidery and soft and his backside rounded out like a woman's. His face took on the pale, pouched, chinless look of the older sopranisti he had found so comical when first he arrived. Some were spared the obvious, physical signs. Farinelli, they said, looked almost like any other gentleman. Almost. Not Lucca. Anyone might see from the most fleeting glance that he was indisputably castrato and offer the ridicule or obscenity they deemed fit. And perhaps because it frightened him, he allowed himself, for the first time, to weaken. He wanted to go home, he whispered into the dark, not caring who heard. He smelt tallow in his nostrils, a sting in his eyes. He wished to see if anyone, anyone at all, would know him as he was now. Over a period of weeks, between the creaking of the masters' shoes as they patrolled the corridors, he heard whispers come back. Surely he knew his family would not wish to see him? Was he a fool? He would be nothing but an embarrassment. He looked like what he was and would never again be fit for ordinary life. Besides, what family would wish to be reminded of what they had done? He could never go back, not now. Not now or ever. Unless he became rich, his family, someone said, giggling horribly, would only cut him.

Lucca did not understand. Not initially. Not until the stories began to piece together, fragments returning like weed through water that he had heard or caught in whispers over the years. One boy, he knew, had the kick of a mule to thank for his condition, another had been butted by a ram or a goat. Two had fallen from trees and one had fallen on a harrow, and several had been told nothing at all. Some laughed till they cried when they told their stories, though the laughter had no joy. It was not till the newest boy, Carlo, arrived that Lucca saw the meaning of the pattern. Carlo, a child with a lisp and a pretty face but no care for singing at all, who had been sent to the Loreto because his parents were dead and his grandfather said he was not fit for anything else, said something that sent a dizziness into Lucca's heart and a chill to his belly. He had been bitten, he said, as a baby. Left alone, a wild pig, bleeding and prayers to the Virgin, too small to remember – the words came out as though from Fazzi's own mouth. They twitched in Lucca's head like a rat with nowhere to run, came back to him again and again at night. All these accidents! A wonder the whole of Italy was not maimed, crippled and otherwise disfigured! Such a quantity of coincidence – enough for the whole of Naples, Tuscany and the Papal States put together. Yet this was only one place, one school, one roomful of boys. What it most likely meant was something terrible and Lucca shared his fears with Carlo. It was the wrong thing to do. Next day, pretty Carlo ran away. Boys ran away from time to time, but turned up again within days, even hours, starving, beaten, or frightened senseless by things they never disclosed. Carlo, however, did not return and the maestri never found him. The whole dormitory were punished and Lucca alone felt it deserved. Deliberately, aware of the choice, Lucca refused to wonder what had become of Carlo and turned his mind tenaciously to his slates, his drills. He did not wonder about being childless and loveless, like Mrs Broschi, or what his own life meant. He did not think about his pitiful appearance or what became of a life that had lost its way. He sang. He dreamed of his mother. She could not see him and closed the door. Through the window, he could see a woman he knew to be his sister pour shells from a jar where they turned to water. On the water was a paper boat, turning on its side like a dying fish. Inside was a boy, drowning.

Final year students might begin to grow their hair a little, accept more freedoms. Some, a very few, might be offered the chance to sing in local opera houses by invitation, ready themselves for the future and meet the right people. Their eyes would be opened to the wider world, the expected routines of the profession. Certainly, they would meet people who would offer a thoroughly bad example – some of our most prestigious castrati were beyond the pale in their boastfulness and craving for all manner of indulgence – but others (the divine Farinelli springs to mind) would provide only good. This is a time of trust, when years of diligence and obedience must come into their own, when God will press each boy to choose. Quiet boys sometimes harbour surprises. Mediocre voices may suddenly come into their own, strong voices bloom into incomparability. Yes, occasionally a boy will run away, even on his last day, but not one such as Lucca. He is dutiful, not a rebel. He understands, from some unknown spring, the nature of sacrifice. Of true giving.

By the time he was seventeen, Lucca neared the end of his apprenticeship with a fine prize for his trouble. A blended, even sound that stretched over three and a half octaves without any strain or alteration, his voice was cool and unsettling and more than Fazzi had any right to. No one would have thought it the same little boy who sang in the island church ten years ago, if anyone there remembered him at all. He had sung small roles in at least two opera houses, and one foreign dignitary had suggested a price and offered bribes for Fazzi's favour. The barber had no cause for complaint. More boys than not came out with nothing of good in the voice at all and, if castrati, were fit for nothing but the church or whoring, preferably in Venice, where one might do anything one pleased for the right money. Fazzi had kept faith and the boy had certainly kept his side of the bargain in return. However. However. If he had to be honest, and he did, something was not quite right. The boy's limbs had taken on a somewhat freakish length – it was a risk of his condition – but this was not an overwhelming difficulty. It would invite ridicule certainly, but theatre managers would not turn away from him on that account alone. Not when the primary thing was voice. And the boy's voice was good. It was true and fresh and not in question. But it had lost something. Spark, maybe. The passion and openness that once took the breath away had dimmed a little, almost as though the boy had lost his goal. Still, Lucca at half-power sang better than most ever would. This was not his main concern. The most worrisome thing was the boy's temperament. He had no cunning, no nous as to the depth of obsequiousness required to make an impression on opera house directors or the right composers. He lacked guile or any desire for it and had almost no lust for success. Telling him to sing for God was one thing; everything else seemed to strike him as passing time. No matter. Signor Fazzi, wielder of the coltello, knew more than most that there were ways to arrange for particular outcomes. He would suggest some expensive pastimes, let the boy enjoy the taste, then make it clear how best to secure the money for more. Ambition could be stoked from desperation fairly quickly. Three houses wished to hear him already. Whatever they offered, he could double it by playing off one against another and things would begin to fall into place. With luck, everyone would make a killing. For the first time, serious return on his investment was not only graspable, but likely. What's more, he liked the boy. He had never had children and saw now the disadvantages, the lack of simple affection that Lucca had brought freely, without ulterior motive, to his otherwise solitary, suspicious little life. It brought tears to Fazzi's eyes to think of the boy, his unexpected saving grace. The least he could do was keep faith. He would keep faith and everything, everything would turn out for the best. Immediately, he took himself off to chapel and gave money to St Damian, the patron saint of barber surgeons. With only the slightest feeling of unease rippling his spine, he lit a candle and thanked God.

On his last day at the Loreto, Lucca let the choir fill his head as though he would never hear music again. He sang with his eyes streaming, and did not care who saw. His eyes were red when Fazzi met him in the courtyard and Fazzi, out of pity, embraced him. It had, he said, been a long journey. He gave the boy an address for lodgings, spoke highly of the landlady and promised to meet him there tomorrow. There was a great deal to discuss. Tomorrow, they should buy him a fancy jacket, a wig. Lucca said nothing. Perhaps the gambling tables, or dancing merely to sample the gaiety of the city? Nothing. At a loss, Signor Fazzi pressed some money into Lucca's pocket and told him he would meet him later that night. They could spend it all if they wished. They would make plans, many plans. Lucca could hardly speak. He kissed his mentor as he had kissed Durante, held him tightly. Signor Fazzi recalled his kiss on that day for the rest of his life, the tears of another wet on his own cheek. He never saw the boy again.

He bought a hat to hide his face from the wind and a warm coat for the rest of him, not caring the sleeves were too short. He bought stout boots like a fisherman's, a thick wool shirt, some leggings to keep out the cold. He counted all his money into a new purse. On the ferry to the island, he threw away his papers from the Loreto, his letters of introduction, his signs and seals, and watched them hit the water with no sound at all. No one saw him, no one spoke to him, for which he was grateful. Strangers were often unpleasant when they heard him speak and looked him up and down, reframing. When they *knew*. Silence felt like consolation and everyone needed that. Everyone in the world. Spray touched his cheek, and the low dazzle of the sun made him crush his eyes tight, so he smiled without meaning to. He had only a few things to do today, not many, then he was, if only so to speak, his own man. Silence and the rocking of the boat helped him think, come to terms. He watched Naples diminish behind him till it looked like nothing much, then turned. The shape of the islands near the rocks, those immediately closest to Isla Tenebre, were coming into view. Craggy but green, home only to birds and bones. Lucca had known since he was a boy that his grandfather had died there, that the tiny beaches, those islets that had them, were spangled with skulls from people who had once been as hale as he was now. They had placed themselves in the way of fate to provide for their families, trusted all to God, and He had brought them here. These people were kin, somehow. They were, even though they would have despised him for a eunuch and denied his helpless affection, like him in a way Lucca could not define. The image of pretty Carlo popped into his head unbidden, his wide, blue eyes. Carlo was kin too. The sky was glowering now, threatening rain or worse, making the distance impossible to gauge. If a wind sprang up now, they might drift closer, closer without noticing. Plenty had before. There was nothing here, when the light grew treacherous, to show the way. He thanked God for sparing him death by drowning and was filled with an ache, more than he had ever experienced in his life, a physical pain to sing. He wanted to turn his face to the water, open his throat and give his greatest gift to God and the unburied dead. He wanted, more than he wanted anything else, to sing for all lost souls, especially those no one remembered, and he could not. He could not. Not here. Sorrow tore at him so he thought he would howl, but he caught his breathing, forced himself to steadiness. He tried to rid himself of blame, and think between deep breaths, of his duty, his destiny, purpose. Calm again, clear of mind, he remembered what he had to do. He opened his music bag. A few arias, his harmony exercises, a copy of Durante's book of paradigms lay inside. Calmly, slowly, he opened the bag wide, let the breeze ruffle the thick pages before he turned them into the sea.

A fresh face, rounded and soft. His eyes were brown, his hair long. He was wearing a green coat and nondescript black boots, nothing showy. Castrato, unmistakably. He had expressed no desire to return to his family. What for? A bright boy, quiet and gentle, if given to introspection. His masters say he asked permission, accompanied, naturally, and only occasionally, to walk to the sea, but made no other demands or desires they could recall. A bright voice, potentially of the first rank, but that would not find him. He would hardly be singing in public. Fazzi, an uncle of sorts, would give good money for news. It was a concern the boy might be in danger, even kidnapped. Or drowned. Whatever the case, Fazzi wanted to know. He would pay. He only wished the boy to come home.

There was swearing and lamenting outside and Mrs Benigno ran to see. Her son-in-law had come to say his boat was stolen, its ropes and nets cast to one side like so much rubbish. No one had seen the thief. He was beside himself with rage and grief. Speranza looked up from the chair where she had been sitting for some time and told him to be calm. That morning, she had found the baby playing with something just outside the door and thought it was a pebble. It wasn't. It was a money-bag, and somehow familiar. She looked inside thinking someone must have dropped it and indeed they had. She gave it to her husband now, let him tip its weight onto the table. A pile of ducats, all gold, and something else. Solitary, fanned with veins, a clam-shell.

Mrs Broschi heard, so it was certain. Fisherman had heard it for some time but no one took them seriously. Fishermen went out alone or with idiot boys who believed in ghosts; they got drunk, they heard things, they told crazy stories. Mrs Broschi was crazy too but not in the same way. So the priest went to the same spot on the beach and heard it too. It happened, she said, when weather was poor. Mrs Broschi was sure it was a dead thing seeking company, a demon or a siren luring sailors onto the rocks in storms. It was, she said, nothing human. The priest said it was also nothing intelligent if that was its plan, since the sound it made, like singing drifting over the bay, did nothing but warn sailors away from its source. This voice, whether by accident or design, was more likely to save life than to destroy it. The suggestion of demonry was entirely absurd. Whatever was true or not true, it came from the little islands, a place where there were no people, only dangerous currents, enough rocks to sink a flotilla. The priest listened hard over weeks to rid himself of the fear it was an abandoned child. But it was not a child for it did not fade or seem anxious. It was, in the fragments and gusts in which it came across the choppy water, measured, even beautiful. It was, he announced finally, nothing malevolent. Indeed, when Mrs Benigno came with her daughter, the girl fainted away as if from shock. But she wept when she revived, calling the voice a blessing, a gift from God. She and her husband lit candles in church for the peace the voice had brought her. She was not alone. One woman claimed it had cured her of dark thoughts, another that it brought her comfort from grief. It was a sound of loss and yearning but filled with a kind of glory. More than anything else, with forgiveness. Sailors came to listen, took off their hats out of respect. It was, and they knew it, beautiful. The priest struggled to rationalise, as he always did. He did not wish to be gullible. It might be the wind, he argued; some new species of bird, a freak echo caused by caves underwater or dolphins. They heard him, but knew even he did not fully believe. For the voice kept coming, sounding repeatedly, more persuasively, like just one thing. It was the voice of a lost angel, an angel about its work in the only way it knew how. Keeping faith with God.

Escalator

Michael Gardiner

There are more escalators in Tokyo than in any other city in the world. Movement from station to store to cafe to station is regulated by the escalator and the moving walkway: a person can go for hours without making a decision with their legs at all, except in unison between escalators. In places people can be carried for several minutes without a footstep. The city silently manages the flow of its human content.

Shinya was making the same mistake he made every day: trying to walk up the right-hand side of the escalator at Tokyo station. The right side is the passing side, but the right side was blocked. It always was, and every day Shinya tried to walk up it.

Last week he had seen a documentary on aikido where a seventh dan had glided through a crowd of people as if no one was there. Minute shrugs of the shoulders and hips and he passed through the crowd like water. Shinya had never done aikido.

And when he reached the top of the moving stairway that hit the general concourse of the station, people were moving in every possible direction, almost comically at random, atoms in a gas. He looked round for a place to stop and think: a place of rest, a place of no movement. He'd done this every day, on this same spot, on every one of the two thousand odd mornings he'd passed through the station, but had never noticed himself doing it.

The deadline for documents for the Section Presentation was last Friday. A month ago an estimate had been promised by a design team which had been chosen by a committee of ten people who took an afternoon to fail to make a decision. The present design team had won by default. But Shinya knew something his Section Head didn't know: the design team was going bankrupt. He looked at his hand as he stepped off the moving stairway. He'd been grasping the plastic rail too hard, and his fingers had black streaks on them.

His explanations to his boss were moving closer and closer to outright lies; his trips of atonement up though marbled lobbies from the seventh to the fourteenth floor were becoming more frequent. He'd started getting stomach pains more often. His wife had bought him a jar of tablets she'd seen advertised on TV: he told her they helped, but, static on the passing sides of escalators, he couldn't notice a difference.

From the ninth floor to the twelfth they played a muzak version of 'Purple Haze' using glockenspiel and strings. All executives had attended a Prestigious University and all were composed and serene. Is this tomorrow or the end of time: they glided across the marble floors like industrial vacuum cleaners. From the boss's office on the fourteenth, you could see from the outer wall of this block of shabby offices to the outer wall of the block of shabby offices beyond.

Shinya stood straight-backed while keeping his head slightly bowed, a practised pose which had seen him rise quickly up to the seventh floor. He hid his blackened fingers behind his back and told Takahashi that design was proceeding as planned. His hair was cemented in place, and he'd left his apartment at six to avoid his suit getting crushed in the train: he looked credible.

He knew that these reports were only buying time, and at rates of interest he couldn't afford. The Presentation would happen at a real time and in a real place. At some point it would fall through. This was a real event which would happen. And yet at the moment he could see no way of not lying except falling on his knees and taking the blame for everything. In the office rumours of layoffs always outpaced the lay-offs, but there were, indeed, lay-offs. Shinya had long since got used to uncertainty.

On the way back down he watched the twelfth floor executives in expensive suits hovering across the floor and looking down-wards politely. From the escalator you could see that every executive had impeccable hair, even from above: some used dyes, some had transplants. It can be hard to tell. Each one had the same worries as him, but with fifteen years' and five storeys' more responsibility. Shinya was said to be headed up here, if he stuck to his tasks. He noticed he was gripping the banister too tightly again, and went to the Gents on the seventh floor to wash off the stains.

On the train to Shinjuku at ten he spotted a seat and ran for it. This is something he never does, run for a seat when there are others standing. But he does. We tell ourselves we don't, but we do. As soon as he sat down, balance sheets started scrolling past his eyes, and he woke only immediately before his stop with his head on the shoulder of a girl of about twenty. She looked at him uneasily. He nodded and got off, holding a hand out to fend off the boarding crowds.

A tannoy announcement was talking about a delay at Asagaya. There were three announcements going simultaneously, leading to confusion on the platforms and in the trains. Some stayed on Shinya's train wearing dinosaur looks, as if the trains would all start up as normal if they waited long enough: most realised that the thing to do was reach Nakano on the slow line then change. Hundreds of people from other lines had also realised and were joining them on Platform 10, where a bottleneck eight people deep had built up around the escalator.

When Shinya got a foot on the stairway, a single announcement confirmed there had been a human incident – a suicide – at Asagaya, which had momentarily stopped express trains. One fat Section Head muttered, 'Selfish bastard.'

'Shocking.' An old woman was squashed in behind him.

'Meaningless.'

Up ahead no one could move on the platform, and the crowd was being pushed dangerously near the track. Sweat prickled underneath each collared neck. About five behind the front runners, Shinya remembered, in a sudden vision, that he'd taken his present job, temporarily, as a step towards what he Wanted To

Do. For the moment he couldn't remember what that thing was, what he Wanted To Do. All he knew, moving slowly upwards with his face in the perspiration of some Section Head, was that all of time had collapsed into a single moment during which he couldn't remember what it was that he Wanted To Do.

There was, though, a Now. This was the Now that dictated his responses to Takahashi. And Now, the thing to do was save, save for the baby. For babies do not come cheap.

On the four-station ride to Nakano he had to lean sideways to get a hand on a strap, lifting his left foot half off the floor and stretching his right Achilles tendon. Maybe the thing he Wanted To Do had something to do with two feet being flat on the ground. Or one.

It was after eleven before he got home. The stairs up to his second floor apartment seemed hugely tall, the only flight of stairs he climbed by foot during a working day. Recently there had been a debate with his wife about a private kindergarten, and he anticipated something along these lines tonight. He couldn't see the importance of this before the baby was even born, but Minami had researched the whole thing, as she did with family matters. And she would remind him of his own history of kindergarten, school, Prestigious University, that had propelled him to his job in the city, his mortgage, his Pretty and Capable Wife. To the last acquisition, there was no possible answer.

Tonight, like every night, the last thing he wanted was cross words with Minami. Minami never really argued anyway: she never saw the need, because she always had the information. When Shinya came home every night she looked so responsible. And so, pregnant. He sat down. Minami brought him a beer and some nuts. Cashew nuts: which neighbour had she been talking to this time?

Shinya realised that he could hear a noise from somewhere.

Speech: he could hear speech. He moved closer to Minami, put his ear to her midriff and made out a sort of a conversation:

'Gee, Yuki. It's raining. I wish I'd brought my umbrella.'

'Never mind, Mary, I have two umbrellas.'

'You do? Thank you.'

Shinya let out an involuntary yelp, composed himself, and lifted Minami's blouse. Over the gynaecological bulge there was a foam pad. When he pulled the pad off her gently, there was mesh underneath: it was some kind of speaker, and conversation was issuing from it. When the foam was off, it was quite loud:

'I thought we could go eat kaitenzushi.'

'What's that?'

'It's just like regular sushi, but more fun because –'

Shinya replaced the speaker and blouse and looked at his wife for a while. He went into the kitchen, got another beer from the fridge, opened it, poured. He drank about half the glass and tried to settle himself. You have to be gentle with the pregnant. The pregnant get funny ideas.

'What is it?' he asked her.

'Remember we decided to try for the kindergarten in Setagaya?'

'I don't remember the actual decision.'

'And so, I thought we should give it a serious try. And that takes hard work.' Minami looked down at her body as if the foetus had the casting vote.

'Go on.'

'This gives him a Head Start. And you have no idea how difficult those tests are these days.'

'For a kindergarten?'

'Absolutely. Some kids have been brought up in America, or in, in, other countries. And look at us, we're just, us. We have to make up for ourselves the best we can.'

Shinya sipped his beer, wiped his eyes. He needed some sleep.

'Those learning theories were disproved decades ago,' he croaked.

'Ah. But on an ad on TV today, this Harvard professor was saying that if you use it to memorise chunks, it can have a beneficial effect on things like language learning.'

'Was he a salesman?'

'Mmn – I think some company was using his evidence. But really. It works. And it was on sale.'

'It was on sale? Meaning, like, how much?' Minami pointed to her mouth, which she'd filled with nuts, to indicate that she couldn't speak.

'Sweetheart, I'm not sure. I mean, isn't it past his bedtime?'

Minami laughed.

'Silly.' She touched his nose. She thought for a while, filling her mouth with nuts whenever he seemed ready to raise an objection. When he was drinking his beer, she said, 'Do you know what the unemployment rate will be when he's twenty-one? Every mother in this block is doing all they can. And if he gets into the kindergarten, he's in the elementary school, and junior high and high school, and then he's a graduate of some place which gives him a chance in life. It's natural that escalator school places don't come easy. It's common sense.'

'Yes. You don't think that now he needs a, a rest?'

'He'd better get used to the studying.' She made a fake-angry face, which, when she did it, was also oddly sexy. It was one of the things that had attracted him to her.

'Dad, you sound like you don't want your child to have all the opportunities you had. And that was what you promised me the day we got married.'

Shinya sighed and picked up the instruction manual lying on the table:

TO GIVE YOUR CHILD THE CHANCES S/HE NEEDS IN OUR INTER-NATIONAL FUTURE SOCIETY, YOU'LL WANT HIM/HER TO GET AHEAD IN ENGLISH STRAIGHT AWAY. AND THAT'S WHAT THE WOMBPHONE PROVIDES. TO START USING THE WOMBPHONE, SIMPLY SPREAD A LITTLE OF THE ENCLOSED JELLY ON YOUR ABDOMEN AND CHOOSE FROM ANY ONE OF FIFTY EVERYDAY CONVERSATIONS THAT ANY NATIVE SPEAKER WOULD –

He shivered, and closed the book.

'Have you asked anyone else about this?'

'I phoned Dad. He thought it was a fantastic idea. In fact, he loaned us the money. He wanted to buy it for us but I told him no, you were earning plenty. He was surprised you hadn't bought one already.'

'That was generous of him.' Shinya rubbed his eyes slow and hard with thumb and forefinger until he saw silver streaks.

Minami went on: 'Get into the kindergarten, and they'll prepare you for the next stage, and then you're on the ladder to –'

'To success. Like I am. You already reminded me.'

'So the kindergarten tests have to be demanding in the escalator schools. They can't just let anyone in. You should know.'

'That's why the fees are so high.'

'Grumpy. Parents should be glad to do everything they can.'

Shinya recognised this as a con-trick played by the pregnant. He knew that she knew that he'd do anything for his son. He'd take the same Achilles-stretching train ride and rise black-handed to fourteenth-floor debt until death.

But now his tired mind had moved to something other than money. The chance of a corner out of the flow of human content. His imagination had drifted into the future, and his son's vision of something he Wanted To Do. He found that the only way he could explain this to Minami was in financial terms.

'And you think we can afford this till he's twenty-one?'

'It'll be tight. But you're doing so much extra work, and – things are looking up, aren't they?'

'I'm having a bath.'

'You can't. The water's gone.'

'Then I'm going to bed.'

'Already?'

Shinya looked at his watch. It was quarter to twelve. If he fell asleep right now he'd still only get six hours.

She said, 'Then I'll come with you.'

Without a bath Shinya's body was itchy, but Minami didn't

seem to mind. She drew him closer as she often did, so that his head was resting on her shoulder and his left ear was near to his unborn son, sometimes near enough to hear his heartbeat. These days Shinya fell into deep and fitful sleeps. And tonight's dream started with a conversation that was strange even by dream standards, since it was in English:

'It's just like regular sushi, but much more fun because the plates go round and round, and you choose the ones you like.'

'That's fantastic. There's so much more I have to learn.'

I Should Have Listened Harder
Clio Gray

It's night at Nertchinsk and here we sleep three deep to keep
ourselves warm. Yesterday, the little man who made a fiddle out of
nails and string didn't wake up with the rest of us. We should have
known better than to put him at the bottom, but there it was. You
have to take your turn. His face was flax-flower blue, his skin like
wet putty, carrying the impress of his clothes and boots and our
fingerprints as we stripped him down. We threw him into Disused
Mineshaft number 15B, saw his pale form twist and fall, disappear
into dark. No use digging ground for graves when it's four feet
deep with frost, no use wasting half-decent clothes and boots. We
let him take his fiddle with him. No one else could get a tune out of
it anyway. It wasn't the worst thing I have ever done and I have
done many things, and there are better places I have been than the
lead mines of Nertchinsk.

The best thing I ever did was meet my Tzrika. The worst thing I
ever did was lose him. I called him my son, but he wasn't. I found
him in a place near Vitim where they said we could build ourselves
a village, plant crops, make a new life. I'd been through the world
and not liked it; I'd come back to Tomsk, soaked myself in good
Russian vodka till my liver began to rot without waiting for the rest
of me, without waiting for the coffin lid to close. I'd signed up for
the New Frontier, got my pass and plot-number, bought my spade
and sack of seeds and set off for the Promised Land. I met some
other stragglers on the road and when we finally made it through
Vitim and reached the place we'd marked with a cross on our
maps, we stopped. We unpacked our baggage, began to set up our
tents, marked out our plots with sticks and string. And then the
soldiers came up from the town behind us, told us the Grand
Scheme was scrapped, though they couldn't tell us why. We could

join the Jews at Birobidzhan, the New Israel a thousand miles to the east, or we could go down to Baikal and scrape a living from its shores. There are the roads, they said, and there are choices: you can go this way or that and we'll be back in the morning. But we'd come too far and could go no further, so we stood by our collapsing shelters, gripping our tent poles sharpened into stakes and refused to go.

'Leave!' they told us and we stood by our pathetic village and shouted back our Noes. They levelled their guns and shot us down, told us one way or the other, we would be gone. And we were. There was me and the boy and two old women who were left to tramp the track to Baikal. We got there, or rather me and Tzrika did. One of the women got sick on the way and the other stayed to look after her.

'Go,' she said, 'we'll catch you up,' but we all knew she wouldn't, and she didn't. And so me and the boy arrived at Baikal, and it was early summer and warm. I found work on the boats and a place to live and Tzrika stayed home twisting ropes into nets and against all the odds, we were happy. We dawdled along its banks, me and Tzrika, when I wasn't working. We got our month of fish, some blubber-oil for our lamps; we smoked fish-skin into leather, traded it for flour and tea and sold Tzrika's nets back to the boats. We took walks, made bows and arrows out of wych-elm, skewered rabbits and marmot for the pot. We told each other stories as we mended our trousers, darned our socks, drank a bit of vodka with our tea. We visited the Caves of the Lonely Sea where the waves will tell a man his future as they lap against the walls on a Midsummer's Eve.

But we were late.

It was autumn.

And we didn't know the Baikal at all.

They call it a sea, the Baikal, and it's like a sea but it isn't. Fifty miles wide from shore to shore and three hundred miles long it stretches: it is London to Paris, Kiev to Odessa, it is the entire width of Iceland. These are all places I have been, but nowhere was so beautiful and blue as the Baikal, with its basalt cliffs running sheer into the water and down to the centre of the earth. It is a windswept width of water – everyone will tell you so. It has from the north the Gara wind which lifts the surface six dark yards into the air, sends the water crashing back again, makes toothpicks out of fishing boats and trees, flings fish overland for a mile. From the south-west comes the Koultouk, milder, wetter, slapping the surface into wet curls, painting it with streaks of white, sending the scree slipping from the hills down to muddy its banks; in between comes the Bargouzine, chasing from east to west like a djinn, hard and cruel, quick and vicious, bringing ice and sleet and hail which cut like cat-whips soaked in frozen milk. And then, when the sun is low and the days are short, when it freezes in its long winter, we think the Baikal sleeps and forgets. We dance with our skates upon its skin, run dog-sleds up and down its back. It is deep, so deep: a thousand fathoms sink beneath our feet as we glide like mites across the surface of its eye. We trade from it, we steal from it, tea merchants from China pass as if it is their Right of Way. But the Baikal knows, and all of a sudden it cracks and yawns a gap of fifteen miles and whoever is there on the ice at that moment, is lost without mercy and gone.

And just when the Baikal was beginning to slumber, when the mercury was already sluggish in the glass, I got the boils down my back like a spill of summer rain. I covered them with creosote, rubbed them with oil, strapped on a babushka of butter and gunpowder, but nothing worked. I'm a foreigner here, I ask advice, I take it. I butcher a Baikal seal down its middle and wear it warm as a cape. The boatman is shouting, 'Last boat out before it's winter!' but the boils are not cured and the skipper demands Tzrika in my place.

'No boy for the boat, no work for you next season,' said the skipper, hard as those Baikal basalt cliffs. 'We're not taking some boil-infested bastard to infect the rest of the crew. It happens,' he'd said, and shrugged his shoulders. 'I can't go out with one man down.'

What could I do? What could we do? Tzrika was eager; I will be a man, he said, and the skipper agreed. I think about that now, what I should have said and done, but it's always too late. I never knew that fiddle-player's name, but he used to say that no man gets to pick his own tune, and he was right. I stayed on the shore of the Baikal wrapped in my sealskin, and the boat went out and with it went my Tzrika. Two days I waited, while the Gara wind growled down early from the mountains like a hungry bear woken too soon from its sleep. Back came the boat in bits, and gone were the catch, half the boat-house, all the nets. And then came that skipper, hard-ridged and red from the wind, death written right across his face, tramping resolute across the shingle. I didn't wait for him to tell me what he had done. I shook that sealskin from off my shoulders and smothered him with it there on those ice-encrusted stones, the clot-rotten seal-blood black upon his face, his gaping mouth the new-dug grave by which I had been waiting. Waiting for the only son I ever had. Or ever would have, and my Tzrika, blown from off the bridge of that skipper's boat like a leaf and swallowed in the blackness of the Baikal. Should I forgive the skipper? Should he forgive me? I don't know. What I do know is it's a long way from Baikal to Nertchinsk: four hundred miles of hard country over the Yat and the Yablonoyy mountains. Take my advice and plan your murder well into the winter, then at least you'll stay at Ullan Ude till the spring. Not so for me. I took those mountains with my hands in fetters just as the winds began to call and the snow was trailing in. I wore my jerkin of sealskin, burned a map into the inside to plan for my escape. But Nertchinsk isn't like Sakhalin where people throw themselves into the sea and always drown. Keeps the prison populations down they say, which is good in a place where there's always more, like rats, to take their place. I used to dream of being sent to Sakhalin, setting off into that sea like so many have done before. I would cling to a raft of driftwood the fifty miles to Japan. That's all it is: two peoples, two continents and only fifty miles apart. Who thinks of that? Only those of us who do nothing but work and sleep, work and sleep, which is what we do at Nertchinsk. We sleep, we work, and sometimes we think. It isn't allowed, but we do it anyway. I think of my Tzrika and know I will never have another son. Not now. Not ever. Not after Nertchinsk. They tell me it's the lead.

We dig the mines the old way, with pickaxes; we smelt the ore the cheap way, on a turnbole, a huge wooden platform raised above the fire. It is mounted on gimbals so we can swing it to the prevailing wind to fire up the flames. It keeps some of us from freezing, makes sure we can work another day. We sit in our heaps next to the turnbole, wrapped in our blankets, no longer caring about the fleas and lice that survive the cold of the night, tell each other stories about how things might have been. I lie there in my sealskin jacket and listen to the wolves. They remind me of the echoes in the Caves of the Lonely Sea. And I think: I think I should have gone there earlier. I should have planted my ear to those cold cave walls the whole midsummer-night through, and then maybe, maybe, we would still be mending nets together and darning socks and drinking tea warmed with vodka and wallowing with seals in the brief summer of the Baikal when the elks come down from the hills and the water is warm.

These are the things which I have done and the places I have been.

It is my turn on the bottom and I have taken off my sealskin jacket. Use it if you find it, for I will not. I see it lying at the edge of fire-light, half in darkness. I turn my head away. I burrow below the shivering bodies of my workmates.

'Pile on, lads,' I murmur, 'pile yourselves high and bury me deep.'

It is dark. Strangely, it is quite warm. I cannot move. I will never move again, except to Disused Mineshaft 15B. My very own cave in my lonely, sonless sea.

We work, we sleep, sometimes we think and as I lie here, I think maybe there is another summer somewhere, maybe Tzrika is already there and if I listen hard enough, maybe I will hear him and better still, maybe, if I keep still enough, he will hear me.

We work, we sleep.

And then there comes the time when we no longer have to think, and this is mine.

Budding

Carole Hamilton

The day is heavy as a coffin. Droves of flies swarm around the cattle. Long tails swish them away. Jack jumps and barks at the beasts that sit like statues on a bed of green. The collie runs this way and that, winding in and out of the animals scattered over the field. Playfully nips their noses. Still they ignore him. Bat eyelashes, flick away flies, continue to chew their cud. Fiona rounds them in, pushes on their guts to get them up. Why keep a dug an bark yersel? Drew says. Fiona closes the gate behind the stragglers. They jump their heavily-in-calf bodies over the poached ground. Wearily she winds her way towards the farmhouse. Stops to brush skitter off the byre walk. Wellingtons stand in a soldier-straight line. Blue overalls, a dark pool spread on the outhouse floor. She sits at the kitchen table fagged out. Eight o'clock, the morning shift done. She goes through her escape plan to a breakfast eaten in silence. The telephone rings. Fiona answers. Drew turns his head to catch the conversation.

– You'll no be here till ten thirty. An emergency. That should be fine. No, they're tied in the byre waiting.

She hangs up.

– He had to go to a breach birth.

– I'll have another cup.

Fiona lifts the large aluminium teapot off the Raeburn. Refills the mugs.

The surly silence of him reading the paper threatens her mood.

Mr Williams and his assistant wear rubberised trousers. They tie white plastic aprons on after removing their jackets. In the small byre Fiona and Drew stand in the bis holding the stirks' heads and flanks to stop them jerking. They haven't been handled before. The vet takes a large plastic syringe, inserts the liquid into the corner of the animal's eye. It tries to grapple and break free. They hold the chain tight. A hoof crunches down on Fiona's toes making her eyes water. In and out each bis till all the beasts are numb. They bellow and struggle at the closeness of humans. Sense what is to come.

– Did you miss this batch then?

The vet nods towards the twenty beasts.

– Aye, I had the flu and the wife here could only dae the milkin, these got missed.

– It's easy to take the buds away from the calves, not so easy now.

– Ah ken.

Mr Williams brings out a hacksaw and lays black plastic sheeting on the ground. He'd been the talk of the town last summer. Had an affair with his assistant nurse, Suzy, young enough to be his daughter. His wife now works as receptionist in the practice and Suzy has got a new job on the other side of the valley. Fiona leaves them to it. She tidies the byre, waits for the water to circulate through the pipeline and milk dishes.

Inside, pots simmer on the stove. Steam circles overhead. The flypaper is stubbed with dark shapes. She opens a window to let one escape with the steam. Lays the table with knives, forks and spoons. Lifts a towel and takes the baking trays from the oven. Sets the rhubarb tart in the middle of the table. The scones, fairy cakes and fruit loaf she spreads on the worktop, then transfers them to a wire cooling tray. Removes the knucklebone from the broth and gives it to Jack. He sniffs it, jumping back from the heat. Paws it around for a bit until it cools. Grinding his teeth on bone, drawing the marrow from it. She slips in and out of the door to watch dinner and to see if the men are finished. Finally, she hears voices.

– A bit of a mess, all right.

– Glad we don't have to do that too often.

– Fiona, bring us something to wipe ourselves wae.

She recoils at the sight of them. Waterproof trousers and white plastic aprons are covered in blood. Hands and arms with sleeves rolled up, a mass of red. The men's eyes are wide and wild as slow drips darken the outhouse floor. Jack wanders round licking the drops that fall. They take turns using the sink. Fiona gets some old cloths and towels and stretches her arm over the bis.

– Are they all right?

– Aye. When the freezing wears off they'll have sore heads.

– Where did all the blood come from?

– When you cut through the horn, you sever the blood vessel. The byre floor's covered.

Fiona loses her appetite, between the heat from the cooking and the sight of the blood. She dishes out the dinner, clatters plates down on the table.

– What will I do in the afternoon, start and muck the small calf pen out?

– That'll dae.

She sits in the garden with a mug of coffee and fruit loaf dripping with butter. The air gets rid of the smell in her nostrils. Sparrows are splashing in the puddle at the gate. A patch of clover on the lawn. She gets down on her hunkers and looks for a lucky one in the tightly packed green leaves. They all have three, unlucky again. Picking some daisies, she makes a chain. She lays it on the table, rinses her cup before going back out.

In the tool shed, she lifts a graip. Looks in the small byre at the stirks. The air is heavy with the smell of fresh blood. The animals are quiet, lying down, breathing heavily. The door to the calf pen is ajar. Seven calves run free in the field beside the house. The straw and dung's piled higher than the doorway. It smells sweet. Their diet's milky. She hasn't lost a calf this year. Sticks the graip into the tightly packed manure, fills the barrow, caked in old shit. Wheeling it to the midden she tips it over. A sheep's carcass lies on top. The shrunken flesh eyeless, something's ravaged the remains. The sun begins to poke behind the row of beech trees up the old road.

Fiona leans on the handle watching the ripples of light dance between the shadows of the trees. Jack still rolls the bone around the outhouse floor.

The daisy chain lies flat and wilted on the kitchen table.

Next day rain pours from the heavens but by evening it's stopped. A flight of starlings making for the city rest on the shed's corrugated roof. Every hour, they take turns to check the beasts. Most of them have stopped bleeding and bellowing. She scoops some extra cake into the troughs. The blood's begun to congeal and go black. Carefully she scatters straw in the grip, cuts open a bale of hay, gives each of them a slice to settle them for the night. She'll put them in the other byre the morn and clean up. Puts the chains around their necks to stop them bashing each other. One cow's separate from the rest, ready to calve. She gives it some extra feed and spreads some soft fresh bedding around it.

Inside, the windows are veiled in steam from tinkling pans. Fiona lifts the beef from the simmering pot. A trail of fat freezes to fondue when it lands on the cold floor. She hands the plate to Drew, who eats the stringy beef with yellow fat. It leaves his fingers and mouth slimy. Taking blotting paper, she mops up some grease from the grey water. Lifting the wooden chopping board, she methodically slices the potato and leek into small round segments. Alternate days she makes soup. Sometimes broth, others lentil. Depending on the cut of meat available. She scrapes the neat vegetable sections into the pot. Flotsam and jetsam on top of the dark liquid. Slings the steeped broth mixture on top with the rest. Carrot grating she leaves till last. Her back hurts from the angle it's bent at. One done, two to go. She stops suddenly as her skin grazes the metal. The blood spurts from her knuckle and mingles with the orange shreds. She examines the fresh marks on her red and callused hands. Rubs cream into the chafed skin and runs her finger under the tap then sticks a plaster on.

Stretching into the chest freezer she takes out frozen stew

cooked last week. Shoulder beef from the heifer that stood at the first bis in the byre. Around four hundred and fifty pounds of neat packages came back. She spent the week before last cooking mince and stew and refreezing it. For emergencies. She sits the block in a pottery bowl to thaw. For the second time that day she prepares vegetables. Her arms rest on the sink as the small of her back gets sore. Drew sits at the large oak dining table marking up the books with one eye on the farming weather programme.

She rinses out the basin and sets the pots on the cooker. Stokes some dross in the Raeburn and turns the temperature down. Lifts the towels from the pulley and folds them into a bundle. From the boiled kettle, she pours water into chipped mugs and carries them through to the living-room. Drew speaks without raising his head.

– We'll need to phone the dead animal lorry. There's a sheep at the byre end and an auld dun cow in the corner field behind the cottage.

– I saw the sheep. What happened tae the cow?

– She wis jiggered. Her feet wur bad and her body was aw shrunk. It happens like that sometimes, they just die. Will you phone?

She lifts the receiver and starts dialling.

– We've got two beasts to be collected the morn, a cow and a sheep. Morton's Farm. Aye that's right, about eleven the morrow. Right, I'll tell him. They'll be around at eleven in the morning. That's the dinner aw set up ready. I'll see tae the reddin up when I get back.

– They two auld mincers that staun at the tap of the byre, the Ayrshires, they'll need to go to the market. They're yell, hardly give a gallon atween them. Costing mair tae keep them. They'll die next. Can you ring the market and get them picked up?

– Are they no in calf?

– I thought they were but I think they're jist past it. They can hardly hirple in and out the field their feet are that bad and their udders nearly touch the ground. Lost the grip of their bags.

– They'll be shut, it's efter nine, I'll do it in the mornin afore I go.

She sits on her usual seat, the mottled tweed sofa with frayed arms. Her brown trousers and woollen jumper merge with the fabric. Everything about her smells of monotony. She pokes the fire and shoves on another log. Sparks fly out onto the fireside rug. Quickly she wipes them away with her hand. Black holes appear on the stained carpet.

– I'm no finished these books yet. Will you check the beast in the byre again?

– Right.

Pulling on boots, she opens the byre door and switches on the light. The bull starts to bellow and shake his chain. From the other end comes a low moaning. The cow has started calving. She's lying on one side with a pained expression. The calf's feet are sticking out. Afterbirth spills onto the grip in a pool mixed with the dung. It hadn't burst yet but its head begins to balloon out towards the cement. Cow's skin is stretched taut. She gets a shovel and clears away some dung. Puts straw bedding around it. The day's work's not over; they'll have to keep checking until she calves. She leaves the byre light on and goes back in.

Next time they check the calf's head's pushed halfway through. The head's so big Drew thinks it's a bulldog calf. After a struggle, she manages to give birth and lies stretched out, wabbit. Insides near ripped apart. The calf tries to stand but it's too slippy, from the slimy afterbirth. Fiona wipes it away and leads it to its mother, for her to lick clean. Guides its mouth to the teat and massages the calf's mouth. Eventually it begins to suck. Fiona stands holding it, to support its wobbly body and prevent it from toppling over. Once it's full, she steadies it towards the pen. Prising her finger into its mouth she pushes its head into the milk pail. Soon it's drinking on its own without suckling her finger. Its head jolts up for air. Fiona gently directs it back into the pail.

The last of the light is leaving the sky as she walks back to the house. The countryside is silent like the night is waiting to pass. Quietly she moves through the gloom, a prisoner walking slowly back to her cell. A fragrance of damp grass hangs in the air with the clattering of water passing down the brook.

Odd Jobbing
Nick Houldsworth

For most of his journey on the Piccadilly line from Wood Green to Leicester Square, Terry sat opposite a fat rich man and his trophy wife. He discreetly eyed them up. The fat rich man wheezed like a penny whistle through his nose when he spoke, and his skin was pallid like wet chalk, but his suit expensive and his young wife tanned and svelte like an otter. She wore a blank expression of kept contentment, which probably cost far more to maintain than anything the man was wearing.

He started to read the Tube adverts instead. Above and slightly to the left of the man's head was a poster for *Jesus Christ Superstar*, Lloyd Webber's latest offering to the West End masses. Charlie must be doing all right out of that, he thought. His old acting-school friend had tried to get him along to the auditions, but Terry had convinced him that it wasn't really his bag of buns. In actual fact, he thought Lloyd Webber produced little more than juiced-up pantomime crowd-pleasers, but he resisted the urge to tell Charlie this at the time, an omission he was glad of when his friend later landed a major part.

The truth, however, was that Terry could neither sing nor dance his way out of a pensioner's homecoming, but his preferred line was to tell people that 'he was only interested in serious drama, film or television'. Still, the steady income would be nice.

The carriage was becoming heavy with the young wife's perfume, and he was glad to get off at Leicester Square and step out into the warm spring air. London had her own smell at this time of year too; musky tarmac, rubber and pipes. Not exactly perfume, but comforting in itself.

He lit a cigarette and walked west through the square, turning right at the end onto Wardour Street. It was April and lighter in the evening now. Neon signs blinking outside gentlemen's clubs coated the cars in a cartoonish glow. Crossing Shaftesbury Avenue he passed a small group of kids in full punk uniform. The girls wore safety-pins in their skin, and the boys, who must have spiked their hair with egg yolks and flour, looked like zombie Roman generals. He admired their effort.

After continuing up Wardour Street to the offices of Absalom Productions at number 87, he passed through the glass doors into the small lobby, and took the brass elevator to the third floor. The office receptionist politely asked him to take a seat then buzzed her boss.

A pretty enough girl, he thought, but too much slap. Shame.

'Terry, nice to see you again!' said a bearded man with a faint Cockney accent, standing in the corridor at the far side of the room. He walked over to Terry, in his matching chocolate shoes and sweater with black velvet slacks. It was a style that almost worked, but mostly didn't.

'Hi Paul, how are you?' Terry said, standing up.

'Good, thanks,' he waved about the room. 'So you found the new offices OK?'

'Actually, I've been here before.'

Paul pretended to slap his forehead. 'What am I thinking? Of course you have. Sorry.' He led Terry past reception. 'Let's go through to the kitchen, shall we? Get you a cup of tea. Suzie's waiting for us there.'

They walked down a long corridor with stucco wallpaper and deep blue carpet. On the walls were framed black-and-white photographs of minor celebrities, film extras, and a man with his hand up an animal puppet. The 'kitchen' was a cramped cupboard conversion at the end of the corridor. Suzie sat at a fold-down Formica table and smiled when they came in. Terry knew her, they'd worked together before. She was cute in a homely way, and the cloth cap and suede jacket she wore made her look younger than she actually was.

'Hello Suzie,' he said. 'Lovely to see you.'

'Thanks Terry,' she said, 'and you. Paul only just told me we'd be working together. I'm glad.'

'Me too.'

'OK, kids,' Paul said, 'there's a pot of tea by the kettle, and coffee in the cupboard. It's only instant, I'm afraid. I'll be back in five with the scripts.'

Terry fixed himself a tea and a cigarette, and sat on a plastic chair opposite Suzie, squashed between the wall and the table. It was an uncomfortable little space. They should rename it 'The Tea Cupboard', he thought, but immediately decided it wasn't funny enough to say out loud. Before he felt obliged to come up with something that was, Suzie spoke.

'I saw the Brillo commercial,' she said. 'I thought you were good. Very funny.'

'That?' he laughed. 'That was nothing serious, just a little cash.'

'A bit like this then?'

'In a way, yes.'

'Well, you were still good.'

'Thanks.' There was a short, awkward silence. 'How's Phillip?'

'He's good, thanks.'

'The kids? They're well?'

'Yes,' she smiled, 'a right pair of tearaways!'

He thought for a moment. 'And are you currently working on, anything . . . else?'

'Not right now, no. But I'll be involved in a play at The Albery this Autumn.'

'Terrific. Who's it by?'

'Some new young star apparently. Harry Lockwood. Have you heard of him?'

Terry made the face of someone pretending to think. 'No, I don't think so.'

'Me neither!' she laughed. 'It's something heavy and dramatic though, I think. You know the type.'

Terry nodded.

'And what about you?' she asked, 'any projects on the go?'

'Well, I'm waiting to hear back from my agent about an audition he put me up for. It's a . . .' but before he could finish, Paul came loudly through the door and sat down next to Suzie.

'OK, guys, here are the scripts,' he said, passing them out. 'There's only two to do tonight, sorry. We're still waiting on the other. Maybe later in the week. We'll call your agents, if that's cool?' They nodded. 'So it's a standard voiceover, you know the drill. The first film's German, the second is Dutch, I think. Not that it matters to us, since the sound will be turned down.' He stopped shuffling his scripts for a moment, and looked at them each with a raised eyebrow, 'Unless, of course, you plan on watching them at home?'

They all laughed, a little nervously. Paul continued, 'You'll be doing two characters in each film. Any more than that wouldn't be believable, according to the distributors at least. If it was my call, I'd have you doing them all, but it's their money, so that's how it is. There are three scenes together in the first movie, and four in the second. Try to vary the voices as much as you can. Your parts are marked out in coloured pen, see?'

They opened the scripts and started leafing through the pages.

'How long do you need to have a read through? Twenty minutes?' he asked.

'That should be fine,' Suzie said.

Paul checked his watch, got up and moved towards the door. 'OK. Meet me through in the sound booth at, say, half seven. You know where to go.'

The sound booth was a larger room down the corridor. It was divided into two smaller rooms by a partition wall and a large glass window. On the other side of the window was the control room, where Paul waited for them at a large mixing console, smoking. Except for the cigarette ember and the glow of valves and meters on his face, it was dark. In the recording room, the walls were lined with egg-carton shaped foam, so that it resembled a padded cell in a space-age lunatic asylum. Having spongy properties, the foam walls were good at soaking up both tobacco smoke and body odour, and the room uniquely preserved the smell of everyone who had ever worked in it. Positioned near the window were two high stools, a pair of headphones, and two chunky microphones hanging from the ceiling. There was a large TV monitor above the window.

Terry and Suzie took their seats, and put on the headphones. Paul spoke through a desk mic, his voice close in their ears. 'We'll be starting with scene three of *Die Liebmaschine*.' They opened out their scripts to page eight. 'Do you want to do a quick run through first?' he asked.

'I don't think we need to,' Suzie said casually.

'Just go for a take,' Terry said. 'If we balls it up we can do it again. Excuse the pun.' Suzie giggled.

'OK, fine.' Paul said. 'Are the levels OK for you?'

They nodded.

'Here we go then.' He reached to his right and pressed the tape record button.

Above the glass, the TV monitor switched on, showing first static, then a flickering film reel. The picture was a grainy, 8mm image of a living room in a modern, Scandinavian-looking house with low ceilings, wood-panelled walls and stone fittings. There was a plush velour sofa in the middle of the room, and beside it a cream plastic telephone on a small table. The volume was low, but they heard the telephone ring. Jerkily the camera cut to a close-up of the phone, then back to the wide shot of the room. A young woman walked into frame, dressed in a skimpy nightgown, with straw-coloured hair and heavy mascara. She sat on the sofa and answered the phone. The camera cut to a close-up of her face, and Suzie began lip-synching into the mic, reading from the script.

'Hello?' Suzie read, feigning a squeaky teenage voice.

Through his headphones, Terry could just make out the voice of the actual actress beneath Suzie's dialogue.

'Yes, this is Mrs Whitehouse . . .'

'That's right, my husband phoned yesterday about the crack in the floorboards . . .'

'Yes, in the master bedroom . . .'

'You can send someone round now?'

'Oh, that is good news, thank you.'

'OK, bye then.'

The scene faded out to black, then faded back to a medium shot on the front door. A doorbell rang, and Mrs Whitehouse answered it, still in her nightgown. At the door was a tall, tanned man in denim cut-offs and a patterned shirt, carrying a little yellow toolbox. He had a big brown moustache and blow-dried hair. Terry had to hold back a laugh for fear of missing his first line.

'Hello, I am Hans,' he read into the mic, hamming up a deep Euro accent. 'Hans the builder.'

'Hello Hans,' Suzie read, 'Have you come about the crack in the floorboards?'

'Yes. That is why I have come.' Terry read, trying to synch the words to the actor's wooden facial expressions.

'Good, then. They are through in the master bedroom. Follow me please.' The camera cut to a wide shot again, and Mrs Whitehouse walked across the living room, Hans following. Their movements were robotic and stiff. The camera followed them unsteadily.

'I am sorry,' Suzie read, 'my husband usually takes care of these matters, but he's at work right now.'

'That is OK,' Terry read. 'I'm sure we can fix the problem together.'

The bedroom walls were painted yellow ochre, and blond wooden slats lined the floor. At the foot of the bed was a large Persian rug. The camera cut again to a medium shot of the actors.

'The problem is under the bed,' Suzie read as Mrs Whitehouse made a weak hand gesture towards the floor.

'You can show me, please?' Terry read.

'Sure thing, Mr Builder,' Suzie read, suggestively now.

Mrs Whitehouse smiled, winked and walked over to the bed. She bent down on her hands and knees, and rummaged about underneath, which caused her short nightgown to bunch about her waist, so that her rear end was staring Hans in the face. The camera cut to a close-up of her face, still under the bed.

'Hmm, that's funny,' Suzie read, 'the crack doesn't look so bad from here.'

Back to a close-up of Hans, smiling, his left eyebrow raised.

'Ja, I know,' Terry read, 'it looks just fine from here.' The camera jumped to a wide-room shot of Mrs Whitehouse on all fours, her head stuck under the bed, with Hans standing near behind slowly unbuttoning his shirt. In the headphones, Terry heard cheap funk music fading in. Hans bent forward and started kneading Mrs Whitehouse's raised behind.

Terry read, 'But I still think it will need a little work, ja?'

'Ooh, Mr Builder!' Suzie read, faking surprise.

The rest of the scene was largely ad-lib moaning and grunting, and, apart from the occasional 'That's good, baby' or 'Ooh, Mr Builder', did not require particularly tight lip-synching with the actors. Terry kept pulling faces at Suzie, and towards the end they struggled to keep from breaking into laughter. A few giggles did leak onto the soundtrack, but on playback they more or less blended into the sweaty action onscreen.

'Nice one chaps,' Paul said, pausing the tape at the end of the scene. 'You want to review it again, or leave it till the end?'

'Let's just move onto the next one, shall we?' Suzie said.

By ten thirty they'd completed all seven scenes, and raced through master playback, stopping only once or twice to overdub mistakes. They wrapped at quarter past eleven, early enough for

Terry to catch the last tube home. He walked Suzie back down to reception. Paul met them there a few minutes later.

'Anybody fancy catching last orders?' he asked.

'Sorry, Paul,' Suzie said, 'I have to wake up early to get the kids to school.'

'Terry?'

'Maybe next time, mate. I've got to dash to make the last tube.'

'OK, guys, no problem,' he said, mocking a sigh. 'I'm going to be here all night anyway.'

They walked to the elevator together.

'So, it's the usual rate. I'll get a cheque out to your agents no later than Friday.' He pressed the button for the third floor, and all three of them watched the numbers light up in sequence as it climbed. 'Good work tonight, by the way,' he said.

Suzie looked sheepish. 'Er, thanks Paul.'

'I mean, it's not exactly Macbeth,' he joked, 'but it pays the bills, don't it?'

'Sure, sure,' Terry said. 'It's good money for a few hours' work.'

'Yeah,' Paul said, 'and we all have to make ends meet, right?'

'Indeed we do,' Terry said, then added. 'Besides, it's kind of fun, I guess. I mean, it could be worse.'

Suzie nodded.

The elevator bell chimed as the doors slid open, and she and Terry stepped in. She pressed the button for the ground floor.

'Maybe see you later in the week then?' Paul said.

'Call me,' she replied as the doors closed.

Outside it was cooler and dark now, but the street was still halogen bright and neon colourful. The air tasted of lager and vinegar chips.

'Good luck on that audition,' Suzie said, then remembering, 'Oh, wait. You never finished telling me what it was for?'

'That?' he said. 'Oh, it's just a pilot for a BBC sitcom. Some comedy set in a seaside holiday camp in the fifties or something. Not very highbrow. I shouldn't think it'll amount to much.'

'Well, I hope it's good news all the same.'

'And I hope to come and see you at The Albery in the autumn.'

'Darling, you'll probably see me here sooner than that,' she said, smiling. 'You know how it is.'

'Oh, right. Yes,' he replied, a little embarrassed. 'See you then.'

'Take care,' she said, kissing him on both cheeks. She turned and walked briskly north up Wardour Street. Terry watched her go while he fished his cigarettes out of his coat. He turned around, lit one for warmth, and walked quickly back down to Leicester Square Station.

A Vision Thing
Paul Johnson

Ten minutes. That was generally accepted as sufficient to make an effective presentation. Ten minutes to sell the idea, and yourself with it. He laughed a little to himself. No, that can't be right. Too much like a prostitute and just at the moment, well, that wasn't a helpful line of thinking. He picked at the corner of a fingernail, glanced at the clock. Soon there would be whisperings and vaguer noises beyond the stained oak door. How many would there be? For this sort of thing you could never tell. He pulled a little at the dark cloth, adjusting it to his shoulder for, on these occasions, appearance matters. So, have a little self-confidence, he urged. At least dark colours suit you, run well with your complexion. Distinguished? 'Well, presentable,' his mother would have said, but she couldn't be here.

Come on, get a grip. He fussed a little with his left sleeve. This isn't the first one you have had to do, even if it has to be the most important. Think what they think, feel their feelings, sense the mood, let their silences and their fidgeting speak to you. As for his own anxiety, his own emotional turmoil, these had to be gripped, had to be managed; a little of both they would expect, a lot and they would be concerned. He knew he was unsettled, unfocused, unsure. I should have prepared better, known better how I am going to say what needs to be said, for he knew that his words would be attended to with care, sifted, scrutinised for many things but above all to identify any shift from established policy, from long-standing certainties. He had wrestled with openings, with phrases, with endings, but had still no clear path to his central message. It was not just his future that depended on the next few minutes. He was certain that theirs did, too.

There was a time, not so long ago, when such a challenge would not have troubled him, the unshakeable, non-negotiable certainty of the official line being the very thing that had attracted him to a leadership role in the company in the first place. It had felt good to be right, to be acknowledged as right. 'Steady', they had apparently said of him; 'Sound chap, interesting, but always safe'. Hopefully, the people who said such things, expected such things, had applauded him for delivering them, would be out there now – not that these people had said those things to him personally, of course, that was not their way, but there was gossip, obliquely repeated, in order to ingratiate, by those who looked to him for status. It was somehow distasteful but true, that petty gossip of all things had given him an assurance that he was well regarded, that the people who mattered thought him right most of the time and, if not always right, then always ready to learn, to master, to obey.

Would he know them all, would he recognise them? He doubted it but that probably wouldn't matter. Would he be able to look them in the eye? Should he even try? Usually he was confident, confident in his public presence, in his style, his speech. He could hold an audience, expect to be listened to. What if he could not convince them? Then what?

He was certain they would be looking for rational conviction because that in turn was how they estimated the wider public, as in a constant search for what was honest and reliable, seeking what was clearly right for themselves, open to intelligent persuasion, to an effective, reasoned, presentation. But he was not so sure. The public, he had only lately come to recognise, moved with its heart not its head, fixing its choice through emotion, not reason. It was not, he supposed, what one might call wise, but it was somehow deeper, oddly more stable, precisely for its vulnerability to mere feeling, for feelings, he now knew, were universal. He confessed himself now to be one of this helpless throng, conscious that to sell in this particular market place one had to be one of them. 'Show' or 'tell'? Everyone at his level and above had been trained to 'tell'. Here was the challenge. He had to show them otherwise.

Caution prompted him to be realistic. A change in approach was unlikely to be universally welcome and it was a fact that he had his enemies. They stored information tenaciously, enduringly, like weapons-grade plutonium. Given the opportunity, and he could see no way of avoiding this, those to whom his ideas were anathema would assiduously polish their choicest recollections, choose the most damning, and delicately introduce the selected memory to those around them. Would it be Braehill? That was bound to be dragged up. His last boss had moved on but no doubt there would be a note in a file somewhere about his various managerial difficulties. Braehill was considered a promotion. His previous patch had been gravel drives and people carriers, gin and credit cards, easy to work in a superficial sort of way, not easy to penetrate to any depth. What had been on offer was much larger, dogs and dole and the social, but a loyal clientele, happy to lodge contact details, to take home calls, even to make the first approach. He had accepted, worked hard, kept the ethos, but opted for a more up-to-date pitch, especially at the youth end and this had naturally meant compromises, some reworking of the traditional way of doing things and saying things. There were letters and telephone calls, no e-mails, of course. They all said the same. This man's approach is compromising the essentials, they said, and so weakening the brand image and, worse still, he is following the tastes and values of the public rather than leading them to the product, but despite the volume of protest, and it had been distressingly bitter and personal, he had survived, for he had his supporters, too, and they had pointed to the significant rise in numbers through the door and the accompanying cash-flow consequences, and so he had been rebuked, no more. For those who had wanted more, this would certainly be their chance.

In truth his whole time there had been painful. His assistant, middle-aged, had wanted the job. He sometimes wondered why they had not given him it. He was dull, boring if truth be told, and had little sense of how to engage with others, but he always upheld the company's values, never deviated from the official line, kept the product in front of the public. The man had had plans of his own, to refurbish the premises, go back to the older style of doing things – which had its constituency, as had to be admitted, and, as also had to be admitted, one which his own policies had lost. Will he be out there? Undoubtedly. Payback time? Well, maybe. Opening times, that was what the row had supposedly been about. Shorter, properly staffed hours had been the demand. The man had gone over his head, had stressed to senior management the security issues and cost implications, but the numbers coming in through the door were good, the revenue base correspondingly stronger and, as he had pointed out in his defence, the longer opening times gave a sense of availability and belonging. So he had got his way. There had been thefts, of course. For a while he had feared trouble with the insurers but they said little that was specific, just raised the premiums. Anyway, nothing I can say now, he thought, will change any of that. Sadly, he accepted that it was unlikely to change his erstwhile colleague either.

The quarrel with Martin he had never understood. Poor Martin. Perhaps they had been too alike, neat in appearance, reliable in habit, alert to the presentational and recruitment possibilities that an expanding younger audience might bring. Martin had joined him towards the end of that first year in Braehill. He brought his paperwork to the office immediately on arrival, typed, stapled, presented in a labelled folder, had shaken hands with a formal greeting, declined the offer of a drink, returned to a white sports car, from which he carefully unpacked two calfskin suitcases, placed them in the entrance and then, without further acknowledgement, had walked away – to familiarise himself with the area, he had later explained. To be fair Martin had been precise in establishing his responsibilities, and, although he had offered little more either by way of conversation or interrogation, he had set about the duties given him with determination and attention to detail. The issue, when it arose, and it arose very early on, had been presentation. Martin wanted the company's line to be set out clearly, uncompromisingly, and on all occasions. Without it he felt the company identity would suffer. He drew senior management in, and they hesitantly sided with him, requiring change, some changes now, some to be phased in, but numbers quickly weakened, the bottom line wavered, and senior management allowed itself to be distracted elsewhere. Abandoned by his superiors and his certainties, Martin reversed his neat little car into his garage, closed the door, and sat there staring until his throat stung and his eyes watered and the coughing crumpled him across the wheel. The note had been left slightly askew within a suitably labelled folder on his dustless desk. Questions had been asked, some of him, but he had had little to say, had felt rather than asked questions of his own. Why had no one been there for Martin? Management didn't ask themselves that. Neither had he – but now he did. At the time he had sensed that everyone had asked the wrong questions, had tried to integrate into a rational whole what was in truth a sorry mess. That was what he had now to make them see – not by talking about Martin, but by talking about what Martin represented, not a personal failure, not a management failure but a whole policy failure. They had to listen.

He must find an arresting opening, accusatory perhaps, specific even. Generalities convinced no one. He would start with John. Everyone was expecting something about John at some point so why not start with him, but not what he had done for the company, or what he had represented, but the way he engaged with anyone on their terms but without conceding his own. Persuasive in himself, John's technique was to draw you in, challenge you, and goad you from your complacency, but never coerce. There was something of the company founder in John.

John would have gone back to managerial fundamentals. Establish priorities, resources, constraints, then develop courses of action, fix on the best and do it – and it could be done, he recognised, momentarily. Just thinking about John made him feel he could do it, must do it. It was, after all, because of John that he was here, though he could not hold this thought as lightly as it came to him. But why take on the problem, why take the risk? They would expect nothing outside the conventional and the conventional might prove every bit as effective. It might not make much impact but 'a safe pair of hands', he could live with, and so he supposed could they. How much did he want this? They would certainly be probing for it, the motivation, the hunger. He had to go out there, get them on his side, build a bridge to link their fears to his hopes, and win them over. Look them in the eye, and, yes, challenge them.

So, a bridge. What would they accept and what could he accept? He and they would agree that well beyond these walls the policy line was known, was long established, and that the brand image was strong. These were the agreed resources and they would expect them to be deployed. So work with this, 'work with this', he could almost feel John's advice reaching out to him. In which case he needed to find a way of drawing the same policy line but have them look at it from the other end. His senses shifted to the gathering sounds beyond the door. His mind leapt back. Yes, that was it. He would admit the endurance and strength of the brand but probe whether longevity or a natural capacity for regeneration had brought this to pass. The product? Well, they would all agree, and he would be wise not to dissent, that the product is good. Yet it was inescapable that there were serious difficulties. Staff recruitment was at best patchy, low in numbers and for the most part in quality. The public base was shrinking, the appeal of the usual icons fading, and it was not local. Things were no better worldwide. They would have no difficulty in hearing such things but they would say that these were just the result of unusual circumstances, transient, of merely tangential interest. It was the dear old mousetrap line; ours is the best mousetrap, let the public come to us.

John, what was it again, what he would have said? Resources. John would have asked them what other resources they had, resources which they had, but were not deploying, would have asked whether different resources would lead to different courses of action. There were, of course, other resources. He could see that now thanks to John, could see that these resources gave the company what it was missing, the curiosity factor, common ground with a feeling public. That was what he had to tell them. Good product, no motivation for the public to engage with it. How? What did he mean, how? How to motivate? How to engage? He tugged at his collar, conscious now of the rise and fall of audible voices beyond the door.

He had to be specific. An example, a story perhaps, might be best, and there was an instance if he could only craft it carefully. It had been their first meeting, well, two meetings really, a formal introduction by the committee chairman; an informal one, at John's initiative, at the mid-morning break. John had offered tea.

'It's OK. I'll get some myself.'

It had been churlish, an ungracious reply he had now to admit, but John had gathered it up and gracefully returned it.

'No, please,' he had said, 'To serve, to serve willingly, is good. Think about it this way, you make contact with people and it's non-threatening. They can even feel superior if they like.'

'They' – a deft word he had realised, a private space created in a public world, shared values assumed. They had talked. It did not matter about what, trivia surely, but they talked.

They had found shared time to go walking, nowhere very special, other couples were ambling much as they. For the most part it was a companionable silence, the occasional observation of a delight to be shared or an object to be savoured. It was not what happened then that he had now to explain to the attentive and the curious. In fact even to mention it would finish him utterly. But here, it now came to him, here amidst the recollection of that brief, brief moment was the sure and certain way to identify the kernel of the present problem, to re-present the case, to draw in not just those sitting out there but the public, all of them, of whatever gender, wealth, occupation, and to win them over, get them back in through the door. He had to talk about this in such a way that they would be caught up in the truth of it, not a moral truth about which there might be confusion, but an inspirational truth, the big idea, the vision thing.

His mind was racing now. The company policy was a social policy. If society shifted, the company shifted but slowly, passively. What the time with John had made him realise was that it would be better, not just more effective, or more desirable, but intrinsically better, to reconstruct the whole pitch at the point of the intimate, the personal. Feverishly he tore at the possibilities. Organisation – fine as it is but change the ethos, first among equals rather than field marshal, cooperation through small teams conjoined not by rank but by a common vision, with goals determined by responsiveness to those same teams, locally recruited, locally deployed, working to a local understanding of priorities. Shift the product emphasis from goods to services. Yes. I'll say just that he decided. They might even laugh. Not usually a lot of humour on these occasions so it should pull them on to my side.

A slight knock and the door opened.

'Is there anything you need, sir, or are you content to start?'

'No, I'm fine. We'll begin.' He adjusted his sleeves one last time and walked out past the sombre-suited man with his receding hair.

A quick glance showed that there were a lot more facing him than he had anticipated or had mentally prepared for, which was difficult as he needed their attention from the start. But he knew he was good at this, knew he could do it. The important thing was to focus on the central figure, gather up the rest in a bodily gesture and let the opening words arrest them.

'Love brought us here, that undivided, undiscriminating love which must be the hallmark of our worldwide enterprise and so, dearly beloved, as we start this funeral mass for John Hansen let us call to mind the times when we have failed to invite, to embrace, to love, and there may well be more of those than we are ready to recognise as a community, let alone to admit.'

The Menu
E. Mae Jones

'You're missing a testicle, son.'

'That a problem?' Walter's naked, chicken-skinned legs dangle from the cold metal examination table. His teeth bite together, into his dignity, so as not to swallow it away.

'Put your britches back on, then we'll talk.'

Walter hikes up his threadbare briefs, and widens the neck of his threadbare undershirt.

'How old are you?' The doctor's eyes study his application.

'Eighteen.'

'Got anything to prove that?'

'No, sir. My mom passed. I dunno where she kept . . . records.'

'Mr Klinuski, much as we'd like to, the army can't let almost-eighteen-year-olds slide by out of our good . . .'

'Born August 23, 1924. I swear.'

'Growth or injury?'

'What?'

The doctor points to his crotch. 'That.'

'Why?'

'That wasn't a mean kick to the groin. You got hearing loss, low blood count; you're underweight and hairless as a Chihuahua. Mustard gas started with the army. We know what it does to you. Regardless of how old you are, the army doesn't take cancer patients . . .'

'But I gotta do somethin'. My brothers – they're only my half brothers – and they a'ready think nothin' of me. They're all a'ready stationed somewhere.'

'You want to do something?' The doctor changes his way of speaking, as if he's decided to tell Walter something confidential. 'Railroads. Don't check health or ages. But why they don't check is it's bad for you in the first place.'

'I don't care.'

'It's mostly negroes and Orientals. Up in Alaska they're laying track to get fuel from the military depot in Whittier. You'd still be part of the effort, if that's what you're after.'

The US Department of the Interior gives every railroad worker one free ticket. Walter's goes from West Pittsburg to where the track runs out.

Anytime Walter's seen a train – whether in person or in pictures – it's always been loaded with a mix of people coming from and going to a mix of places. Some men, some women. Some dressed nicely, some dressed so you wouldn't want to sit next to them. This train's carrying row after row, and then car after car of men dressed similar, acting similar, staring forward, all going to the same place. No one looks like they're in any hurry to get there.

With more than a day left in the journey, he presses his head against the chilly window glass, and tries to get some sleep.

'Hey.'

Walter comes to, sees a black man sitting backwards in his seat.

'You know when they gonna feed us?'

He shakes his head.

'I'm Taylor and this is my son, Lonnel.' Taylor sticks out his hand. Walter takes it. 'Walter Klinuski.'

'Klin– what? What kinna name is that?'

'Polish, my dad thinks.'

'You got a family then?'

'A dad livin' and a mom died three years ago about. And five half brothers and a dead father a' theirs.'

'Ah, I'm sorry. Lonnel don't have a mom neither.'

'Yeah?'

'She died having him. Happens more than people think, you know. We're supposed to be living in modern times where that don't happen, but still does. I don't want to say this, but I wonder sometimes if it happens more to certain people, you know?'

'Yeah,' Walter says, wondering if he means black people or poor people or sick people.

'Know what you're doing?'

'What?'

'You know what you're doing?'

'No, but I can take orders,' Walter says. But then he's embarrassed for saying it to the person he said it to.

A food cart starts down the aisle, pushed by an Indian with two leather-bound tails of grey-streaked black hair. Smiling at each man, he hands out triangular half sandwiches with thin portions of chipped meat between flimsy slices of bread.

'Looks like dinner's served,' Taylor says. 'I'll talk to you more later.'

By the time the train gets to no-town-yet Alaska, Walter has befriended and shared a flask with a white man from Ohio named Vernon, a Mexican named Manny, the Indian, plus Taylor and Lonnel. The group decides they'll bunk up in one of the worker cabins, which the Indian told them holds six, and there are six of them so that works out like luck, Taylor says.

What isn't lucky is that work starts as soon as the engine stops. The rows and cars of men are herded straight to the job site, and Walter can see now, as he watches them spill onto the snow, that they aren't just hundreds of the same man. They have nothing in common but the look of fatigue, hunger, and prior misfortune.

The first day of real work is surreal, as if manhood is some mind-altering disease Walter's contracted. His whole skin perspires and his mostly empty stomach sloshes worse than when he had the treatments. Either time is going slower or life is going faster. Not to mention, he doesn't fully understand most of what he's supposed to be doing.

He takes as much direction as he can from Taylor. Even Lonnel can handle his load. He's never seen men doing work before. Not like this. Peering down the line of bodies – arms and legs, backs and necks, hearts and lungs, straining to their limits – Walter thinks work like this must be the guilty secret of the country's prosperity.

The dim morning turns into flaming white noon, and then into cold pink and blue evening. From six to six, the screams of pounded stakes repeat. The thud of falling cut timber and the less frequent muted boom of moved earth finish the rhythm, which gets slower and slower, until the foreman adds his voice and the pace picks up.

There isn't talking. The Indian told them they'd all get on better if they 'found the loop'. The loop, he said, meant to make time a circle and not a line. He said not talking helped with that – but not how the foreman said to shut up, like an order – but like a friendly piece of advice.

And it was wise advice, even if it took Walter months to figure out what he meant and how to do it.

The Indian became Chef, a simple nickname started by Manny the Mexican, because part of his job was cooking for the sixty men in his crew. Before the sun went down, he got to stop hammering and start supper. Manny says that maybe the loop works for him because his loop is a lot shorter.

'I am fuckin' sick of this shit,' says Vernon, the Ohioan.

'What's wrong?' Chef asks, sipping his chicken broth.

'That we eat this shit every day. Fuckin' watery soup and fuckin' stale bread fuckin' every day.'

'Okay,' Chef says. 'What do you want?'

Vernon seems confused, like he's never been asked what he wanted before. 'You know what we have good in Minerva is ham. With cloves and maple syrup.'

'That sounds good,' Taylor says. 'Hey, Vernon? What you think of Ohio? You think me and Lonnel'd be welcome there?'

'I dunno.'

'Land expensive there?'

'I dunno.'

'Well, you from there. What? You got a problem with us? Don't want us buying land?'

'I just dunno.'

'Sure you don't,' Taylor says, disgusted.

'I don't fuckin' know!' Vernon takes a swig of the flask they're passing around, now half-full of fermented apple juice, then stomps out of the cabin.

The ten-by-ten foot sleeping and eating cabin stays pin-drop silent the rest of the night.

The next morning comes as fast as Walter's head sinks into his limp pillow. Vernon's back in his bed, looking as if he's had a troubled night's sleep.

'Hey, Taylor?'

Taylor ignores him.

'I don't know 'bout Ohio cause I was locked up. Before this. OK? Don't got no real problem with you all. Not no more.'

Taylor nods to him, in apology and solidarity. Walter imagines what prison must be like, and what Vernon might have done to end up there. He feels bad for him, but he's still a little nervous having him just two bunks below.

Now that he's found the loop, work is just a matter of losing his mind in the screaming metal. It's just a matter of adjusting his body, like Chef also taught him how to do. When one set of muscles starts to burn, he uses the other. Walter loses himself and adjusts himself so well, ten days go by in a single effort.

The loop breaks when the men, stumped and thrilled, see a small ham, dripping in syrup and dotted with cloves, on top of their folding dinner table.

'I never tasted ham like this before,' says Walter. Neither has anyone but Vernon, who's busy folding slice after slice of the stuff into his mouth until it's so full he can't chew.

Walter notices that Vernon never bothers to thank Chef, and

nobody bothers to ask where the food came from. He's pretty sure the Department hasn't listened to Vernon's complaint and sent a ham to every cabin.

'I gotta piss,' Walter says. He walks out behind a lone evergreen and does his business, then walks further on to the next cabin over and taps on their plywood door.

'What you want?' the door swings halfway open. Walter sees six men drinking soup out of handled tin cups.

'Nothing. Wrong cabin.'

'Drunk son of a bitch,' the door closes in his face.

Through the thin wood walls, he can hear the crew, still talking about food.

'Carolee used to make me pizza pie – tomatoes, cheese, greens piled thick as my fist. She made the bread and everything. I used to go over her momma's and watch her learning how to cook for when . . .'

'I never had that,' Vernon says. 'Can't be good as this ham.'

'I'd die twenty years before my time to see her punching that bread dough again.' Taylor takes a slow sip of the community bottle of beer and passes it to his son, who has learned to turn his face into concrete every time his father mentions his mother.

'Only fourteen.'

Walter remembers being fourteen and hearing his father sneak into the house after a long night at the hospital. He heard the squeaking screen door, and his father's slow steps and long breaths, and he knew. Losing his mother then was harder than seemed fair, but Taylor losing his wife – or the woman who would've been – seemed more unfair than anything he'd ever heard.

'If Carolee hadn't . . . we'd already be at the end a' the plan, you know. Cause she coulda stayed home and taken care of Lonnel and I coulda gotten a job just like normal. But I can't leave him for how many months at a time. Plus this way we get two wages, so we can buy some property sooner. I guess life works out sometimes.'

'You call that working out?' Manny says. 'Lonnel, how old you?'

'Fifteen.' Lonnel's dad shoots him a look like he broke a rule.

'None of us gonna tell. What you think, Lonnel? Mom dead. No education. You gonna be working in frozen middle of nowhere forever, and is OK?'

Taylor stands up. 'I'm making the best of things, man. We'll get some land, and when Lonnel has a kid, that kid'll get an education. And then that kid's gonna do better. And then on. Carolee . . . just set us back one generation.'

'Some American dream you got.' Manny straightens out in his bed, as if to say he doesn't want to fight anymore.

The next two weeks pass through the loop and not much happens, except Manny takes to nicknaming more people. Taylor and Lonnel become American Dream One and Two. And Walter, who's sprouting fuzz-fine hair all over his skull, and even some on his chin for the first time, becomes La Barba, which means the beard in Manny's language. Vernon doesn't have a nickname yet, but Manny says he's working on it.

By afternoon – Walter isn't sure what day it is – whispering sweeps through the gang like tornado winds.

'What happened?' Walter asks Lonnel.

'Think somebody got in the way down where they blasting.'

'Lonnel!' his father scolds him. 'We don't know that. Keep working.'

'I heard somebody took off their arm at the elbow,' says Vernon.

'Accidents happen,' Manny says. 'Right, American Dream?'

Walter's curiosity about the accident has split the loop wide open, and the next four or five hours of work seem to last longer than the whole time he's been in Alaska.

Taylor's lip is quivering, but Walter's not surprised to see a pizza, bubbling and steaming with cheese and greens, right where the ham had been two weeks before.

'I wouldn't a' thought, but I just might prefer this to the ham,' says Vernon, eating more than his fair share.

'Got it,' Manny says. 'Estomago. Stomach. There. Well, Estomago got his wish, and Dream One and Two. Is me and Barba left. Hey, Barba? What your momma make you?'

'I dunno.' Walter wants to tell them about his mother, like Taylor talked about Carolee. But it'd only be another sad story, and it seems like having a sad story is practically the test for getting work on the railroads.

'Pierogies.'

'What's pierogies?' Chef asks.

'Well . . .' Walter tries to remember days when he ate them, sometimes ten in a sitting. He tries to remember the last one his mom ever scooped out of the frying pan. But their pleasing taste seems imaginary now. 'Like dumplings. Half-moon noodles, fried up. With potatoes inside.'

'I'll try 'em,' says Vernon.

Before quitting time the next day, a foreman gathers the workers around a cinder block platform.

'Attention.' A Department man speaks from a handful of papers loud enough so the first few rows can hear. 'Let's get right down to it. We're asking the Alaska Railroad Workers to take a fifteen per cent cut in pay, as the war effort requires it. Materials are getting more expensive and resources have to be . . . preserved. Also, your time and a half Sunday wages will be reduced to . . .' he drops his head, '. . . time.'

Then his tone becomes threatening. 'Anyone displeased can leave. Anyone meaning to keep on will do so without argument.'

'75 cents. But not even, which means 74 cents.' Weeks later, Manny is still arguing with himself about it.

'They ain't doing this on purpose. It's for materials,' Taylor says.

'Is exactly right. You know what problem is . . . man is something that grows back. Like weeds. What you think is more value? You or metal. What gonna work harder, last longer. You? No.'

Vernon's had enough of the debate. 'Walter? This what pierogies supposed to taste like?'

'Close as I can remember.' His teeth squish into another fried half circle and the warm potato escapes into his mouth. 'Can't say they're the prettiest ones I ever seen. But that don't matter to me.'

Manny picks up right where he left off, holding out his chapped hands as evidence. 'Skin crack and rot. Arms cut off. Get exploded.'

'Nobody got exploded,' Taylor argues.

Walter hands the flask, half-full of vodka, to Chef.

'No.' Chef keeps it moving.

'No?'

'I don't. The mind . . . the loop works better without it.'

'And your loop,' Manny says. 'Your loop don't help the worker. Your loop fools the worker. Time is not this circle. Time is six o'clock, then seven o'clock, then more and more and six o'clock again, and we still working. Time is yesterday, and today, and tomorrow, and . . .'

'We're getting paid, man.' Taylor has had enough.

'Listen, American Dream. In Mexico, we are slaves, too. We are slaves now. Don't use same word, but is the same.'

'I thank God that none of us ever had to live through that.'

'Well, I come here so I don't live through that. But is same. What is this freedom we have? Is just idea. Is not real. Yes, make money. Yes, buy home, be happy. But can never make enough. Can never be happy. In my home . . .'

'Where is your home?' Chef asks.

'Chihuahua,' Manny says. Walter laughs to himself.

'What is your favourite food in Chihuahua?'

'What? You make me some fish, make everything better? In Guadalajara they are making it better.' Manny sips the vodka. 'Hey Barba?'

Walter perks up. 'Hmm?'

'You want more than this loop . . . you come to Chihuahua. You come to Mexico with me. We make it better.'

As the rest of the food and vodka disappears, Manny tells Walter his ideas – ideas that Walter doesn't entirely understand. Taylor tells Walter that Manny's crazy, and that they already got a union.

Walter can't find the loop again, and work feels like work. He gets used to it – both sets of muscles burning and time's changing speeds – but getting used to it doesn't make it go away.

Two weeks have gone by, stubborn and hard, and Walter's expecting a decent meal of Manny's native food. But Chef and Manny are both missing from the dinner table, which holds only a lukewarm pot of broth.

Vernon checks the kitchen and the other cabins. He doesn't find them, but he learns of something unfortunate, for which he feels partially responsible.

'Chef's gone. They cut him. Found out he was paying that supply guy from Whittier extra. Making stuff that wasn't on the menu.'

'Somebody turn him in?' Taylor asks.

'Prob'ly that cabin one down. Prob'ly smelled it.' Walter says, thinking about the men who slammed the door in his face. They don't have to wonder about Manny. He'd been talking about Mexico, and the movement, with growing excitement to anyone who'd listen. But Manny and Chef, and the prospect of good food, being gone in the same day? Walter feels like his happiness is being hammered away.

'I never thanked him for the pierogies. That was good of him to try and make those for me. He did good,' Walter says, looking at the dirt floor, counting the number of hours until work begins again, and guessing at the number of days he's got left in Alaska.

When You Wake Up
Peter Likarish

One day, you will wake up in a different world. Let me be more precise: an *alien* world. Who knows how you'll first figure this out. It's possible everything will be very similar to your world but also ever so slightly incongruent; maybe it'll be something as simple as banana-like fruits that taste like guavas and a sun that's red instead of yellow. Or, it could be something bizarre – maybe they've figured out a way to literally have 2.5 kids as opposed to our figurative half-child. You'll know them when you see them. Oh, and you'll also know you're in an alien world because the room you wake up in will not be the same as the one you just went to sleep in. I'm sure you'll have questions like, 'How the hell did I get here?' and 'What's going on?' and 'Has it all just been a dream?' Let's address them:

'What's going on?' Evidently, you are now living in an alien society. I know little more than you do at this point. Or maybe you've gone crazy? I certainly hope not.

'How the hell did I get here?' I don't know. Maybe, just maybe, your body experienced a quantum shift and suddenly the entire thing – or nearly all of it, enough for the sake of argument anyway – jumped into an alternate dimension. Quantum physics tells us this is so unlikely as to be impossible while remaining not entirely un-possible. It's bound to happen at one point or another. Maybe, instead of wasting our time with questions, you should consider yourself lucky. After all, you landed, against astronomically fantastical odds, on a planet where you can breathe, and your eyes haven't popped out while you asphyxiate in the near-infinite vacuum of Almost Anywhere Else in the Universe.

'Has it all just been a dream?' Doubtful. You've tried waking yourself up, haven't you? I'm sure all your friends and family will

be wondering where you've gone. Feel free not to believe me but I, for one, can't think of a reason I would lie to you.

Everyone in this alien world will be terribly surprised that you have appeared out of nowhere but it's not really surprising that they will be surprised because who wouldn't be surprised by that? But, to your surprise, their surprise is centred on the error in their census the previous day, rather than the fact that a human has appeared, apparently *ex nihilo*. You see, unlike our census, theirs has been completely 100% spot-on since day one. Until you showed up, that is. Evidently humans do not make a habit of spontaneously de-combusting, even on alien worlds. As a result of your appearance, the person responsible for counting everyone in the city will be put to death (the de facto punishment for misreporting a number to the Comptrollers). Surely the discovery you have been, indirectly, responsible for a man-alien's death will weigh heavily on your conscience.

Outwardly, everyone here may look and act much like your friends back home (except for some minor differences, such as the Genitalia SNAFU – I'll leave it at that, there's no reason to be lewd) but, unlike you and your pre-quantum fluctuated friends, they really, really like counting. Really, really is an understatement. Imagine eating, sex and any third thing you love to do all wrapped up into one giant package of joy and you will have some idea of how much they dig counting. Why? If I had to venture a guess, I'd say it's probably because some freak occurrence caused the gene we associate with mild forms of savantism – particularly with the ability to count a large number of objects seemingly instant-aneously – to be over-expressed in an entire population. Who knows? It's possible – and significantly more likely than you being there in the first place. So, you find yourself surrounded by people whose primary occupation seems to be counting. Social standing and worth are all dependent on how good you are at counting. The deceased census worker? A minor underling. People are large, easy to spot and the total doesn't tend to vary much from day to day.

The truly important people are the ones who count the tough stuff. Sands of grain on a beach. Anything of that nature. Those change from moment to moment so it takes a brilliant mind to manage it. In fact, the task is so mind-bogglingly difficult that you and I can have no conception of how it's done.

After your arrival, you'll be tested in a variety of counting-oriented ways. And, sadly, it will be apparent you are not only a very poor counter but actually retarded (they are not much for political correctness) by the standards of this society. This is not good news. Further complicating a situation that – we can both agree – needs no additional wrinkles of complexity, you will have noticed your entire adventure has been narrated by a disembodied voice echoing from inside your skull. Namely, moi. I will be a superciliously self-indulgent narrator, knowing precisely as much as I intend and no more. At this point, you will undoubtedly have more questions, along the following lines: 'Who are you?' and 'Why are you in my head?' But you've had your three questions and everyone knows you only get three. Expecting anything beyond that is pressing your luck. I suppose though, since I am feeling magnanimous – and because the mathemagicians on this world have proven, beyond a reasonable doubt in their court of law, that three is perfectly capable of masquerading as a four – I can do my best to equivocate.

'Who are you and why are you in my head?' As far as I can recall, I have always been here, maybe you just haven't noticed until now? I'm probably a side-effect of your improbably faster-than-light flight through time and space and subsequent appearance on this alien world: a defence mechanism to prevent ourself from going insane? Perhaps.

Regardless, it appears you're stuck with me. Let's get on with our job. Or your job, if it disconcerts you when I conflate us. We've established that schoolchildren on this planet are more adept at counting than you. Accordingly, you've been assigned a job that roughly equates to the Earth equivalent of working the graveyard shift at a convenience store, something to keep you occupied while limiting your interaction with 'regular people' to the greatest extent possible. It's not that they think your mental condition is contagious per se, actually, your semi-isolation stems from their generous desire to spare everyone, yourself included, the vast amount of embarrassment inherently generated by interacting with such a rudimentary being. Your job: count a single statue. Singular. One. Unchanging. Ever. I only hope that you can handle it.

You'll certainly become far more acquainted with this statue than you ever cared to be. The statue in question depicts a famous Comptroller, holding aloft his purely symbolic calculator – only a plebeian such as yourself would require its aid – and it rests on a large hill overlooking the city in which you will find yourself – a city that looks disturbingly like Budapest, that fortress of mathematical genius.

Here's an excerpt from your counting journal: Monday: # of statues: 1, Tuesday: # of statues: 1, Wednesday: # of statues: 1 . . . You get the idea. Oddly enough, as time flows on you'll come to the conclusion that this job is no more insultingly repetitive and simplistic than any of your Earth-based employments and it takes far less time. While these aliens are self-important Literalists who would surely climb the hill every day to make certain that the statue is still physically there, you, in all your mentally deficient glory, are content to glance through a pair of binoculars at noon each day and duly report the count in your journal: 1.

Uncertain what else to do with your new-found freedom, you take to drinking alcohol – some things truly *are* universal – and indulging in the various licit drugs common to this society. It's during one such binge that the Genitalia SNAFU occurs. You have been drunkenly attempting to woo a paramour and, unlike numerous other encounters, this time your efforts are rewarded. Apparently, the alien attributes your idiotic behavior to intoxication rather than mental deficiency. Lucky you. It's not until you two are in rather more ... intimate circumstances that the incompatibility becomes apparent.

Then, in a moment of outstandingly brilliant inebriation, you attempt to defuse this so-embarrassing-it-is-physically-discomfiting situation by reciting poetry. But as you finish the second stanza of Byron's 'She Walks in Beauty' you're forced to stop out of concern for your no-longer-potential mate's well-being. She seems to be seized by some sort of debilitating paroxysm and it takes a minute for you to realise that she is laughing uncontrollably. You'd be surprised if this wasn't a fairly standard female reaction to your attempts at wooing.

The rest, as they say, is history. Albeit history that has yet to transpire as far as you're concerned. News of your newly dis-covered ability spreads faster than the latest counting theorems. Before you know it you've been proclaimed the creator of a first – a form of entertainment completely divorced from counting – you don't have the heart to explain metre to them. Your every move-ment is dogged by thousands, all waiting for a single couplet to fall from your honeyed lips. The Comptrollers arrange for perform-ances and every one sells out. You leave them rolling in the aisles, knock 'em dead, so to speak. After a while, having exhausted your mental stores of poetry, you are forced to write your own. Luckily, quality of verse does not seem to be a factor. The only problem? You have a strong suspicion that your comedic stylings might have an Earth equivalent in a 1980s comedian named Gallagher, a man whose routines inevitably involved smashing fruit with a big hammer, showering his audience with pulp and seeds.

You're something of an enigma in this rigidly hierarchical society; by virtue of your dismal intellect you should rightfully rank with the lowest of the low but none of the aliens would be willing to heap adulation on someone so far beneath them. You begin to feel like a rebel, even an early civil rights leader, bucking the arithmetical control of society. Things may well have con-tinued in such a manner for a satisfactorily long time if you had not run afoul of two well-documented side-effects of new-found popularity: a swollen ego and a bit of blasphemy. Don't forget that, even while on tour, you were required to continue your statue-counting duties. Given your popularity, you could have ordered a lower-class member to do your counting for you – they would do so purely for the novelty of being associated with such an eccentric – but you decided against such recourse as 'a condemnation of the discriminatory practices of the government'. Needless to say, your rhetoric did not please the Comptrollers.

In the end, it's unclear whether you blasphemed knowingly or out of pure ignorance. Some even claim you were framed. Millions pleaded you were mentally incapable of being held ac-countable for your actions, the old insanity defence. All to no avail. I assure you, your sentencing and execution were most moving spectacles, chock-full of high drama. When they announced your sentence women wept and clutched children to their breasts while men stoically held tumblers and muttered. All this fuss over one little line in your counting journal: 'Wednesday: # of statues: e.' A crime against humanity, using one of the Endless numbers for such a mundane task. Congratulations on successfully violating every aspect of their faith. At least you can take solace in the knowledge that your execution cemented your status as the best comedian of all time. Upon being asked if you had any final words, you recited, with flair and gusto, a most stirring rendition of Hamlet's 'To be or not to be' soliloquy and left everyone tuned in to your execution with tears of laughter in their eyes. You never really liked maths that much anyway.

A Concrete Dream
Sangam MacDuff

'Hey, Boss – how long you been workin' these roads?'

'I don't rightly know, Nathan, if truth be told. My whole life, seems like. They tell me I must be past retirement age, but I ain't got no birth certificate.'

'Don't you know your own birthday?'

'No, never did have no birthday.'

'Ev'body got a birthday, Cuth,' Nathan said kindly. 'Come on, we gonna take y'out 'n' celebrate tonight.' He turned to the other men on the team, all Latinos, except Charles, who was black, like him: 'Hey, boys, guess what? It's Cuthbert's birthday, an' he's officially retiring from the team. We gonna go out 'n' have ourselves a party, right?'

'You really leaving this time, Boss?' Gustavo asked.

'Looks like it,' Cuthbert said. 'I told 'em I didn't wanna leave, but they said I was getting too old for paving.'

'It getting dangerous, man,' Elveraldo said. 'You guys hear about that guy got hit on Richmond Bridge the other night? Killed dead.'

'Killed dead,' Charles repeated. 'God bless.'

They all looked at the steady stream of bullets flashing by. It was only one o'clock and already there was rarely a gap across the lanes.

'Happens more and more,' Nathan said. 'Ain't no wonder. Nobody obeying no speed limits, and no cops or nothin'.'

'Who taking your place, man?'

'Can't tell you that, Gustavo. Ain't nobody can, 'cept the supervisor.'

'What's the bets it's gonna be another white man, huh?' He spat on the dusty tarmac.

'Nathan should get the job by rights,' Charles said. 'He been here longest, after the Boss.'

Nathan shook his head gravely. 'Don't work like that. Them boys in the office don't care about the likes a you an' me. Hell, they don't even care whether the job gets done right. All they care about's their forms, so's they gets their gov'ment money. That's what it's about, son.'

Cuthbert took another slice of corned beef from the tin and chewed it thoughtfully.

'When I first started there weren't no Highway Maintenance Association – there weren't hardly no highways then, not like we know 'em. Back then, people still took the ferry to San Francisco. Matter of fact, I spent my first three years working on the Bay Bridge. That's how I got a job, not having no papers or nothin', cause they was desperate for labour. After that came the 580, then the Richmond Bridge.'

'So how come you got made manager if you didn't have no papers?' Gustavo was indignant: twelve years of labouring on minimum wage, watching lesser men pass him to promotions.

'Back then it was like Charles said: if you served your time and you weren't no criminal, you got promoted. I was in the building department then, not pavement or repairs. I learned my trade on the bridges. It was all ri-bar and flexipoint construction. That whole there bridge is resting on balls of steel. Pivots, they called 'em. You had to be real careful . . .' His eyes glazed over for a moment and he cocked his head towards the road, as though listening to its muffled roar. 'All to do with flexibility – withstanding the wind and the trucks . . . Anyways, when it came to expanding the highways, especially over in Marin – you know, where the ground's soft – they wanted to use the same kinda method, so guys like me got made foremen.'

He finished the corned beef and took a slug of sweet coffee from the flask. He looked up at the sky: February, and the sun was blazing. He drained the cup and wiped it with his handkerchief before screwing it back onto the old silver thermos.

'Alright, men, let's get back to work,' he said, getting up.

Elveraldo wiped the sweat from his brow. 'Too hotta work, Boss, and it your last day. What you say we take th'afternoon off?'

'I won't report you if that's what you want to do, but I got to stay and finish painting these lines.'

Elveraldo glanced at Juan, 'Eh, chingon, el Madderlóde, recuerdes?' They both sniggered. 'Hey, boys, there's this bar down Laurel called the Mother-Lode – real nice, real cool. You guys gonna come down?'

Gustavo eyed the youths. They were young; he had a family, he couldn't afford to lose his job. Black fumes were still rising from the bitumen, though. All morning he'd been rolling new tarmac in the filthy heat, killing his lungs for eight dollars an hour. He needed a drink.

'Go on, enjoy yourselves,' Nathan said. 'You're through with the resurfacing, right? I'll help the Boss finish the seals then we'll join you. Where is it? On McAuley?'

'Yeah, you know, by that RV place?'

'Yeah, I know. You goin' with 'em, Charles?'

Charles looked nervous. 'I . . . I can't, sir. I'm not allowed to drink no alcohol. I'll just stay with you guys till we're finished an' help put away the cones 'n' that.'

The Latinos loaded up the big truck with the jackhammers, steamroller and mixer.

'So long boys!' Gustavo shouted out the window as they rolled by, laughing. They lumbered up the Works lane, gradually picking up enough speed to join the race on the Freeway.

All afternoon they worked in the blazing sunshine, sealing each section of the new surface with a snake of shiny black tar. Three weeks they'd been on the 580, relaying the whole of the outside lane and parts of the central division, all the way from Mill College to 35th St. The lane had been ripped up, dug up, packed with new hard core, laid and sealed. It was finally ready to re-open. All they had left was the hard shoulder between eastbound and westbound traffic, which they were spot-patching where the cracks were worst.

'I don't know why they bother,' Cuthbert had said. 'It don't save nothin' cause you just have to do the same thing 'gain next year, and the year after. Then the next tremor gonna come, or the land shifts, you know, when the rain comes down especial' heavy, or we get an especial' dry spell – open up the whole freeway 'gain. They oughtta lay pavement right if they gonna lay it at all – proper diggin' an' foundations, deep hardcore, reinforced iron lattice, high viscose tar.'

Still, the cracks were drilled open in nice straight lines like rectangles of peeled skin; new sand and gravel were pounded into the joints and a layer of boiling tar was poured over the wound. Three weeks of surgery and the repairs were finally finished. All they had left were the seals, like butterfly stitches round new grafts.

It was too hot, though, and the road was dirty, and the tar was too thin; it slid over the repairs, bubbling and spitting, unwilling to join the surfaces. Nathan and Charles wanted to leave the job for the night shift, when it would be cool and the tar would go down easily. But Cuthbert refused to wait; he would finish it alone if necessary. Nathan and Charles couldn't leave him on his last day, so the three of them worked together, Charles sweeping ahead, Cuthbert guiding the line marker, Nathan smoothing down the strip.

The stretch had been cleaned when they started, but it was already littered again with the debris of disposable life – glass, paper, plastic, polystyrene, those little marbles of worn tire rubber, and a film of thick grey dust. It was amazing what you'd find along the highway: single shoes, bags of clothes, rolls of carpet, broken chairs (not to mention razors, condoms, pornographic magazines, underwear, photographs, scraps of journals and letters).

'There's white folks livin' on these freeways,' Nathan said, when they stopped to refill the hopper. 'Dem SUVs their homes, man! They got hotels, motels, travel inns, happy inns, that's if they

A Concrete Dream   151

wanna sleep, else there's restaurants, coffee-shops, burger joints, sushi bars . . . Used to be you could only get drive-through burgers, now seems you can get drive-through most anything – drive-through laundromats, drive-through ironing service, drive-through banking; next they gonna get drive-through crematoriums!'

'My mama says I shouldn't be working on the freeway – Free Way to the Devil, she says.'

'Why's that, Charles?'

'Cause they's bringing ca-sinos and houses-a-ill-repute down from Nevada, on the 80.'

Nathan laughed. 'Son, we already got 'em here: they just call 'em gentlemen's clubs.'

'When I started there weren't none o' that,' Cuthbert said. 'Oakland, Piedmont, Berkeley, they was all separate towns then. There weren't nothin' on the 80, 'cept maybe one, two gas stations and a couple diners. Alameda County was still farmland. This here was dairy fields, all the way up to Berkeley Hills.'

They stopped and looked up at the continuous bank of development, stretching several miles up to the tree-line.

'This ain't nothin'!' Nathan replied. 'Remember I was down in LA not long ago for my sister's wedding – she married a preacher? Well, matterafact, her husband was from Santa Barbara, an' we drove down there for the wedding. My, oh my, you would not believe it! There must be at least fifty miles of automobiles, one showroom after another: thousands and thousands of brand new cars laid out like cakes in a bakehouse. You'd've thought they was the only thing you ever needed – like you'd get yourself a new one for the weekend. An' in-between the cars, a solid mall all the way to Santa Barbara. I don't think there's a single thing you could even need that you couldn't get within a quarter-mile o' that freeway.'

''Cept trees,' Cuthbert said.

'An' family.'

They went back to the seals and worked in silence for a while, surrounded by the hum of the freeway. Eventually Cuthbert straightened up, looking older than Nathan could remember.

'I'll never have to listen to a jackhammer again,' he said, suddenly despondent.

'Well, you earned yo' rest, anyone has,' Nathan declared. 'We gonna take y'out 'n' celebrate tonight!'

'Naw, I don't deserve no rest . . .' Cuth replied, his voice drowning in the traffic. Charles glanced nervously at Nathan and they both looked over, trying to figure the old man, but Cuthbert was busy looking down the freeway at the rush of oncoming cars. Their windshields glinted flashes of anger as they roared by, rocking the bollards. They all turned back to the road. Inside the cordon, the ribbon of pavement where they were working seemed nothing more than an endless pattern of random rectangular patches, each a slightly different shade – mauve-grey, violet-grey, charcoal-grey, silver-grey – like the scales of a sleeping serpent.

'I saw a painting like that once,' Cuthbert said, after a time.

'Yeah?' Nathan asked.

'Sure did. In the Museum of Modern Art, in San Francisco. We were doing a job on Geary, as I recall. Yes, siree, Abstract Art, they called it . . .'

He remembered tracing the shapes of the painting – like two miles of shiny black tape, two inches wide, stitching the ground together.

The shift ended at four, but what with the heat and the dirt, they were less than halfway through. Cuthbert made no move to stop.

'Come on, Boss, let's knock it off. You been working long enough.'

'Can't do that, Nathaniel. I gotta finish my job. Taylor's team's movin' out tonight and they ain't letting me back tomorra.'

'Why you don't want leave?' Charles asked.

'Ain't got nothin' else.'

'Ain't you got no family?'

'No.'

'No brothers, sisters, nothin'?'

'I had a sister once, she died. My mother died with her.' Cuthbert straightened up again. 'My father, he was lame.' The old man seemed to be thinking back, and the other two looked respectfully at the road, which shook with every passing tremor. Vehicles roared by, harrying the wind and the cones, but it was strangely still in their circle.

'What happened?' Nathan asked.

Cuthbert started. 'Oh . . . he . . . he was a stevedore, Port of Oakland. Lost his leg in a crane accident and couldn't work no more . . . 'ventually they put him in the poorhouse, in Albany, and I went to an orphanage, all the way up in Walnut Creek, where the rich folks lived. I liked it there, 'cept I missed my dad, but they didn't seem to like me, cause they threw me outta that school . . . said I was delinquent. They sent me all the way down to San Luis Obispo, where they had a school for feeble-minded children, run by Catholics. I hated that place. They didn't teach me nothin', 'cept religion and obedience. But they didn't do that too good neither, cause I ran away soon as I could and jumped a train all the way back to San Francisco.'

'You were in a nuthouse?'

'Yeah, but I weren't crazy. Practically none of us were, least when we got there . . .'

'Where'd you live, when you got out?' Nathan asked.

'Oh, I went down the Mission, there still was a Mission then, a real Catholic Mission. They gave me a job as janitor, till I got my first construction job, on the bridge.' He thought back: it must be fifty years and he'd never told anyone. Yet it didn't seem strange. It was easy, when you started, like confession. Tomorrow he'd be gone.

'You want to know the one good thing 'bout the home?'

'What?'

The old man savoured Charles's eagerness. It gave him a new sensation, a glow of pleasure to confide in his companions.

'The library. The nuns had them a magnificent library – thousands and thousands of books, all bound in leather – green and brown and red, with gilt lettering on the spine. Books on most every subject you could imagine. They had so many books, there was a balcony round the walls, just so's you could get at them, but even so sometimes you needed a ladder . . .'

'How come you didn't get no book job, being white an' all?' Charles asked.

'I don't know. One day – I think I must have been about fifteen – I got a letter from the poorhouse saying my dad had died. That hit me verra hard. I hardly ever read a book again. I hardly even spoke no more.'

He thought back over the years of silence. How long had he known Nathan? Ten years? Twenty?

'It wasn't long after that I ran away,' he replied to Charles. 'I joined the HMA and that was that.'

'So what'll you do when you're done?' the boy asked.

'Don't know,' Cuthbert said, letting go of the line marker he'd been leaning on.

He thought for a moment, head cocked to the side, staring vacantly at the distant trace of the footbridge.

'Come on,' he said suddenly, laying down the marker.

The two men put down their tools, glancing at each other quizzically, and followed the old man. He led them slowly back up the freeway through the gathering dusk. Every so often they looked back and saw tail-lamps flashing like fireflies into the cerulean arch of the sky.

Without warning Cuthbert veered to the right and began clambering over the low wall which divided the freeway.

'Where you taking us, Boss?' Nathan asked, uneasily.

'Come on, you'll see. Help me over.'

The three men bundled over. Cuthbert was excited. For the first time in years he felt a boyish thrill as he looked across the freeway. Six lanes of continuous traffic: there would never be a gap long enough to make it in one go, but it was still rush hour and the current was relatively slow, especially where it bottled at the exit.

'Come on!' he yelled, half running, half hobbling across two lanes, as vehicles screeched behind him, blowing their horns.

'Come on!' he roared again, raising a clenched fist at the torrent of on-pouring cars, like horizontal rain. Their hoods glowed back menacingly in the orange streetlamps and their glassy eyes were darkly reflective, flashing iridian scans as they passed.

But the old man was overcome with adrenaline. He no longer looked at his pursuers; he no longer cared. He walked boldly down the exit lane, with a line of cars tooting behind him; without even pausing to look, he jaywalked across the busy carriageway at the bottom, bringing cars skidding to a standstill, and marched straight on up the other side, chicaning left and right up the little hill to the overpass. There he continued his march out over the freeway, on the narrow concrete footbridge. Originally, it had been completely fenced in, but now wire hung loose from the struts where a great hole had been ripped in the netting.

Cuthbert stood before the gap in the fence and looked at the river of cars: a flock of white geese flying towards him; a stream of red fish swimming away. He could see the line of lights shining steadily, one after another, thousands and thousands of them, stretching all the way back to Berkeley on the right, and Oakland to the left. Beyond that, he could see the junction of the waters: the mass of flyovers where five freeways crossed their paths of pulsing light – like the laser lights at the Arena, he thought – suspended impossibly high in the air, a network of artificial veins and arteries circulating red and white cells through the city.

Suddenly he felt himself being pulled backwards.

'What you doing, man?' Nathan snapped. 'You gone crazy or somethin'?'

Cuthbert smiled. 'Aw, just thinking.'

He turned back to the endless city, its skyline looming dark against the last of the sunset, its blinking lights already reflecting a lurid, brilliant fuschia off the man-made clouds. The human machine rolled on unerringly, red and white.

'You know, I been thinking, this city ain't nothin' but a concrete dream . . . Whole country maybe . . . Ain't nothin' but tin cans in a concrete dream . . .'

The two men stood and wondered as the Boss leant out over the road, his rough hands pushing back the gap in the fence.

'Come on back,' Charles said, trying to get a grip on him.

'No, son, my time is up. I ain't never goin' back.' And without so much as a backward glance, the old man dropped through the hole.

Brittle

James Mavor

Penny sits on the train, first class, heading north. The meeting with her publisher has gone well, certainly better than she had anticipated.

She loves going to the Faber offices, the buzz she gets from waiting in reception, flanked by the author portraits – Eliot, Auden, Ted and Sylvia, Dylan Thomas – and, among them, her own: Penelope Walton, poet.

She has known Charles for twenty years. He is always charming. He takes her hand and kisses it. He is always so positive.

'We are all very excited,' he gushes.

'Are you?' she asks him. 'About what, exactly?'

'About *Moss*,' he tells her. 'I may have some rather good news. Where will you be this afternoon?'

She will be on the train, she tells him, going back to Cambridge.

'How is Geoffrey?'

'He's broken his leg.'

'Oh dear.'

'He's in plaster. Can't move. He's so pissed off.' She smiles, enjoying the words. 'Pissed off'. She'd never say that with Geoffrey.

'What is he again?' Charles is asking.

'A bryologist.'

'That's it.'

'Mosses and liverworts.'

She is happy to talk about Geoffrey (even though the subject is one neither she nor Charles feels passionate about). It keeps Charles off the subject she is dreading. The thing she has come to London to discuss.

But here it is. There is no avoiding it.

'How is the next one coming along?'

'Swimmingly,' she says, and not a flicker of doubt crosses her face.

'We did have a title, didn't we?'

'*Brittle.*'

'*Brittle,*' Charles echoes. '*Brittle. Brittle.*'

He seems to roll the word around his tongue, like he was tasting wine.

'You don't like it?' she asks.

'I don't know,' he says. 'It's rather difficult to tell without having read the actual poems.'

'Well,' Penny says, still holding the smile. 'You will just have to wait.'

The train moves on. Her telephone rings. She presses the button. It's Charles. He tells her the good news. Penny disconnects. The ticket collector comes through the carriage. Penny hands him her ticket.

'I've just been shortlisted for the Whitbread,' she tells him.

'Is that good or bad?' he asks, clipping a small circle from the ticket.

'It's a major literary prize,' she explains. The man opposite has looked up from his newspaper. Penny feels foolish and vain.

'What do you win?' asks the ticket man.

'I have no idea,' says Penny. 'Money, I suppose.'

'You don't look too cheery about it.'

And it's the truth. She doesn't. Doesn't feel cheery at all. She hasn't really felt cheery for a long time. What she has felt is brittle.

The train banks slightly and her pen rolls across the table. She puts out a hand. Stops it. Lifts it. The pen is named after a mountain and Penny can see the way its designers have given it qualities of weight and solidity and power and competence. It feels thick in her hand, almost too heavy.

She sets the pen down, next to the notebook which Geoffrey bought her at the shop for artists. It's really a sketchbook. The pages are thick and white like freshly fallen snow. About a year ago she wrote the title on the first page – *Brittle* – and, since then, not a word. Not since Hay.

It's not a long journey from London Liverpool Street to Cambridge, but it's long enough for a poem. In the halcyon days, she often managed two or three. Much of *Moss* was written like this, heading north, facing the direction of travel, coming back from a good lunch with Charles, say, or a trip to the V&A or the Royal Academy, and looking forward to being home and hearing about Geoffrey's latest taxonomic triumph, the flatlands whipping by.

First *Moss*. Then Hay. Now *Brittle*.

Or rather not. Not *Brittle*. Nothing. A void. A heavy pen. The fountain dry. The virgin paper undefiled. Nothing to say. No words. The flatlands whipping by.

A year ago and Penny is on the platform at Hay-on-Wye. It is the nation's leading literary festival and she is a leading poet. To her dismay, she discovers that her fellow speaker is not to be – as advertised – the dashing, rugged and handsome Jonathan Barley (*Fields of Love*) but Max Williams. The Old Soak. The Has-been. The One-hit Wonder.

Two years before, they had met at a Faber Christmas party. Max was, naturally, drunk. Penny was, characteristically, sober and judgemental. Charles introduced them.

'You may think I'm mad,' he fluttered, 'but I really think that you two might just get on, you know?'

Max was rude. He told Penny her poetry was constipated. Penny was flushed (it may have been the champagne). She told Max that, as a young woman, she had been swept off her feet by *The Burning Man*. Everyone was, back then. For one shining year, Max had literary London at his feet. Editors wanted to commission him. Newspapers wanted to photograph him. Girls wanted to sleep with him.

'And what exactly have you been doing since then?' Penny had asked.

'This,' Max told her, raising his glass and knocking it back and then taking another, smiling at the waitress as he lifted the drink from the tray, taking in her figure, her breasts, her potential availability, her desire for attention, her need for paternalistic love, while simultaneously weighing up his own desire, degree of inebriation and energy for the chase.

'This,' he said. 'I've been doing lots of this.'

At Hay, the readings went well. Penny read from *Moss*, Max read from *The Burning Man* plus some of his recent, unpublished work. They were asked about the future of British poetry. They were asked to name their favourite poems. They were asked where they got their ideas from. The afternoon passed slowly. Penny had an argument with a young woman who was angry that she could not understand some of Penny's poems, even after reading them dozens of times. Max was attacked by a different, older woman who accused him of phallocentrism and misogyny. The chairman brought the session to a close. There was a general sense of disappointment that Jonathan Barley had failed to show.

Later on, after they had made love, they talked about poetry. Max told Penny that he admired her work more than that of any other living British poet. Her work was buttoned-up and held-in and unforgiving but so what? So was Elliot's. So was Larkin's. That was her voice.

And then, after they had made love for a second time, she quoted from *The Burning Man*, words she'd had by heart for thirty years:

I am the hungry man, the angry man,
The yearning man, the burning man.

She held him in her arms. Max had the soul of a poet. He was passionate and sensitive. He saw things that no one else did and he saw them clearly, as if they were illuminated from within. He believed, along with the Russian formalists, that the purpose of art was to make stones stony. And he could see this – the stoniness of a stone, the tigerness of a tiger, the womanliness of a woman. He had the gift.

The trouble was that when he came to write these things down – these messages from God – he fumbled. He was not an artist.

Max had learned to live with his mediocrity, scraping a modest living from the odd bit of literary criticism, occasional tutoring on creative writing courses – though he was not often invited back again – and the occasional payment of royalties from *The Burning Man* which was still in print and still sold well, particularly, for no good reason that Max could work out, in Poland.

Penny ran her hand over his chest. There was a scar on his side, just below the rib. A war wound, he told her. She laughed, 'Which war?' He kissed her for an answer and, again, they made love and, again, Penny felt more alive than she had felt in her entire adult life.

They woke the next day, jumbled in each other's arms. The sun was coming in the window and, with it, self-consciousness. Max asked when he would see her again. Tomorrow? Next week? The Edinburgh Book Festival? (Max was on standby in case a well-known Chilean radical poet's anticipated release from prison did not come through in time for mid-August: the odds were looking good.)

Penny turned her face – the sun bothering her eyes – and told him that they would not meet again. She is married. She is a mother. It is over.

But Max had not left it at that. He was, after all, a *romantic* poet. He had phoned. He had visited ('There seems to be a chap at the door,' Geoffrey had said. 'Looks like some actor.')

And Max had written – poems, of course. Poems which, as poems, were not great art but, as declarations of love, they were extraordinary.

But still she said no. She was married and there was Geoffrey to consider. And she was a mother – although Tom had long since gone, living now in Tasmania – about as far from home, Penny often thought, as he could possibly get. And, above all, she was a *poet*.

Penny was frightened of this person she had been with Max – languid, uninhibited, loose, vivacious, raunchy, abandoned, free. Who was that person? Was that the real Penelope Walton?

(Or was it the champagne? It must have been.)

And would that person write like Penelope Walton? Would she write at all? Or would she just lie in bed all day, making love and being happy. What kind of life would that be for a poet whose work was founded on misery and repression?

'Where do you get your inspiration from?' they always asked.

'Oh, lots of things,' she always said. 'Long walks. Train journeys.'

She never told them about the stone inside, the lump that grew in her chest like a tumour.

Maybe one day, she'd tell them: 'Guilt. Pain. Despair.'

The train moves north. The sky is grey. The flatlands whipping by. Penny remembers coming back from Hay, coming home on the train – this train, she thinks, this train. The whole journey she's been thinking of him, of Max, and him inside her and then she sees a young woman opposite and she's reading a book – her book. The girl is reading *Moss*. The book has that photograph on the cover – the one everyone talks about, the picture of moss, but it's not quite moss, it's something else, something you can't quite put your finger on, something mysterious and, well, poetical. It's a great picture. Charles maintains that the picture alone has at least doubled the sales figures, perhaps more.

And then the girl looks up and does that frowning thing, and Penny watches as the girl realises that the person she's looking at is the person who wrote the poems she is reading. She even glances at the author photograph, just to check. Penny feels a wave of guilt. The girl smiles.

'I love these poems,' she says.

Penny nods. Her neck is stiff. 'Thank you,' she says.

The girl folds back the cover of the book.

'Would you sign it for me?'

Penny signs with her favourite pen, the one that's named after a mountain, the pen that has since run dry, her hand shaking, and then she goes to the back of the carriage where there's a lavatory. Someone's inside. Penny realises that she is going to be sick. She can actually feel the bile streaming into her mouth. She clamps her teeth together. The door opens and a youth comes out. He smiles. He looks a bit like her son Tom.

'It wasn't me,' he tells her. 'Honest.'

She goes in and closes the door. The floor is wet with urine. In the toilet, there is a large turd, shaped like a croissant. Penny retches, vomiting the guilt back out again, onto her dress and her stockings and her shoes. She spends the rest of the journey locked in the lavatory, cleaning and dabbing and mopping, trying to put herself back together again before Cambridge.

She remembers Geoffrey meeting her at the station. He kissed her on the cheek. 'How was Hay?' he asked. 'Tiring,' she told him. He lifted her bag and they headed towards the taxi rank.

The train heads north. Spots of rain. Some cows in a field.

Something has broken.

Penny lifts the pen. It had been a gift from Charles, or perhaps, more accurately, from Faber – Charles's lavish generosity was always on expenses. Now that *Moss* was on the shortlist, they wanted *Brittle.* They needed to get it out there. The pressure was on.

The man opposite set down his newspaper. He looked at her and Penny could tell that, having heard her tell the ticket man about her recent nomination for a major literary award, he was trying to find a way of starting a conversation. Perhaps he felt embarrassed on her behalf – that she blurted it out like that? Perhaps he was a poetry lover? Perhaps he too was heading home to his partner and hoped to find out more about Penny, exactly who she was, in order to have a funny story, an anecdote, to share with his wife, rather than have to tell her that his day at the office had been largely similar to all his other days and that he was bored with the commute and had begun to formulate plans that they just quit the whole thing, sell up and buy a house abroad, probably in France.

In fact, he just wants to borrow her pen. It is his daughter's birthday – she is five – and he has just remembered that his wife had told him to make sure to buy and write a card.

Penny has seen the newspaper, folded roughly on the man's table.

'Would you mind?' she asks. He hands it over. She flattens it out.

Obituaries.

Born in a small mining village . . . the shadow of Dylan Thomas . . . the boldest and brightest of his generation . . . The Burning Man.

Max is dead. Penny reaches for the phone and calls Charles.

'Why didn't you tell me?'

'I didn't know you knew each other.'

'You introduced us.'

'So I did.'

'And then we met again at Hay.'

'I never knew.'

'It says it was cancer.'

'Yes. It had been going on for years. He'd had nearly everything taken out, I think. A kidney. Half a lung. The last couple of years can't have been much fun, poor bastard. A total drunk, of course, and a terrible ladies' man but, still. Quite a character.'

She finishes the call. The man hands back her pen. The train approaches the station.

'Keep the paper if you want,' he says. 'I'm done with it.'

She looks again at the picture of Max. It's from Soho in the 70s when he was in his prime, a cigarette in his mouth, a drink in his hand, a girl on his arm and the world at his feet. Thick black hair. Smooth skin. Confidence pouring out of him like a natural force.

The man nods at the paper.

'Did you know him?' he asks.

'Yes,' she says, 'though we only met a couple of times.'

'Good-looking fella. Who was he?'

'He was the love of my life.'

The train pulls into the station with a sigh. Penny watches as the man hurries to collect his car from the Park & Ride. She reaches the automatic barrier and searches for her ticket. A queue forms behind her. She senses their impatience. Stupid old woman.

Penny tells the railway official that she did, of course, have a ticket but that she must have left it on the train. He tells her she will have to buy a new ticket in order to pass through the barrier. Normally, she would argue, she would feel indignant and abused, she would make a fuss and the man would, having made his point, nod for the guard at the barrier to let her through. 'Just this once, OK?'

But today has been a special day and Penny hands the man her credit card and tells him to charge her for a new ticket, first class, from London to Cambridge. He takes the card, swipes it and shrugs. 'I don't make the rules.'

She passes through the barrier. Geoffrey is waiting for her. His leg, of course, is still in plaster and she can tell that it will have taken him considerable effort to dress and to organise a cab to come to the station to greet her and to welcome her home. She wonders why, today of all days, he has done this.

'Congratulations,' he says. 'I am so proud.' And he pats her – he actually pats her – on the back.

She stares at him. What is he talking about? She would like to hit him. She would like to kick his leg – chip some of the plaster off onto the tiled station concourse.

Geoffrey looks happy, like a schoolboy with a frog.

'Charles called me. About the Whitbread. Well done you.'

Penny smiles. Geoffrey takes her arm. They walk towards the taxi rank.

Her eyes are wet but she will not cry. Instead, she feels something forming in her chest. A hard lump, like coal. She knows what it is, this feeling, and that, in a day or two, if she leaves it alone, it will become a poem.

Strange Fare
Brian McCabe

It was beginning to get dark and he was thinking of packing it in for the day when he saw the guy standing outside Sandy Bell's. He'd stepped off the pavement and was leaning out into the street, holding an arm out as if he meant to grab hold of the wing mirror rather than just hail the taxi. He was a tall guy with shoulder-length brown hair and a heavy beard. He wore jeans, a black leather coat and a grey scarf wound round his ears, and he had a plastic carrier bag under his arm. Even before he pulled over he could make out the guy's bulbous, purplish nose – and the nose of the bottle sticking out of the carrier bag.

When the guy got in he put the carrier bag on the seat next to him. He was too old to be a student, but maybe he was a teacher of some kind – there were books and papers in the bag along with the bottle. Maybe it was the way the guy's lips kept moving, as if he was talking to himself, or talking to somebody else who wasn't there, that made him think this. Then again, sometimes you just had a hunch about whoever was in the back before they said a word. When he was bored, he sometimes played at trying to guess what people did for a living, or why they were going where they were going, or what they'd just been doing, then he'd get talking to them and find out if he'd got it right. More often than not, he hadn't – but it made the job more interesting.

– Where to?

The guy didn't answer immediately. He was gazing into the distance and his lips were moving, as if he was talking – no, not talking, but singing. He was singing something under his breath.

– Where to, pal?

– Oh, yeah. Ah, Raaslin.

– Roslin?

– Yeah, the castle.

– Roslin Castle?

– Not Roslin Castle. I forget the name. It's around there somewhere. We'll find it when we get out there.

He put the meter on and pulled out.

He didn't much like the sound of that. He knew there was a castle in Roslin, down on the Esk somewhere, but although he'd grown up in the area, he'd never been to see it. He had never liked castles. They gave him the creeps. What was the point of going to see a castle? The only castle he'd gone to see on a guided tour had been Edinburgh Castle, on a school day out, and all he'd found out about it was that it had been a place where people were imprisoned, tortured and put to death. He had never liked castles for that reason, and he didn't want to go to Roslin Castle on a Saturday night. But it wasn't Roslin Castle. So which castle was it? He hadn't heard about any other castles around there, and he'd spent his childhood there, crossing the Esk every day to go to Lasswade Primary School, which was perched on top of a hill above the valley, a grim wee castle for the poor kids they had been, surrounded by high walls and high fences. Who they were trying to keep out, when he thought about it now, was beyond him.

The sound of the name Roslin brought back other memories he would just as soon not remember. As a boy, he'd been scared of Rosslynlee, the lunatic asylum in Roslin. Rosalene, a patient from Rosslynlee, sometimes roamed the streets of the town he grew up in. Though he had never seen her, her reputation – and the rumour that she was out – had been enough to make him stay in the house on bonfire night instead of going to the bonfire. It was said that she sometimes chased cars, or people on bikes, or children. It was said that her eyebrows met in the middle, and that she was stronger than a man. As a young boy, he'd had nightmares in which he was being chased by Rosalene and caught. What she would do to him then was never revealed, because he had always woken up sweating and shouting at the moment he was caught.

The guy had settled back in the seat and looked out the window, singing something to himself in a low voice. Okay, so he was a bit tipsy and he was going to Roslin. Judging by the accent, he was American. So why would this guy be going out to Roslin at this time on a Saturday? It was a cold night, and he could understand that a visitor – mind you, he didn't really look like a tourist – might find it difficult to find out about buses. Anyway, he must have some money – enough not to think twice about a taxi to Roslin. Maybe he was going to a wedding at this castle and the guests were being put up for the weekend. Maybe he'd arrived earlier and had gone into town for a drink or three.

He looked at the guy in the mirror. No, he wasn't going to a wedding. A funeral, maybe. Now that he eyed him in the mirror, he did look a bit the worse for wear – and maybe he was going to fall asleep in his cab. He'd slumped in the seat and his eyelids were drooping. He thought about trying to strike up a conversation with the guy, to keep him awake if nothing else. He stopped at the lights.

– You're not part of the film crew or the cast out there, eh?

The guy didn't seem to hear him, but went on staring out the window at the shop fronts and tenements they were passing without really looking at them. He was singing to himself, some kind of folk song, every so often coming out with the line: *Ready, steady, Jenny Lasswade.*

When the lights changed, they moved on.

Jenny Lasswade. He remembered the story from childhood. This woman who ferried people across the Esk for a price, before there had been a bridge. And sometimes, according to the story, she stopped halfway across and asked to see the colour of their money. If they didn't have enough, she dropped them in the rat-infested river. At least, it had been rat-infested when he'd had to cross it to go to school every day. Older boys had told him that if you fell into the river the rats would eat you. He'd seen rats running along the banks and that had been another source of nightmares.

In the mirror he watched the guy lean forward and pull the bottle from the bag, unscrew the cap and take a swig. Drinking in the cab was something he'd put people out for before now – it wasn't allowed – but this guy was in his fifties and he wasn't giving him any bother, so he decided to turn a blind eye.

It had been a bit slow for a Saturday and finishing with a fare to Roslin would help. It had started off okay with a call-out to the airport. Two young guys – going to Prague, they'd said, for a stag-night – had emptied their pockets of British coins to pay the fare – it was a bare fare, at that – then he'd been lucky enough to find a businessman in a hurry to get into town who hadn't gone to the official taxi rank. Those airport drivers had it all sewn up. In fact he was contravening their code by picking up a stray fare at the airport. If any of them had seen him and taken his number, it could result in a problem for him. They'd complain about him to the firm. After that it had been slow – a couple of fares to Waverley and Haymarket, then he'd taken a call-out to the shopping mall at the Gyle. A woman with a full trolley of shopping. After that nothing for a while, then a guy taking his son to the Hearts-Hibs game at Easter Road. Getting back out of there had taken a while because of the crowds. The tips had been pretty poor all round. Even the woman with the shopping had given him just fifty pence on a seven-quid fare, after he'd helped her in and out of the taxi with her bags.

Everybody assumed you were making good money. You were a taxi driver, with a meter that showed a price that got higher by the minute, and higher still by the mile. They saw the wad of notes you tried to hide in your wallet or your pouch and they saw the collection of coins you rifled in for their change – slowly, so that they might get impatient and say forget it, just keep the change – and they assumed you were cashing in. They didn't take into account the cab hire, the petrol, the percentage you paid the company; they didn't know that the Inland Revenue assumed that you were cashing in as well – earning more than you were declaring and averaging tips of fifteen per cent. Fifteen per cent! On a ten pound fare, that would make the tip . . . one pound fifty! When did anyone give a tip of over a quid? The reality was different. On a ten-pound fare, you rarely got a quid. On an airport run, you sometimes got a quid, but not always. Usually a big tipper was in company, showing off. There were exceptions. Once he had been given a fiver by an American lady who was going to the Sheraton from the airport, here for a conference, but he suspected that she had given him the fiver because she wasn't used to the money.

Even Diane, his wife, assumed he was making more than he was, and he went along with this, exaggerating his earnings and his tips because it was clear that she was making a lot more at the nursery. .

The time he'd been investigated by the Inland Revenue still rankled with him. Okay, he'd maybe been a bit lax in his first few years about his accounts and his tax returns – he'd submitted estimates – but the investigator had told him with taxi drivers they did it as a matter of course. He'd been driving for six, seven years at that time, so it was time they took a close look at his accounts. Now he always made a point of doing his accounts and submitting his tax return promptly, hoping that his promptness would look like honesty.

Sometimes he wondered what he was doing, what he was really *doing*. Ferrying people from A to B – but what did it mean? What was his work, when it came down to it? He didn't produce anything. He didn't *make* anything. He wasn't as necessary as a plumber, no question about that, although sometimes people did need to get home, or away from home. That was it. Maybe, when you thought about it, getting from A to B was as important as anything else. But then, what was his job when he got a fare like this one – someone who didn't know exactly where he was going? Anyway, it was work. Work was work and you had to do it. You had to earn a crust somehow. That was what work was, by definition. Something you had to do – something you wouldn't choose to do if you didn't have to. But if you didn't have to work, what else would you do?

He decided to cut over by the Braid Hills road. It was good to get a stretch where you could go up to sixty and leave the streets behind, but as soon as he got on the road and the houses disappeared, the guy cleared his throat and spoke.

– Hey, where is *this*?

– Braid Hills. It's a short-cut. Takes us out Fairmilehead, then we're on the way out of town to Roslin. It's a skoosh. That's quite a good golf course over on the left. Play golf yourself at all?

– Uh-uh.

That killed that one dead. Sometimes they didn't want to talk. They wanted to be left alone. You could sense it. He moved up a gear and put his foot down. The Braid Hills Road was one of his favourite long short-cuts, because it felt like driving in the country. He tried again.

– Where d' you come from in the States?

In the mirror he saw the guy shaking his head, taking a slug from the bottle and wincing.

– Saskatoon, Saskatchewan.

– Oh, Canada. Sorry. That's like you calling me English, eh?

He thought he heard the guy say under his breath: or worse.

– What's that?

– I said, it's worse.

– Maybe you're right there.

He didn't like the turn the conversation was taking and he didn't want to rub the guy up the wrong way – he was big, and maybe he was drunk – so he turned the radio on low and let that take over. The news came to an end, then the football results came on. In the middle of it the guy just started talking.

– I tried to get to that soccer game in Edinburgh but it was sold out.

– What's that?

– That soccer match, it was full.

– The game at Easter Road? It would be. You like the football?

– A bit. I went to a local game, somewhere out where I'm staying. You know what they did at half-time? They tarred and feathered a girl.

– They what?

– They led her out to the middle of the pitch, shaved her head, put some black stuff all over her head and stuck all these feathers to it. Do they always do that at soccer games here?

– Never heard of it.

He was beginning to think the guy must be nuts when he added:

– Then they announced how much money she'd raised. I guess it was a charity stunt.

– Ah, right. Where was this?

– Bonny, ah . . .

– Bonnyrigg?

– Yeah, that's it. Bonnyrigg. Bonny means nice, right? Pretty.

– Eh . . . yeah.

– There's nothin pretty about it.

– No. You're right there.

He was on the point of telling the guy that he'd grown up in Bonnyrigg, and that he'd gone to watch Bonnyrigg Rose as a boy, but he'd never heard of such a thing happening at half-time at any football match, and he started to wonder if the guy was the full shilling. But maybe it was a stunt for charity like the guy said. Now that he was talking he tried to keep it going.

– You on holiday or here for work?

– Bit of both.

– You're not working in the place they cloned Dolly are you?

– No, sir.

There was just the hint of a derisive laugh before he took another swig from the bottle and went back to looking out of the window.

He drove up through Fairmilehead and then they were out of town. Though the fare to Roslin would put up his takings, it added another hour before he'd get home, and he wished he hadn't bothered.

Tomorrow was Sunday, but he was so used to rising early that it was impossible to have a long lie, and most Sundays he decided to take the taxi out at least for a few hours. Before he started work on weekdays, he had to run Diane to her work in the nursery school, Joe to school (it was on the way) and sometimes he would also take Helen to college, if she was running late, even though she had a student bus pass and could get there in plenty of time if she spent less time doing her hair and her make-up. After the family run, he sometimes went home and had a little time on his own, when he made himself tea and listened to radio and made a first stab at the crossword. People often said to him that it must be good to be a taxi driver because you were your own boss. To an extent it was true, but people forgot the slack times, sitting in a long queue at a rank and waiting to move to the front, chatting to the other guys or just doing the crossword. A lot of your time was spent just waiting for the next fare. Sundays were worst for that, although because there were fewer buses you could sometimes go looking for fares at bus stops, getting ahead of a service that ran only every half-hour. It was a bit of a carry-on, that, but you did it because it was something to do. Even if you weren't getting a fare, you were trying.

The guy in the back had closed his eyes and seemed to have nodded off. Would he have the money to pay the fare? Maybe he should do a Jenny Lasswade and stop here, on this dark road winding out past the Pentlands, and ask him to show that he had the cash. He'd sometimes done it in the past – with bunches of young girls or young guys on a Saturday night – but before he'd started off on the journey, not in the middle of it.

When he came to Roslin, he slowed down and tried to rouse the guy, but there was no response. He'd slumped in the seat on the way out and hadn't stirred since.

– This is Roslin, sir . . . Hello!

No response. He pulled over, put the light on in the back and chapped on the glass. Still nothing. Jesus – the guy wasn't moving. Was he dead? He got out of the cab and opened the passenger door, then leaned in and shook the guy by the shoulder. The guy grabbed his arm and sat upright, his eyes wide open, then he seemed to remember where he was and let go.

– We're here. Roslin. So where's this castle?

– It's not here, but it's near. It's around here somewhere. Turn round and go back up the way some.

He climbed in and turned the taxi round and moved up the main street.

– Down here, I think. It's over by a place . . . it's near Lasswade.

Then the guy leaned back and started singing in a low voice:

– Ready, steady, Jenny Lasswade . . .

The last thing he needed was to be driving around here in the dark looking for a castle, but he followed the road winding down into the Esk valley, then up again. When they came to a crossroads, the guy told him to go left. They were heading down towards Polton and Lasswade when he shouted to stop. He pulled in at the side of the road but couldn't see anything that looked like a castle.

– It's back the way. We passed it.

There was just a big iron gate in the wall beside the road that looked like it hadn't opened in years.

– That's where the castle is? Do people live in it?

– It's a retreat.

– What kind of retreat?

– A retreat for people who need a retreat. I'll walk from here.

He stopped the meter and waited while the guy fumbled in his pocket looking for the money.

– Here, keep the change.

Before he could say anything the guy had passed him some notes and was out of the taxi, heading towards the big iron gate. He counted the notes. It was just enough to cover it. Another bare fare. He heard the gate squeal open and looked back to see the guy disappearing down a dark driveway.

When he drove down into Lasswade something made him pull into a side street before the bridge. He got out of the taxi, walked halfway over the bridge and leaned over the iron railing to smoke a cigarette. He could see lights on in the old primary school on the hill. It had been converted into private flats for people who commuted into town. He looked along the banks of the river but didn't see any rats. Then he watched the dark water rolling and frothing under him.

A retreat for people who needed a retreat – what was that meant to mean? He was a strange fare, a strange fare altogether.

On with the orange light again. There wouldn't be anyone on the way back to town, not at this time. Then again, that was the point of this job: you never really knew. You never knew who was out there waiting for you in the dark, waiting to go home.

Not in the Home
Lynda McDonald

Jumping from the barn roof with the dog had been the first thing. I'd wrapped my body protectively round him like one of those meals people ate centuries ago where there was one meat stuffed inside another meat and so on until you had a whole bison on the outside and a pygmy shrew on the inside. This was just me, Cliff the dog, velocity and gravity. Cliff loved it. His tail wagged as if he wanted me to try again, only from something more exciting this time – a pylon, perhaps. I've done several pylons now. Cliff never got his chance – he was a long time ago dog. But I know how to fall well – to fall, to drown, to be consumed by fire. Stunts. You name it, I've done it.

There's my brother and me. Twins. It's amazing being a twin. Like an out-of-body experience. Whatever you do, you can see yourself doing it – and how you look while you're doing it. We lived in a village and there was only one school, so we had to be in class together. When we went to the big school, we chose the same subjects. Our minds developed along the same lines. We wanted to do the same job – one that maximised on the potential of twins – like the CIA or the FBI. Jobs with initials, not job descriptions. Stealthy sorts of jobs. One day we'd write a novel and a sequel simultaneously.

Somebody like Steven Spielberg came to the village one day to film. He had the same first name anyway. He was Steven Shaw-cross. He was the location scout. If you're still there at the end of the credits, you'll see his name. On this occasion, he'd probably been given the brief to look for a farmer willing to rent out a field, barn, cows, wife and hens (watch out for the stampede), a village store that dated back to the time of *The Waltons*, a main street (ditto). He also needed two boys who could pass for look-alikes. My brother and I were playing dust football in what we call Main

Street one day. He gaped at us, then looked up to heaven as if his prayers had been answered. We were in.

He walked back to the house with us and Mam told him about our long silver-screen tradition. It had skipped Mam and Dad's generation, although she does remind me of Meryl Streep. Her face has humanity, humour and a certain windswept quality. Dad was rugged but introvert. When he wasn't farming he mended toys for the village children.

We sat and listened to Mam tell the scout about Grandpop. How this countryside we lived in and the joy of the parallel-ploughed furrow had not captured Grandpop's imagination in the way it gave Dad deep personal joy. How Grandpop had been impossible to pin down – as if he were a butterfly that refused to be impaled. Which he was in a way. So he'd left the farm to make his fortune.

He'd crossed the Atlantic and earned his passage by entertaining the passengers with tricks. He'd taught them to Louis, our Dad, when he was a boy. Dad had shown us in turn. So, our particular DNA link was through tricks – the missing thumb, the ear that sprouted pennies, the disembodied hand. It was in our make-up. On board that liner had been a film producer. When Grandpop smashed the man's pocket watch and produced it not only whole, but gleaming, Gramps was a made man. He took his tricks far beyond anything our Dad would have considered necessary for enjoyment.

We had a collection of those silent movies of Grandpop's. We knew every trick, knew where the famous actor bowed out and Grandpop came in. We analysed the moves and tried them out after school. Kirk, my brother, would do something like jumping on top of the car and I'd do the same and we'd decide who was the famous actor and who was stunt double that day. Then one of us would jump off the roof of the car, the other – for the sake of verisimilitude, would slide off the back onto an old mattress we'd put there. We'd swing from the highest branch of the tree or dive into the icy water of the bottomless burn as it swirled round like a cup of stirred milkless tea. We'd lie under the water and hold our breaths as long as possible. Kirk always won that one as if everything in twins is the same except breath. Kirk was learning to smoke so he could double for the bad guys eventually, so I guess that would take care of the breath anomaly.

Our first film was disappointing – we just had to appear side-by-side while the cameraman shot us with a silky filter. I wanted to ask why they didn't just do a split-screen effect, but I guess we had to start somewhere. But our names appeared on the credits: Ghostly apparitions played by Kirk and Clark Block.

Anyway, back to Grandpop. Mam was telling our new friend Steven Shawcross about Grandpop and his dislike of routine, of the predictable. Dad chipped in that he'd never understood that. So much in life was beyond our control that we should be thankful for those things we could rely on. Steven looked interested at this point (perhaps he knew he had to get Dad's permission for us to film). When pressed, Dad said a lot of oh's and well's and that it was only his opinion, but he liked to know that here, rain was predictable . . . things like that. Though Steven leaned forward in his seat, expectantly, we knew from experience that was it. Mam looked at Dad as if he'd once more said the profoundest thing in the world, but Steven looked a bit disappointed. Kirk said Dad valued order. The same words were on my lips even as he spoke.

Anyway, Mam went on to say how Grandpop joined a big studio in Hollywood and perfected his craft.

'What about your grandmother?' asked Steven. It was a natural question, after all.

Dad left the room. He had to check out the clouds, he said, you could learn a lot from clouds.

'Did I say something wrong?' asked Steven.

'It's kind of . . .' I started.

'Sensitive,' Kirk finished.

'The idea was for Grandpop . . .' I said.

'To send for Grandma,' said Kirk.

Steven's head was going from one to the other of us like at a spectator sport. We felt sorry for him and I nodded to Mam and she nodded back, ready to tackle the story.

'He got very famous in his own right, you know. He doubled for so many famous people – those that didn't do their own stunts. My father-in-law, the boys' Grandpop, became great pals with them. And he was doing some amazing work.' She went over to the drawer and brought out some bills from several films. Steven said he'd seen them all.

'He could freefall before it was invented,' said Mam. He could ride three horses at once, jump from train to train, stay underwater for several minutes.' (Here, I nudged Kirk who coughed and exhaled the smell of an Embassy cigarette.) 'In this *Tarzan* film,' – she held up a poster – 'he had to be Johnny Weissmuller when he got ill one day.'

'I saw that one,' said Steven. 'I thought there was something slightly different about Johnny – couldn't put my finger on it. So it was your father-in-law who jumped from that cliff-top into that rock pool, who got pulled behind the stampeding herd of buffalo and wrestled with the crocodile?' (Oh boy, were Kirk and I longing to do that one.)

Mam nodded. We realised she had been evading the question of Grandma, but Steven was smart.

'He didn't call for her?'

'Didn't call?' said Mam, innocently.

Steven nodded.

There was a silence.

'Ah.'

Nope, Grandma had never, as Steven put it, been called to join Grandpop in Hollywood. But what Mam didn't go into was Grandma's Revenge – for never seeing Grandpop again, except in celluloid.

Kirk and me would go and visit her nearly every day. We'd sit on the rug at her feet and we'd talk about school and how we'd been put on opposite sides in games and how the teams always drew when they did that and everyone said that was more disappointing than losing. She'd rub our hair in a kind of circular motion – distractedly – in different directions, like that trick you can do rubbing your head and stomach at the same time, but going opposite ways. Then we'd ask for an old film of Grandpop's – before we knew what he'd done, anyway.

Or not done.

Dad talked from time to time about sins of omissions, but his references were smaller-scale than God's. Dad's faith was rooted in smaller things generally than God's, or most people's for that matter. Dad was the most content person we knew. It gave him joy to repair a Dinky car for a village kid, to see the first shoots of a new crop, to sharpen the prongs on his pitchfork until they gleamed like forked lightning. His father's absence was probably the only Sin of Omission he thought of with capital letters.

'I played the piano for the silent movies,' Grandma told us one day. We'd turned simultaneously to her old piano, which we'd never heard her play.

'It was what was done then. When people didn't speak in movies, the music told the audience what to feel . . . what to prepare themselves for. And I did the background music for your Grandpop's movies. I would sit down in the pit of the cinema, with only a candle light and it would be just me and your Grandpop together again. I was so close to him, I could see every pucker from a sleepless night or bloat from bad eating.'

We'd been about twelve and emotions were beginning to bite. Despite what we considered to be our bourgeoning worldliness, words like lonely, abandoned, betrayal were not yet in our active vocabularies.

One afternoon much later, Grandma sent us to the dresser to find the film called *An Afternoon in New York*. We knew Grandpop had doubled for a very famous, if not notorious, actor for that one.

Though it sounded innocuous, it had involved some of his most daring stunts. If I say the words skyscraper and missing girders, Times Square and a pilotless plane, the Statue of Liberty and Wellingtons, you'll know the film I mean. We watched the beginning, read the words, sensed, rather than experienced, the action. Grandma got up.

'Start it again.'

Kirk rewound the film on the projector, which squeaked and clicked and had its own dialogue even if the films were silent. We watched in awe as Grandma went to the piano and lifted the lid. As the film started up, she played. Slowly at first and rhythmically, then more discordantly – sometimes the *pianissimo* announcing the pattering of rain, or the famous actor walking through the streets alone and thoughtful-looking. Then the *fortissimo* announced a crescendo of action and this would be Grandpop about to do something daring and breathtaking. The piano would imitate a drum roll like they do at the circus. It all made sense for us. We asked for it all over again. Grandma smiled, then winked. We'd never seen Grandma wink before.

There was something wrong this time. The music was different when Grandpop appeared. It was out of sync. Nothing seemed to accord with his movements on the screen. Something was very, very wrong. Though he seemed to be doing scary things – scaling the outside of a skyscraper or jumping in front of a train, there was a strange time lapse that made his movements – usually so graceful – clumsy and ponderous. And there was a humour about the music at the most inappropriate moments.

'It was my revenge,' said Grandma. 'I could make him look as silly as I liked in front of people in the town.'

She never played the piano again as far as we knew and we never watched any more of Grandpop's films. The closest we came to Grandpop for many years was in the séances Grandma's house-maid had with his bowler hat, which had been left behind.

Grandma didn't know, of course, and we didn't tell. Dad thought of sweets as something not to rely on – you may enjoy them, but they would, in the end, rot your teeth. We were given sweets by Millie if we said we saw the bowler move, thus signifying our Grandpop's presence and her amazing powers. No problem. There it goes again.

We got to Hollywood, Kirk and I, thanks to being twins and those appearances as children. It opened up a whole new range of possibilities for studios we were told. Stunts are different now – I don't know whether to say they're more demanding than they were at the beginning, in Grandpop's day. That would diminish the sheer bravery of those pioneers. But audiences now demand more from their entertainment. They expect people in films to act in improbable ways. They know it's not really Brad Pitt or Harrison Ford out there. They would prefer it if it were, so that gives them a strange ambivalence towards the stunt person. Me, I suppose.

Kirk eventually went into mainstream and, guess what?, I became his stunt double. I developed a liking for the subtle, the low profile, for anonymity. We complemented each other in a way Grandpop and Dad did, though no one would ever acknowledge that. Remember I said our village was like something out of *The Waltons*? You know, everyone did their own stunts in that. Oh, very funny, you might say – handling a dangerous cookie cutter maybe. When I watched the re-runs, I realised our Dad was a bit like Paw Walton. Things they said on that programme were often quite profound. I'd been impressed once when Paw said to John Boy, 'Son, you can't blame yourself for the things that happen in life. You can't put yourself in the centre – you got no business there. What you've just gotta do is take things as they come and just keep going.' True.

Kirk and I finished a film together – a remake of *Apocalypse Now*, with additional helicopter stunts. Vietnam films always make my blood run cold. I've never seen one through. After it, we had some time on our hands. We went in search of Grandpop.

*

It seemed that, in the end, he'd acquired a philosophy and a peace not dissimilar to Dad's, only more so. He'd joined the most obscure sect he could find. It was a sub-sect of a sub-sect of a reclusive, unworldly sect that could foretell all sorts of events in the clouds. I remembered the day when Dad went out to look at clouds, all those years ago, when Steven Spielberg came to the farm (that's what we tell our Hollywood friends). I wondered if they had both been looking up at the same time and some sort of communion had passed between them.

I wish Dad knew how close they finally became. In his Paw Walton sort of way, he'd have pondered that news. I see him standing in the doorway of the barn, pitchfork or spade in hand; and eventually he'd nod his head and say something really deep like, 'Well, I guess Grandpop's previous experience would have come in really handy for all the dangerous things a sect might have to do.'

Which is not the end of the story.

It seems Grandpop was called out of retirement one last time. Some New York executive wanted him to talk about his life to new stunt artists. Being in the sect had not dulled his curiosity and he set off for New York. One last trip to the outside world he'd promised them at the sect branch meeting. Although he'd gone, his response to the hurly-burly of life in New York has never been recorded, because the sect denounced all forms of personal writing as egotism. But it seems that on his first afternoon there, a man called Norman Clutsky III, a man from a stable and run-of-the-mill job in a bank, had leapt from the tenth-floor window, not as a stunt, but in deadly earnest; and Grandpop had been underneath to break his fall.

'It gets you in the end,' Grandma had said on hearing the news. Whether it meant life, work, or one's just desserts, no one liked to ask because her eyes were closed and she was playing a weird sort of tune on the piano at the time.

Coastal Business
Duncan McLean

Hokey Pokey's perches on the promenade, its sky-blue door opening directly off Bayview Road, ten steps from there taking you to its back windows and the grey and wormy sands stretching out beyond. That's at low tide. At high, the North Sea flicks at the rimy panes like a wet towel on a schoolboy's bum. It could take your eye out, that sea, it really could, and just for looking at it.

It's the only building on the sea side of the prom. The others on Bayview – whitewashed fishermen's cottages, three B&Bs, a Baptist kirk – are sensibly crouched on the dry side. Sand only gets in their sugar bowls on days of exceptional gales. (Cromarty; north-north-east, Force six; one thousand and five, rising; three miles; *poor*.) But Hokey Pokey Tony's grandad had started off parking his ice-cream tricycle at that precise point in 1937. Then Tony's old man had banged up a wooden shed around the trike in the 1950s. And Tony himself, with business booming one last time before Benidorm and Malaga burst the Moray Coast's bubble, built his Deluxe Refreshment Salon around the shack in the early seventies.

Retrospective planning permission was mentioned more than once, I've heard, but the council, having carried out their requisite surveys, decided that the whole place was likely to fall into the sea at any moment, so there wasn't much point in wasting time and money on paperwork. (Not often you hear a council say that!) They'd only have to produce a whole lot more when the thing tumbled into the waves. Anyway, owing to the vagaries of planning law, Hokey Pokey's was still officially classified as a Temporary Retail Outlet – a tricycle, to be exact – despite the twenty-by-forty foot pink and sky-blue concrete extent of it, the lavvies emptying out through big rusty pipes kinking seawards, the ice-cream maker, the deep fat fryer, the beautiful rows of beautiful boiled sweeties in beautiful big glass jars.

'That's all just window dressing,' Tony would say. 'Look, we really could move the whole damn thing any minute.' And he'd point to the skeleton of his grandad's tricycle hanging from the rafters amongst looping strips of plastic pennants and Dairy Maid ice-cream posters.

'It's got a flat tyre,' I'd say.

'That's how my grandad ended up in Portduff,' he'd reply. 'He was actually heading for New York, but got a puncture halfway down the prom. And here we've been ever since.'

And what about the next generation? Tony's son and heir, Anthony the fourth? Wouldn't he labour like Hercules to avoid such a collapse in the family business? Wasn't he already planning to further accessorize the ancestral trike with a twenty-first century Wi-Fi Enabled Lo-fat Juice Bar Chill-out Emporium? Actually the young fellow had such faith in the booming future of the Moray Coast tourist industry that he had run away to sea, and was working as a dancer on the lucrative South Georgia/Falkland Islands/Tristan da Cuhna cruise triangle. (Best not to mention the boy in Tony's company, I'd learned.)

All of which filled my head as I drove out to Portduff for my first appointment of the week. That and me trying to work out how much commission I'd get in various permutations of sales for the month. And whether it would be enough to pay the rent, the credit card, the pension plan, the petrol, the child support, the gas people who somehow managed to pump electricity through their pipes into my flat . . . allowing me to sit up way into the night poring over the strategies, the sales analysis, the hot and cold leads, the maps of Scotland (north and east), the commission reports . . . and so back to the bills again. That was my headful for the day, as it was most days. However, the evil hour couldn't be put off forever: there was a living to be made. At least I hoped there was.

I parked outside the kirk, lifted my samples from the boot,

pressed the key to lock it (which made all the lights flash – not once or twice, but continuously), pressed it again, which stopped the lights but unlocked the car, pressed it a third time, *hard*, which locked and . . . made the lights flash just the once. New car due from the company in five months' time! (Highlight of my year, every third year.) Till then, no non-essential repairs allowed.

I strolled over to the sky-blue door (which is a strange name for a colour in north-east Scotland in mid-March. Sky-grey would be more like the fellow, though admittedly not so cheery on a sweetie shop's exterior.) I walked in, setting off a jingle of bells sewn into the net curtain that swung on the back of the door.

'About time!' cried a voice.

'Good morning, Mr Tony.'

'Good? From what point of view exactly?'

'Well . . . good to see you again.' Though I couldn't see him actually: he was through in his miniscule back shop, observing me through his security glass, no doubt, scratching his private parts, picking his nose, giving me two fingers quite likely – but all hidden to me. 'Don't you know, it's always good to see you.'

'I was expecting you yesterday.'

'Yesterday was Sunday, Mr Tony. I don't go out on a Sunday.'

'Alright for some! Sitting with your feet up eating free samples that should be *mine*! Some of us have to work for a living. You've no idea of the life of the little man.'

You wouldn't have described Tony as a little man. Very few folk who spend their days amongst chips, ice-cream, doughnuts and beautiful boiled sweeties manage to stay little, even if they started that way.

'Surely you weren't open yesterday Mr Tony?' I said towards the security glass, seeing my frown of almost genuine concern in its strips of mirror. 'Not much Sunday trade yet, eh?'

'Not much trade at all. It's hard times. I hope you're not expecting me to buy anything from you.'

'Not expecting, Mr Tony, but hoping. I live in hope.'

'We all do. If we didn't have hope we'd have nothing.'

A heave of a sigh came though from the back shop.

'I have a hope actually, Mr Tony.'

'Oh aye?'

'Aye, I hope you'll come out of your cubby hole and talk to me.'

There was a silence.

'Do I have to?'

'Only if you want to see the most stunning selection of new confectionary ranges from Sweet-tooth Sweeties. Only if you want to get your hands on some generous samples that will tantalise your taste buds and send your pleasure centres spinning. Only if . . .'

'Okay, okay, I'm coming, cut the crock.'

The customer is always right. I cut it.

Tony came out from the back shop, yawning and stretching, and we shook hands. Then he cleared some space on the counter and I started to pull out my new launches.

'Tandoori Bon-bons, Tony. Curry is now officially Scotland's national dish, so what better way to build sales success than a luscious chewy caramel sphere, lightly flavoured with chilli, then lovingly dusted with a mixture of icing sugar and curry powder. Delicious! And a national advertising campaign to follow from Easter, featuring that Glaswegian off the telly, the Indian one who runs the shop – very funny, bound to get a lot of airplay. Tandoori Bon-bons: a hot tip for the summer, you might say!'

I laughed. Tony didn't.

'No,' he said.

'Very sensible,' I said. 'Actually, it's a bit gimmicky, eh? But wait till you see this. A new twist on the established family favourite, Soor Plooms. These days, with the rise of juice bars and smoothies, consumers are ever more familiar with exotic fruits that would have been beyond the imagination of kids a generation ago. So, to meet this growing sophistication, Sweet-tooth Sweeties are launching Soor Mangoes, Soor Kiwis, and Soor Pomegranates. Sure to be a hit with . . .'

Tony waved his hands, cutting me off.

'Nobody wants that kind of thing any more, Andy,' he said. 'The kids don't want boiled sweeties out a jar in a wee paper poke, they want the big names.'

I gasped. 'Big names? You don't get a much bigger name than Soor Plooms! There's a chapter of Scotland's history in that name. When the English raiders rode over the border, little did they realise that the defending Scots were hiding up in the trees in the orchard. So when they rode underneath, clippety cloppity over the cobblestone paths . . .'

'Stop!' cried Tony. 'I ken all that: you told me last time, and the time before that.'

'It's my favourite story,' I said. 'It's our heritage! And now Sweet-tooth Sweeties is bringing Scottish history right up to date with this multi-ethnic range of multi-flavoured fruit boilings!'

'Will you shut up if I buy some?' said Tony.

I smiled, smoothed the top page of the order pad, and pulled out my pen. I hadn't lost the old touch, not completely.

On my way to my next appointment, I sang a wee song to myself, or a rhyme, maybe, cause it didn't have much of a tune yet: 'Hymn to Coastal Business, or, How I Stopped Worrying and Learned to Love the A98'.

> Findochty, Portknockie
> Portsoy and Rosehearty
> A little bit breezy
> But not a bit clarty.
>
> St Combs and St Fergus
> Balmedie and Boddam
> You can't sell them sweeties
> If you've not got 'em.

Or maybe I should call it 'Get Your Kicks on the A96'. But then I'd have to change the towns, and anyway, I never really liked that road: too many tractors. Not to mention timber lorries. And caravans in the summer. And that would just remind me of the A9, which was the last place I wanted to be reminded of: I'd be going there soon enough. In this business, when you hear the Call of the Wickers you've just got to answer it.

All in all, not top-ten material I suppose, but it cheered me up. And the appointment wasn't too bad either: sold an enormous quantity of Sherbet Dabs to the dame: Maud of Maud's Tearooms, Maud. 'What's going on?' I asked her. 'How come Dabs is the flavour of the month? It's not exactly sweeping the nation.'

She opened her eyes wide, looked over both shoulders, scoured the far corners of the shop (though no one at all had been in since I'd arrived half an hour before) then leant towards me.

'I reckon it's they druggies,' she said.

'Eh?'

'There's this one guy comes in on a Saturday morning, nice-looking chap. And ken this? He buys a dozen Sherbet Dabs. Every Saturday. Suspicious or what?'

'Maybe he just likes the stuff. Or his kids do. Or . . .'

'Wait. So one Saturday night I was locking up, and I happened to look off towards the rubbish bin in the car park. And guess what was lying in a wee heap by the bin?'

I couldn't guess. Maud's was famous in the trade for a period in the late eighties when, so the legend had it, a dog turd was stuck to the front window of the place. Some kid who'd got banned had thrown it there, and either to make a point, or else because she didn't care, Maud had just left it where it stuck. For two years.

'I can't guess,' I said. 'What did you see?'

'It gars me grue,' she said. 'But it was . . . twenty or thirty liquorice sticks. From out the Sherbet Dabs!'

'Eh?'

'Mr Nice Guy must have been sitting in his car every weekend, picking out the liquorices from his big bag of Dabs and flinging them towards the bin. And then, and then . . . then he heads off down to Peterhead to sell the sherbet to the junkies . . . *as Class-A drugs*. It's evil!'

'Or maybe he just doesn't like liquorice.'

She leaned back, shook her head, looked at my pityingly. 'It's an evil trade,' she said. 'Preying on our kiddies. Aye, them and the trawlermen. Evil.'

The customer is always right, even when they're completely barking. So I just nodded. Then she leaned towards me again.

'Better give me a dozen cases of Sherbet Dabs. And do you have any without liquorice sticks in them? I hate to see waste.'

When I stepped outside Maud's the greyness was blinding. Buchan's fine on a fine day: the sky blue above Mormond Hill, the miles of flat green fields, the faces of the folk scarlet with wind and crabsticks smuggled out the back door of the Broch factory. But on a grey day it's flat grey land, louring grey sky, grey-skinned people. It could make you go blind, all this greyness, it could suck the sight right out of your eyes, Buchan. I blinked and paused at the edge of the car park.

From somewhere out of the grey glare came a whistle: the theme to *The Good, the Bad and the Ugly*. I blinked again and screwed up my eyes to look across the chuckies. Of course: Eddie Fish, slouched against the bonnet of his vermilion Vauxhall Vectra, Lambert & Butler in his clenched lips, sample cases at his feet like panniers of bankhaul.

'Draw!' he said, then twirled his hands, stuck them in his jacket pockets, and pulled out . . . a PDA. 'Bang!' he said, 'You're dead.'

'That would explain a lot,' I said, and started across the gravel expanse. 'And how about yourself Eddie? Still living? All set for the season? How's business?'

'Splendiferous, Big Man,' he said, 'Absolutely stonking.' He poked nicotine-tanned fingers at his PDA, or pretended to, then flicked his eyes back up at me. 'Ten per cent up on last year, six per cent up on target, sell-through exceptional, stock turnover down to six weeks, reorders up by a factor of four, customer satisfaction soaring, all goals booted home, all targets bull's-eyed.'

'And best of all,' I said, 'All pigs refuelled and ready to fly.'

'Aye!' he frowned, spitting the end of the fag from between his lips. 'It's crap basically, shit, the whole business is going to shit, the whole world is going to shit. No one appreciates the art of the fucking fine chocolatier any more. Handmade Belgian chocolates, handmade in Belchland by Belches! And who cares? Nobody. Pearls before swine, Andy boy, little brown pearls, little brown handmade Belchland pearls, 70% minimum cocoa solids. But who cares?'

'What are you doing here anyway?' I said. 'I was three o'clock. You can't be three-thirty. Maud would never head to tail two of us.'

'Aye, she needs to go and sleep for half an hour after seeing you, ya bas.'

''Cause my dynamic sales pitch has worn her out?'

'Nah, cause you've bored her to sleep. What've they given you this season? Come on, stun me, what's the latest innovation from the Sweet-tooth boffins?'

'I'm not telling you. You'd be straight on the phone to Brussels.'

'Ha! What's Flemish for Hawick Balls? I think not, Andy boy.'

'Well I'm not telling you, I've got to have some trade secrets.'

'Never worry. Maud'll tell me ten seconds after I'm through the door.'

I looked at my watch. 'So when is that, Eddie? 'Cause I've got to get on.'

'Four o'clock, man. So what've I got? Twenty minutes? Ach, I'll give her ten then go in.'

'I can't believe you're that early, Eddie. What's going on? Can't get the appointments to fill the day?'

'Nah, it's the GPS – we all got issued with them just before

Christmas. They're the biz, I'm telling you. Never get lost again, man, on the way to some crappy little café in the back of beyond. See how far you've got to go, how long it's going to take. And I've got it linked up to the old Bluetooth, so it gets traffic updates and that, roadworks ahead, fantastic. Though I have to admit most of the updates are for the M25 and the M11: not too much is heard of the good old B999 Potterton to Pettymuk, where I've just been, let alone the famous, nay infamous, Unclassified Road with the Wiggles from Ordiequish to Craiglug, down which I had the pleasure of dawdling this very morning.'

I opened the boot of the car with only a couple presses of the key button, the lights flickering half-heartedly then going back to sleep. 'So they're still looking after you, the Belgians?'

He watched as I slotted the cases back into the boot amongst the jars of mouldy returns and the boxes of counter standers and window stickers.

'I've always said, if we look after the customers, then the company looks after us.'

'And do you still say that?'

He gazed across at Maud's for a moment. 'Times are hard, Andy boy. Now I say: as long as the company's looking after you, you look after their customers. But if they stop looking after you . . . fuck them. Time to move on.' He shrugged, crouched down to open up one of his sample cases. 'So they try to keep us sweet. GPS, PDA, OTE – all the alphabetti confetti you could ask for.' He lifted out a couple of golden, ribbon-wrapped boxes, then from under-neath them a cellophane bag-ette with a rubber band round its neck, and a pile of red marble-sized chocolates inside. 'Here,' he said, and tossed them to me. 'On the house. Ginseng truffles. Take them home to Mrs Andy and put a bit of pep back into your life. This season's big idea.'

He obviously hadn't heard about me and Sheila. And that was something I wasn't going to tell him, or it would be round every confectioner's, tobacconist's and roadside tearoom in Scotland overnight. So I just laughed. 'Thanks. You're a gent. A gentleman of the road.'

'Is that no a tramp, Andy boy, what are you saying?'

We both laughed again. Unless, of course, he was double bluffing and he *had* heard about me and Sheila, and that was exactly why he was giving me aphrodisiac sweeties, in a typical Eddie Fish pish-take.

He snapped shut his case and stood up, looking me in the eye. 'Seriously,' he said, 'we've got to stick together, it's us against them.'

'Oh definitely. Eh, against who? The supermarkets?'

He shook his head.

'The customers?'

'Nuh.'

'The public?'

'No! The company! Just cause you don't see them for three months at a time doesn't mean they're not out to screw you. And they think they can buy me off with a fucking GPS!'

He lifted his cases and started off across the car park towards Maud's. Halfway there he turned to shout back to me to me, 'I'll tell you something though, it's great for finding your way home to the hotel at midnight when you're completely bladdered. Type in the address while you're having your first pint then switch it off till it's time to go home. Splendiferous!'

My last appointment finished just after five. An hour and a half to get home, I reckoned. I headed back westwards, the sun already setting behind clouds up ahead, a gloomy end to the day. And only three ginseng truffles left to keep me alive, or at least awake.

Round about Buckie the locks on the car doors started acting up, clicking and knocking, locking and unlocking, settling eventually on locking me in. Then my headlights failed. Well, my dippers did, the beamers were okay. So I was fine while nothing was coming, I could whack on full beam and see way down the road. But when anyone appeared coming towards me I had a choice: stay on full and dazzle the hell out of the oncomers, or switch to dip – darkness – and drive blind into who knows what up ahead, guided only by the strategy of aiming just a little to the left of the approaching headlights.

For a while I favoured the full beams, reckoning on safety. I had to see where I was going for Christ's sake! But after a while I was swithering: screwed up and sweating. All these oncomers flashing their lights at me! I couldn't stand the anger, the disapproval, the rejection. It was the old story with me: got to keep everyone happy, the customer is always right.

So I changed my strategy. Next time someone came round the bend towards me – not just one car, but a whole stream of them, as it happened – I switched to dip, meaning *nothing*, and I drove on, plunging ahead into the darkness.

What Question?
William Sutcliffe

Amy is an extraordinary young lady, with qualities too numerous to list here. She may not appear, at first glance, to be what is known as 'a catch', and her conversation may be a little sparse, but excitement is precisely the sensation of which the long-term investor should be most wary. To explain it in simple language, she's a blue-chip girl, not a make-or-break high-tech venture.

If that comparison appears a little vulgar, I can only inform you that when one deals on a daily basis with sums of money so vast that the general public can barely conceive their magnitude, one is forced to redraw certain boundaries of *politesse*. There are many things that would appear obscene to you, but which appear perfectly natural to the likes of me. My salary, for instance.

I'm joking, of course. My remuneration is entirely in line with such peers as there are in my field. I have worked like a dog to obtain my current position. However it may look to the jealous eyes of five-figure earners, there is no lazy route to that extra digit on the salary.

But I digress. This is a love story.

One of the great ironies of my work is that although it gives me a financial and social status that places me in at least the ninety-fifth percentile of eligibility, the hours demanded at the office render my bachelor status strangely hard to shed. There are, however, introduction agencies specialising in resolving this conundrum for men such as myself, to whom there is, I believe, no shortage of female subscribers.

I see nothing unromantic in the notion that my potential suitors were statistically sifted before introduction. After all, where would we be without statistics? I shudder to think.

If my desire is for a 5'6", blonde, public relations or magazine publishing professional, 20–23, with a non-Oxbridge second class (or lower) degree, I see no reason why I should waste courtship time on anyone else. That Amy is of American extraction amply demonstrates my willingness to yield on non-essential factors. (My knack for the sensitive weighting of variables in complex statistical models is, if I may flatter myself, admired throughout the financial community.)

The success of my relationship with Amy is proof – if proof be needed – that a rigorous approach is a great time-saver in matters of romance. I shan't bore you with the old boy-meets-girl, boy-spends-astronomical-sums-on-ostentatiously-overpriced-theatre-tickets-flowers-and-restaurant-meals, girl-dispenses-sexual-favours-of-sufficient-meagreness-to-denote-wifely-potential stories that lie behind every successful courtship. I shall simply say that both parties in the developing passion were entirely content for a full three months, after which I took it upon myself to propose marriage. Her response, 'Ask me again when you're sober,' came as a surprise.

On our succeeding date, I again requested her hand in marriage. Her reply was the same.

After two failed attempts to win Amy's hand, I resolved upon a different approach. It appeared distinctly possible that her rejections were rooted in some cause quite other than that she had stated. Women, as you may know, are notorious for speaking in elaborate codes. Drunkenness seemed an improbable reason to turn down a man of my status. I am in no way dependent on alcohol. Were I an alcoholic, it would be impossible to perform a job as powerful, responsible and stressful as the one I currently hold. My career success alone is sufficient to show that I have no problem whatsoever with alcohol.

I therefore gave further thought to Amy's uncharacteristic refusal, and proceeded to analyse her personality and background for clues as to the true nature of this mysterious obstruction on the path to our impending marriage.

For her to turn me down (albeit in terms that hinted at future acceptance) signified that my offer contained the miscalculation of a factor in the relationship containing hidden value. My task was to picture the proposal from her side of the table, in order to unearth the variable that had received deal-breakingly divergent valuations by opposing parties.

Using a simple logic tree, I laid out all the chief attributes that I perceived she might desire in a marriage and proceeded to analyse the data for the area that I had neglected (see *Figure 1.0* below).

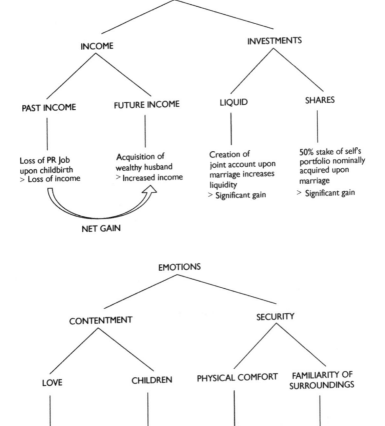

Figure 1.0 Analysis of loss/gain inherent in proposed marriage (from female perspective)

The problem immediately made itself known. Amy's American lineage was the stumbling block. That she had chosen to reside in Britain of her own free will diminished the likelihood that she would prefer to marry an American. Indeed, at several stages of our courtship my Britishness had shown itself to be something of a selling point. It seemed more likely that a cultural gulf, product of our widely differing upbringings, had led me to omit an element in the courtship ritual that held high value for an American, and such little value for an Englishman as to be casually overlooked. Customs out of which we Europeans have long since grown still hold sway over the New World psyche.

I pondered for days over which cultural *faux pas* I could have made, then, in front of late night television with a pugnacious little bottle of Italian plonk, while thinking about other matters entirely, the answer came to me. I had failed to ask Amy's father for his blessing.

This, I concluded, was the true source of Amy's resistance. The only other area of doubt on the entire logic tree was that of my as yet unproved potency. Providing a certificate of sperm count would have presented little problem, since I had no doubts whatsoever on that front, yet it struck me that to leap to such a conclusion, and to provide the relevant document as part of the next marriage proposal, could come across as somewhat *gauche*.

No, Amy's father, it seemed, held the key to her heart. His arrival, on a transatlantic business trip a month or so after my logic tree epiphany, presented me with a perfect opportunity to rectify my omission.

In terms which hinted that it was to be some form of 'occasion', I invited him to a dinner, which I ensured was thoroughly and expensively lubricated by taking immediate command of the wine list, explaining that I had chosen the restaurant not for the food but for the excellence of the wines. This is the type of pretension that impresses Americans. Personally, I prefer other types of pretension, but my sole duty this particular evening was to charm my future father-in-law. (Would I one day be expected to call him

Pop? This thought made me feel rather queasy. Infantilism is the American disease. I could expand on this theory at length, but, as I have already stated, this is a love story.)

I chose a Gigondas 1986, whose obscurity and £60 price tag would, I felt, impress without appearing flashy. I'm no expert on the niceties of viniculture, but I find that choosing the sixth most expensive wine is a reliable method for passing oneself of as a *connoisseur*. Anything from the top five comes across as a novice ordering on price.

In part thanks to the Gigondas, the early formality of the meal dissolved into easy conviviality, the conversation skating happily from topic to topic (see *Figure 1.1* below).

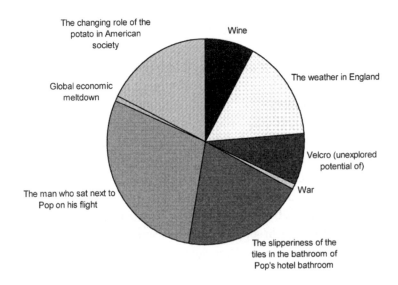

Figure 1.1 Breakdown of dinner-table conversation (early stages)

By the arrival of the main course it was apparent that the evening was a success, the only annoyance being Amy's grating attempt to prevent me ordering a third bottle of wine. However, a logistical flaw in my plan emerged. 'Pop', or 'Mr Wenbourne', as I had sycophantically chosen to dub him, would be leaving by cab immediately after the meal. Amy would be sitting with us throughout. I would only be alone with him if Amy retreated to the toilet. To make my request in her presence would undermine the entire exercise, and risked the possibility of Amy reiterating her decline in front of a witness, thus cementing it still further.

I proceeded to ply her with liquids, topping up her wine and water glasses after every mouthful, yet even as the waiters removed our dinner plates, myself and Mr Wenbourne having relieved ourselves twice each, Amy remained stolidly in her chair. One of the many fine qualities possessed by la Wenbourne, which I have had occasion to admire in the course of long-distance drives, is the capaciousness of her bladder. Yet on this evening I was silently cursing her for it. She drank and she drank – a glass of water for every meagre sip of Gigondas – yet nothing, it seemed, could stir her from the table. Would I have to resort to spilling coffee onto her dress? In the circumstances, I was reluctant to resort to such ungallant measures.

Then, moments after ordering dessert, my opportunity came. Without so much as uttering a syllable to interrupt her father's anecdote of the journey to a 1978 job interview during which a shoelace had broken, she slid from her chair and made for the toilets. I leaned forward. I coughed. I tapped my cutlery. I shuffled backwards and forwards in my seat, nodding faster and faster, willing the anecdote to a conclusion, yet the shoelace story went on and on.

I glanced at my watch. Although I hadn't checked the time when Amy left the table, looking at my watch seemed the only way to assess how much time I had left to salvage the simple reward I desired from this costly evening. She must have been gone three minutes, and Mr Wenbourne still hadn't arrived at the interview. He was still in reception agreeing the price for the loan of a shoelace from a security guard. I glanced round at the toilets. *She was coming back! She was on her way back to the table!*

Interruption was the only option. 'MR WENBOURNE!' I said,

cutting him off mid-flow. 'I'd like to ask for permission to marry your daughter.'

He stared at me. He blinked. His mouth opened and shut a few times. Then Amy took her place at the table.

Mr Wenbourne looked as if he had been slapped. I, presumably, looked no less agitated. From Amy's expression, it was clear that she immediately detected the strained atmosphere at the table. I had to cover, fast.

'Oh, yes!' I said. 'Yes! That's wonderful. You wouldn't believe it. He . . . he gets the shoelace . . .'

'. . . from the security guard,' she interrupted, with a tired sigh. 'I know. And that one breaks on the way up the stairs.'

'It breaks on the way up the stairs?' I said, my intonation way off. 'I mean, it breaks on the way up the stairs! Yes! Amazing! You wouldn't believe that was possible. Two laces! Ha!' I was over-compensating disastrously, but it was hard to stop. 'Ah, dessert!' I heard myself saying. 'Dessert! The waiter's bringing dessert! Good, good! Dessert! For us! Er . . . dessert wine? Anyone? Yes? Oh, we must. Just a half-bottle.'

And so, with the consumption of an exquisite Baumes de Venise, followed by coffee and a round or two of brandy, the evening was dragged back on course. I can remember little of what it was we talked about during the extended latter stages of the meal, but I do recall that I was arm-in-arm, not with abstemious Amy, but with Wenbourne Senior as we tumbled from the fug of the restaurant out onto a chilly London street.

Amy hailed a cab for her father, remembering the word 'taxi' and the name of his hotel with mental dexterity that struck me at the time as vastly impressive. It was unclear by this stage whether I was supporting the weight of Mr Wenbourne or vice versa. Together we navigated a course from the restaurant door, over a daunting expanse of paving stones, to the kerb, from which I heaved him into the cab.

'Wait!' he barked, as he clambered onto his seat, before lurching forward and sliding down the window. 'Son, I've thought about your question,' he said, gazing at me fondly. 'The answer's yes.'

I gazed back at him, and though I couldn't quite focus on his eyes, which seemed to swim around alarmingly within the frame of the taxi window, I aimed an amicable smile in his general direction.

'What question?' I said.

Authors' Biographies

John Aberdein lives in Hoy, and is working on his second novel. Early short stories were published in *Ahead of Its Time* (ed. Duncan McLean, Cape, 1997), and the tales 'Moving' and 'Imprint' were listed in the first two *Scotsman* & Orange Short Story Awards. His novel *Amande's Bed* (Thirsty/Argyll) was voted Saltire First Book of the Year (2005).

Sally Beamish moved to Scotland from London in 1990. A member of Stirling Writers, she writes fiction, drama and poetry. She is also a composer, and her poems, *Trance o Nicht,* part of a concerto performed by Evelyn Glennie, have been published by Poetry Scotland. Her musical, *Shenachie,* co-written with Donald Goodbrand Saunders, reached the finals of the Highland Quest.

Kate Blackadder was born in Inverness and now lives in Edinburgh with her husband and two children. She is a freelance editor. Her story 'Another World' was inspired by the view one summer's day across Loch Meig in Strathconon, Ross-shire.

Lynsey Calderwood rebuilt her life through creative writing following a traumatic brain injury at the age of fourteen. Her autobiography *Cracked* was published by Jessica Kingsley in 2002. She continues to write, mostly about life, love, brains and the underdog.

Linda Cracknell was born in the Netherlands and came to Scotland in 1990 via Devon and Zanzibar. She now lives in Highland Perthshire. Her short stories have been widely published, and include her own collection, *Life Drawing* (2000). She also writes radio drama for the BBC. 'In and out the windows' is a story from an episodic novel she is currently writing.

Morven Crumlish was a finalist in the 1998 *Vogue* Talent Contest for young writers and in 2004 she was awarded a New Writers' Bursary from the Scottish Arts Council. Her work has appeared in *Shorts 4*, the Macallan/*Scotland on Sunday* short story collection, and has been broadcast on BBC Radio 4. She lives in Edinburgh with her daughter and is currently writing a novel.

Morgan Downie is one of the many and varied islands of the mythic archipelago of Scotia. Its people believe in the guiding power of cats, love unconditional, the blue Smartie, the clean beauty of a perfect breaking wave and the notion that at least one in six statements should be untrue.

Sophie Ellis studied for an MA in English Literature at the University of Edinburgh, graduating in 2005 with first class honours. She has enjoyed travelling and teaching in Eastern Europe, and plans to start a postgraduate course at the University of Newcastle in September.

Jackie Galley is joint editor of the new publication *Southlight*, which is now on its second edition. Her work has appeared in magazines including *Markings* and *Chapman*. Jackie runs creative writing workshops as part of an adult continuing education programme and also as themed workshops on environment and creativity. She lives in Dumfries and Galloway.

Janice Galloway was born in Saltcoats, Ayrshire, and read Music and English at Glasgow University. Her award-winning novels include *The Trick Is to Keep Breathing* (1989), *Foreign Parts* (1994) and *Clara* (published in 2002 and winner of the Saltire Society Scottish Book of the Year Award.) She lives and works in Glasgow.

Michael Gardiner has studied in Oxford, London, St Andrews and Tokyo. He is currently honorary researcher at Aberdeen University. His previous publications include *Modern Scottish Culture* and *The Cultural Roots of British Devolution*. His short story collection *Escalator* was published by Polygon in 2006 and he is currently working on a biography of Thomas B. Glover.

Clio Gray was born in Yorkshire, and now lives in Easter Ross. She has won several awards for her short stories, most notably the Harry Bowling Award, which has resulted in the publication of her first novel, *Guardians of the Key* (Headline, 2006).

Carole Hamilton won a Scottish Arts Council New Writers' Bursary for a short story collection, *Heart's Desire*. Other publications include 'Dissy', 'No Excuse' and 'Let Me Take You Down', in anthologies from Glasgow University, where she studied Creative Writing. She is currently writing her first novel, *If You Leave It Too Long It Hurts More*.

Nick Houldsworth lives in Edinburgh. Amongst other jobs, he has worked as a NHS physiotherapist, an office IT technician, a barman and a shelf stacker in a weight-loss clinic. Now, he is a full-time musician with the Scottish indie-folk band Hobotalk, playing guitar, mandolin and harmonica. 'Odd Jobbing' is his first published piece of writing.

Paul Johnson was a history teacher before he retired, during which time he wrote a seriously dull book on a medieval duke. As a retirement job he drove a taxi. He now aims to explore through a novel the lack of narrative we are able to give to our understanding of ourselves in social groups.

E. Mae Jones is currently completing her postgraduate Creative Writing dissertation at the University of St Andrews. She holds an undergraduate degree from Carnegie Mellon University in English and Drama. This autumn she will return to her native Pennsylvania to live with her new husband, Al, in the home of her grandfather, Walter from 'The Menu'.

Peter Likarish was born in Littleton, Colorado. He studied English and Computer Science at Grinnell College, graduating in 2004. He is currently completing a MSc in Creative Writing at Edinburgh University. 'When You Wake Up' is his first published story.

Sangam MacDuff was born in India and brought up in the sannyasin communities of Bhagwan Shree Rajneesh. After Rajneesh's arrest, in 1985, Sangam moved to the Findhorn Foundation Community in north-east Scotland. He read English at Trinity Hall, Cambridge, graduating in 2000. He is currently completing a MSc in Creative Writing at Edinburgh University.

Bernard MacLaverty was born in Belfast and now lives in Glasgow. He has published five collections of short stories, including *Walking the Dog and Other Stories* (1994) and *Matters of Life and Death* (2006). He has written four novels: *Lamb* (1980); *Cal* (1983); *Grace Notes* (winner of the 1997 Saltire Scottish Book of the Year Award; shortlisted for the 1997 Booker Prize for Fiction and the 1997 Whitbread Novel Award) and *The Anatomy School* (2001). He has also written for radio, television and film.

James Mavor is a scriptwriter whose television drama credits include *The Acid Test, Split Second, Monarch of the Glen* and *Doctor Finlay* (BAFTA Scotland Best Series). He has also written for theatre, radio and opera. His play *Terminal* won a *Scotsman* Fringe First Award in 1990. James teaches screenwriting at Screen Academy Scotland and for the Arvon Foundation. He is married with two teenage children and lives in Edinburgh.

Brian McCabe was born in a small mining community near Edinburgh. He studied Philosophy and English Literature at Edinburgh University. He has been a freelance writer since 1980 and has held various writing fellowships. He is currently Writer in Residence at Edinburgh University and editor of the *Edinburgh Review*. His published poetry includes *Body Parts* (Canongate, 1999). His most recent new collection of short stories is *A Date with My Wife* (Canongate, 2001) and his *Selected Stories* was published by Argyll in 2003.

Lynda McDonald enjoys the short story form and has published stories in magazines and anthologies, including *Shorts* (Polygon) and the *Scotsman*/Orange 2005 anthology *Secrets*. Her poems have appeared in *New Writing Scotland* and *The Interpreter's House*. She lives in Edinburgh, and is now writing a play.

Duncan McLean was born in Aberdeenshire. Since publishing his first book, *Bucket of Tongues* (1992), he has lived in Orkney. He has also written two novels, a collection of plays, and a travel book about Texan music. He is currently working on perfecting a new recipe for Horehound Humbugs.

William Sutcliffe was born in London in 1971. He is the author of four novels which have been translated into eighteen languages: *New Boy, The Love Hexagon, Are You Experienced?* and *Bad Influence*, all published by Penguin. He lives in Edinburgh with his wife, son and cat.